About Brian Dawtrey

Born 1928. Married with a nuclear family of 14.

12 years family farming in England.

24 years organising agricultural land development schemes and building rural roads and dams for African governments under the British Overseas Services Aid programme and The World Bank.

16 yrs Hon.Wildlife Ranger.

Past Chairman of the Wildlife Conservation Society of Zambia.

Dedication

To Cicely (Jo), without whose love and courage there would be no story to tell.

Brian Dawtrey

WILD AFRICA, ODYSSEY IN A FORD CORSAIR GT

AUSTIN MACAULEY
PUBLISHERS LTD.

A CIP catalogue record for this title is available from the British Library.

ISBN 9781785545955 (Paperback)
ISBN 9781785545962 (Hardback)
ISBN 9781785545979 (E-Book)

www.austinmacauley.com

First Published (2016)
Austin Macauley Publishers Ltd.
25 Canada Square
Canary Wharf
London
E14 5LQ

Acknowledgments

I am greatly indebted to, family friend, Oliver Delany OBE for proof reading and assisting with his in-depth knowledge of Tanzania; also to dear friend Gina Antczak for her valuable creative assistance with the cover of this book.

Contents

PREFACE   13

CHAPTER ONE   15
From Dar es Salaam To Norwich And Back Again

CHAPTER TWO   25
From Cape Town to Mbeya

CHAPTER THREE   33
In The Mountains with Elephants, and Wool Sheep

CHAPTER FOUR   71
Usangu: Teeming With Wildlife

CHAPTER FIVE   94
The Oxfam Run Around

CHAPTER SIX   139
Up-Sticks for a New Life

THE CHART   167

ROUTE MAP   168

COASTAL AND NORTHERN REGION   168

CHAPTER SEVEN   169
Mountains, Beaches, Railways, and Amboseli

CHAPTER EIGHT   196
Life in Tanga and on the Serengeti Plains

CHAPTER NINE   226
Philosophy

CHAPTER TEN   255
Escape?

POST SCRIPT   299

Preface

The British Empire and its impact upon its Colonies is characterised by its critics almost exclusively as a regime that took and did not give, serving only the interests of the United Kingdom and ruling over many backward peoples whose welfare was ignored while the UK benefitted from the natural resources of the their Colony. The reality is that the Empire introduced education, health systems, built infrastructure, developed townships and villages, and designed institutional structures to enable the people to govern themselves after they gained independence.

The influence of the UK continued to very good effect in post-colonial times under the British Government Overseas Service Aid Scheme, and British people of goodwill gave many years of devoted service to public services in Africa, India, the Far East, and many other parts of the World.

One such person, who with his wife gave 24 years selfless service to Africa, was Brian Dawtrey. Brian and Cicely were later recognised for their immense contribution to Nigeria when The Attah of Igalaland a province of Nigeria gave recognition to them in the words of the citation "for the benefits they brought to the people of his (the Attah's) kingdom and especially constructing 1050kms of gravel roads connecting his villages to markets and by helping to clear land for increased Yam production".

Undoubtedly such contributions to the Nations of Tanzania, which this book is about; Zambia, and Nigeria, live on and have improved the quality of life for many people there. In writing this preface it is an honour for me to recognise the impact that Brian and Cicely had on their chosen countries, and it is apparent from this and other books that Brian has written, that both of them loved

Africa and its people, and gave themselves wholeheartedly to serving their fellow men.

Both gave much to Africa, and their love and their relish for life in helping the people, shines through the very entertaining pages of "Wild Africa, Odyssey in a Ford Corsair GT". Brian writes in a very easy, humorous and at times self-deprecatory style. This masks a very serious and dedicated life on both their parts.

I commend this book and I applaud two lives given to serving others in Africa and helping nations to grow. There are too few such people and they have reached out to, and enriched many lives.

Ken Thornber CBE, Former Leader and Chairman of the County Council of Hampshire.

Chapter One

From Dar es Salaam To Norwich And Back Again

"Wow! *East African Airways Comet Four*. This is going to be a bit quicker than the 'steamer', Cicely, should give us an extra three weeks' leave. She's beautiful isn't she?"

This exciting innovation in travel hummed towards us confidently as we waved goodbye to Dar es Salaam and climbed into absolute luxury; plenty of room to stretch our legs, waited on hand and foot by smiling air hostesses. It was like first class on the Steam Ship Kenya Castle which took us all out to Mombasa, two years previously on our last tour of duty in 1962.

"It must have to carry a lot of fuel on board to get us to London." observed our 12-year-old Richard.

The first leg got us to Entebbe in Uganda, then a peaceful, happy nation with a prosperous agricultural industry as yet untroubled by the internecine tribal conflicts precipitated by Idi Amin in 1971.

The next leg saw us touch-down in Benghazi, Libya, in order to refuel to carry us to next stop Paris. It had become instinctive with me to check soil texture everywhere I travelled on safari in Tanzania as an agricultural Land Use Planner. I bent down and plucked a handful of Benghazi airport soil.

"Loamy sand." I muttered to our disinterested three children. Benghazi's position as Libya's second city owed its position to being a strategic port rather than its agriculture. The discovery of oil, more to the point, after the Second World War had driven the Libyan economy ever since. However in 1964, a jet propelled passenger plane landing in Libya, was news, and the noisy jet engines attracted a large crowd of waving, welcoming locals. The latest Western technology had arrived in their midst.

Later we felt like Gods, gazing down upon the snowy peaks of the Alps and finally the exciting aerial view of London. All a wondrously new era for 'common folk' like us in those days. Our previous journey to Tanganyika had been a leisurely three weeks by sea through the Suez Canal, in the company of colonial dignitaries and missionaries.

I had ordered a new Ford Corsair GT, a tax-free export, to be delivered to Heathrow for our onward drive to Leamington Spa. The UK list price was £859, including purchase tax, £728 to me for export. The Ford Corsair GT was the latest model Ford and a leader in its class, with the beautiful styling of its wedge-shaped bonnet and long slender body, a fashion model with bucket-shaped leather seats. Its 1600cc engine gave exhilarating acceleration with its twin carburettors. This model had just swept to fame in the Monza Rally beating the World Speed Record over a three thousand mile run at 101.7 mph. It was also noted for its comfortable suspension, which I expected to put to the test on African corrugated dirt roads on my next tour of duty.

We were deflated to find a Ford Zepher 4 awaiting us with an apology letter from the Ford factory, "Sorry Mr Dawtrey, our computer, that controls the paint shop, produced the wrong colour. Your grey Corsair GT will be delivered to your Leamington Spa address in 10 days' time."

"Oh! So, nobody to blame then! The computer's fault," Cicely has never been known to accept excuses, "oh well, this is England after all; no urgency. World leader in aircraft design though, that De Haviland Comet IV has been a fabulous experience, Brian, a new world dawning. Ford needs to catch up. With a bit of luck we could possibly get our car in ten days' time; AND possibly even our baggage!" The Dar es Salaam baggage handlers had obviously caught the British car manufacture's 'disease'.

"Your baggage has gone to the wrong airport. It will arrive later. We'll forward it." the airline official said.

"Get the camera, George." My sister Joy gave me a hug, something I hadn't had for years, when we drove up to their house in Leamington Spa in the Zepher 4. "I expected to see you in bush khaki, Brian, a big hat and a rifle over your shoulder, not that Persil-white outfit. What's that all about?" she smirked.

"Oh, it's standard coastal government officer rig in Dar es Salaam, where we have just come from. It's devilish hot out there you know. White reflects the heat and helps you keep cool."

"Oh, really. How come the Africans are black then?"

"Ah … Well …" I responded, struggling to discover the answer to that riddle.

My mother broke in with a smile, "You look quite white-skinned considering you've come from Darkest Africa! What are they like, those black people? I've never actually seen one in the flesh." In UK at that time only 1% of the population were black-skinned and they mostly lived and worked in Birmingham.

It seemed as though Africa was still an enigma to my family. We handed around our African gifts; Zanzibarian filigree earrings made from solid silver Marie Theresa coins, a moonstone from Sri Lanka, Zebra skin wallets, elephant skin shoes and a native fly whisk made from a Zebra tail.

Our new car duly arrived. It was a joy to behold, and we felt proud to be able to own such a fast smart car. Our next stop was Cicely's family in Nottinghamshire, Sister Jean and her father Arthur Marriott, a war horse veteran of the First World War. Cicely's father was the love of her life, next to me of course! Sadly he seemed edgy, and unwelcoming. Jean said he hadn't got over his wife Eva's premature death last year. They had been an utterly devoted couple. He had always been jovial company, and a leg-puller, but no more, it seemed. We all went to our well-known 'watering-hole' the White Post, for supper. Cicely's dad declined to accompany us and she was greatly saddened and confused. *I've lost my Dad, why? I shouldn't have gone away to Africa with Brian, that's why.*

In Tanganyika we had grown accustomed to friendly conversational people surrounding us, happy people. We thought, *Maybe it's the new medium that everyone seems to be obsessively glued to wherever we go – TV.*

They say that Africa grabs hold of you and never let's go. We felt estranged. We decided to abandon our relations and head for our old home, Norfolk. We had hired a beach chalet named Seaholme at Walcot by the sea, for £7.00 per week. The main topic on BBC Radio News was football, Mods and Rockers, and crime. Peru had played Argentina and the umpire had disallowed a goal. There was a riot – it wasn't a game, it was war, 350 people died. Despite the news we were happier in Norfolk, there was still 'The Archers' and 'Gardeners Question Time' and 'Any Questions' on the radio.

We visited our Norfolk friends from our farming days, all lovely people and finally to our beloved Home Farm where we were warmly welcomed by the owners, well-known Norfolk aristocracy. Our three children were really 'farm kids', now aged 14, 12 and 9. They were deliriously happy to be back on the farm. Caroline met up with her old pony riding friend Suzanne Parkinson who then came to stay with us at Walcot, by the sea. The baking hot summer weather, so typical of Norfolk, turned the girls into brown water-babies.

We renewed our love of the beautiful historic city of Norwich, with its oft visited Maddermarket Theatre, the very ancient Elm Hill street, the gorgeous Tea Rooms, the Assembly House restaurant, the colourful market in the flint stone Guild Hall Square, the great castle art galleries in the city centre, the Cathedral Close and, of course, the River Yar. We always believed that there was no finer city in England than Norwich. However, during our absence, changes here too, the cattle market had been moved out of town and replaced by an overabundance of cars. In 'our day' the cattle market was in the centre and the road into town used to be blocked with driven cattle on Saturdays, not cars.

We were advised by our young friend Rodney Boast that the "Methane pollution has been replaced by carbon dioxide pollution".

"What?"

"Oxen defecation versus motorcar exhaust, polluting the atmosphere." We were none the wiser as to the significance of his explanation. Something about "the weather".

We hadn't had access to a dentist since 1961 and so we visited our trusted dentist Mr Castle, in Norwich, who played the NHS system to give us all the treatment quality we would normally have had to pay for privately. He fixed us all up with; we thought excessive, 'drill and fill' "Keep you going for another three years," he declared.

Derby Day came and went, leaving our horse fanatic, Cicely, eight shillings and nine pence better off.

We had managed to persuade my mother to come with us to Walcot and she loved it really but was reluctant to admit it, she was a bit of a 'Mrs Bucket'. She was a person who had arisen from a coal miner background and aspired to become 'upper class', by marrying a young Coventry motor engineer. She never approved of her only son marrying Cicely, "a common village girl" and becoming a "farm labourer". On one occasion, when visiting our lovely teacher friend Hilda Neale, she refused to get out of the car and sat there blowing the horn whilst we had supper. Once again, we had that feeling that we did not quite understand the 'old folks'. She threatened to go home by train. We were not sure about the merits of the modern phrase Senior Citizen status either.

We returned to the Midlands and 'tried again'. I 'allowed, reluctantly' Cicely to drive the GT Corsair, after some unwelcome instructions! She absolutely loved it. She described me as "pompous" and the car as "exhilarating; a compaction of speed and compact comfort, as compared to our sloppy old Zodiac."

Sister Joy was very welcoming but television over-rode us in the end, not to mention my diminutive mother who proved very dominating at times, and earned the jovial title 'Mighty Mouse' from 'Uncle George'. We used our status as Overseas Visitors to get seats at Stratford Theatre and then fled back to Norfolk to an old cottage built in 1628 overlooking the marshes at Cley-next-the-Sea. This was wildness, with which we were more familiar, especially the walk out to Blakeney Point to see the seals, and collect winkles and cockles for supper. We had invited Cicely's father but he again declined despite his countryman background.

Our two boys woke up one morning and peering through the tiny windows towards the sea, "Hey, Dad, look at this – Gypy Geese." Egyptian Geese were a common sight at Lake Rukwa in South Tanzania, so we all felt at home. They later trapped eels in the dyke. We met Mr Bishop, the Warden of the marshes who told us that the Egyptian Geese were escapees from Holkham Hall the local coastal manorial estate, once owned by the famous agricultural innovator Samuel Coke. Another excuse for Cicely to do some "exhilarating driving", along the north Norfolk coast.

Caroline, age fourteen, needed a boarding school in England due to the imminent 'Africanization' process of her High School in Iringa, Tanzania. She had not taken the 11-plus examination so had to be interviewed by the Norwich Education Committee psychiatrist. Caroline's response to this interview was, "He is the nuttiest man I have ever come across. He asked me the stupidest questions, nothing to do with education at all." He, Mr Lawrence, advised us "In my opinion Caroline is not Grammar School material." We decide not indulge in a confrontation over the fact that she had passed an entrance exam into a Grammar School and had been there two years already. She might not have been their 'Star pupil' but she was certainly a Star amongst the fraternity of St. Michael's and St. Georges School, Iringa.

We already had a British Government Overseas Aid three-year contract for Tanzania so we had the sad prospect of leaving Caroline behind at a boarding school. Local government would pay the fees and central government provide air fares for the pupil to visit parents for two school holidays per year. So this was how the post-colonial Overseas Service Aid Scheme, OSAS, worked, replacing the old colonial service permanent and pensionable, and lifetime career, of government employment.

Cicely and I were 36 years old and looking to our future in Africa despite that deadly question posed by Granddad Marriott, "Now, you two boys; which place would you prefer to live?" We felt that our destiny was in peril. After a pensive silence, parents all ears, the joyous answer came, "Home Farm!" Cicely and I looked at each other, tears rising in our eyes.

My sister Joy had just returned from Ibiza looking like a cocoa bean. She committed herself, thankfully, to look after Caroline whilst she was attending Walton Hall boarding school in

Warwickshire. Joy and husband George undertook to drive her to the airport for her twice yearly flights to Tanzania. A happy life-long relationship between Caroline and Joy evolved from this, for us, somewhat traumatic, phase.

13ᵗʰ August 1964: Our departure was scheduled from Southampton on the R.M.S. Windsor Castle to Cape Town, plus our Ford Corsair GT and our two boys. The Suez Canal was closed.

The Steam Ship, S.S. Kenya Castle, on which we had travelled to Mombasa in 1962 had more crew than passengers to wait upon us and we felt more like aristocracy than passengers, whereas the Royal Mail Ship, R.M.S Windsor Castle, was a big, faster, modern ship of some 45,000 tons and its services were more automated, no more running our bath for us and laying out our clothes for evening dinner.

Carnations appeared in our cabin at Southampton docks − our relations did love us after all − or were they pleased to say good-bye! Of course one bunch of flowers was from Caroline. Human emotions did ultimately supersede the television. We were happier now and so were our two boys. Sister Joy was very happy to have the care of Caroline as her responsibility whilst she was in England at school. Caroline also enjoyed Joy's company.

Our route sailing south took us day by day to ever bluer skies and to sunny Las Palmas a volcanic island. We took the tour up to the volcano crater, "The next time she blows," the guide told us, "New York will be destroyed by the tsunami shock wave."

Cicely won the on board 'Derby', thank goodness. She is a winner by nature, especially picking horses, like her father in his younger days. She had a new Nottingham Lace dress in which she looked ravishing. We danced every night on deck, into an eternity of love and happiness under a moonlit, star spangled sky.

There was an on-board fete in aid of the blind. Richard made 800 flags and sold them for £8. I recall that as a small child on the farm Richard always played games that would be useful unlike many children who just amuse themselves. His brother, Philip, aged 9 years, found a fruit machine which he said was "a bit bonkers!" He raised twice as much as Richard with minimal effort, which also was appropriate to his nature. He was not over keen to hand it over for the blind!

The other passengers were heading for R.S.A., Republic of South Africa and Rhodesia. The idea of driving to Tanzania filled everyone with dismay. "Why would you want to go there to that uncivilised place? Do you realise how far it is!" I knew the answer to that question, 3600 miles to the border, mostly on unpaved dusty roads full of hazards.

Our South African route was to swing round the southern country of the continent following the famous Garden Route and then head due north through Pretoria to Southern Rhodesia en route for Northern Rhodesia, shortly to become Zambia. Zambia is a vast country the size of Europe with a population equal to that of London so that part of our journey would be long and somewhat hazardous, with scarce fuel supplies. We were advised that, carrying jerry cans on board ship might be viewed with suspicion, so we intended to make a purchase in Northern Rhodesia.

Over-night stops in Southern Rhodesia, we were told, would be comfortable with plenty of garages and mechanical services available. In Northern Rhodesia such services would be more distended to say the least. We had a bivouac for emergencies and a camping cook pot in which to boil the odd few maize cobs, available everywhere, in the absence of a restaurant or food store. Once we hit the rough roads in the north punctures would become the main mechanical hazard. I habitually always carried a comprehensive tool kit in Africa and certainly had long experience of its use, especially with punctures and brake fluid leakages with my previous secondhand Mark II Ford Zodiac. Ford is famously good on spare parts, even in Africa which is why I stuck with Ford. I was a dab-hand at removing a tyre and patching the inner tube with a 'hot patch', not forgetting to carry a box of matches of course. My Ford Corsair GT was new, and hopefully more reliable than my old Zodiac. With no such thing as AA Rescue one had to be totally able to fix a car, however basically, so as to move on. I still carried an old nylon stocking in case the fan belt broke.

27th August 1964: Cape Town looked magnificent as we approached in the dawn sunlight, one of the world's geographical and historical icons. We enjoyed a day exploring the town and trying the chair lift to the top of the mountain. "We could retire here couldn't we, Brian. It's a beautiful place, surrounded by sea."

"I've got a few things I want to do before I retire. Ask me again in twenty years' time."

Chapter Two

From Cape Town to Mbeya

27th August 1964: It was freezing in Cape Town when we disembarked. We slept in our clothes for an early start next day, just as soon as our Ford Corsair GT was off-loaded from RMS Windsor Castle. We first installed our venetian blind in the rear window to repel the tropical heat ahead of us and loaded our roof rack with baggage and our bivouac. Following the renowned Garden Route took us to Highgate Farm, Outshoorn where the farmer of 3,000 acres had 900 Ostriches. We learned that they were monogamous and lived for 50 years. The farmer told us that he plucked feathers every nine months and sold them for mops, stoles and film scenery for £22 per bird, which would be £400 in Millenium money. They said that they could run as fast as race horses, hence our race horse fan, Cicely, made an unimpressive attempt to compete with the Ford Corsair GT.

We thought England much more scenic than South Africa as we drove across the Karoo and judged the farming as pretty backward. However, the rural Africans enjoyed a much higher standard of living than did their Tanzanian equivalent social group. The African townships were relatively modern as compared to the shanty townships of Kenya and West Africa. The fact that the Africans were compelled to live there, rather than from choice, did rather take the 'cream off the cake' for them, it was more akin to barracks living. Separatism, better known as Apartheid, was the embarrassingly rampant ethic everywhere. This, we learned, had evolved from an interpretation of the Bible that Africans were condemned by God to be 'hewers of wood and drawers of water'. This was the Gospel according to the Dutch Reform Church of the Afrikaner nationhood.

The Afrikaners at that time made it plain to us that we British were a hated race, a legacy of their defeat, over sixty years earlier, by the British in two Boer Wars. Lord Kitchener's 'scorched earth policy' of destroying Boer farms and placing families in concentration camps – where some 26,000 Afrikaner women and children were said to have died of disease and malnutrition – caused generations of bitterness. We experienced boorish teenagers in the streets, linking arms across the pavement thus driving us into the gutter. The hotel manager deliberately gave us a bed with broken springs and I punctured my thigh quite badly that night.

We visited our ex Mbeya friends in Newcastle in northern Natal Province. They were now living in my father's Coventry Knight 48 caravan that our friend Frank Larlham had restored in Mbeya. I had rescued it from the infamous failed post-war British Government Groundnut Scheme at Kongwa in Tanganyika. Driving out of Newcastle we slowed down looking for turnings. This produced an offensive police motorcyclist in my own open side window pointing a revolver at me. The curled lip uttered, in a broad Afrikaans dialect, "Git movin' digger, yer hear!"

We collected a sack of oranges in the Transvaal for a few shillings but had them confiscated at Beitbridge, the border post that took us over the Limpopo River into Southern Rhodesia now known as Zimbabwe. The problem was Disease and Pest Control Regulations efficiently applied, something else we were not used to! So, no fruit for our sustenance.

The drive through South Africa on tar roads was mechanically trouble free and our engine now well run-in after deviating slightly to East London and Durban to reach Newcastle, we had clocked 2,000 miles to Beitbridge.

The atmosphere in Rhodesia was wholly different; Africans black and white were welcoming. The countryside looked rich, with commercial farmers producing maize and Virginia tobacco, both for export. This was shortly before UDI, the Unilateral Declaration of Independence from Britain, by Prime Minister Iain Smith, which led to catastrophic change.

We finally pulled happily into Robins Camp in the Wankie Game Reserve for two days' game viewing. The Rhodesian idea of game viewing was not quite in accordance with our wildlife experience – no element of risk, luck or adventure or the 'intrepid explorer' attribute to which we were accustomed. In the evening we filed out to join a large group of 'whites' on a stadium style seating arrangement overlooking a water hole. In the background was the throb of an engine pumping water into the water hole. The substantial numbers of antelope, zebra and elephant were fearless of humans and so we were somewhat put-off. This was not the wild Africa that we had been accustomed to.

We crossed the astonishing Victoria Falls Bridge, reaching across an 840 feet deep ravine in the landscape, built by the Edwardians in 1904. This forms the border into Northern Rhodesia. We had stayed at Victoria Falls before, on our previous contract of service when on vacation from Tanganyika and so after having taken a photograph of Cicely with Dr Livingstone, a fellow 'stuck his neck-out' traveller, we drove onto Livingstone town where we knew of a lovely swimming pool. We enjoyed a refreshing swim, followed by a café lunch. With darkness at 6:00 p.m. we drove on.

Wankie Game Reserve had endowed me with a legacy; a large tic, with a caving instinct. It seemed to enjoy the safety of my naval. We had earlier 'pulled-over' and procured our torch, as it was about 7:00 p.m., and dark. Tic-ing by torchlight with tweezers proved as exciting for the boys as hunting for *kwali* with my .22 rifle. Actually African tics will grow to grape size if left, and removing them complete with head and mouth-parts was the tricky bit. On this occasion we failed in the half light and did not get the mouthparts.

We were now in Southern Province of Northern Rhodesia. The surrounding 'bush' was all fenced in with barbed wire, something unknown in Tanzania. Freehold land owners had taken over; this wild country was now, sadly, 'owned'. Whilst this had the merit of keeping wild animals off the road we still faced another hazard. The monotonous unchanging scenery for the dozing boys in the back seat suddenly changed on the tar-strip road! We were now meeting trucks, at high speed, head-on, on the narrow tar strip. This was just wide enough to accommodate a vehicle with banking either side of, sometimes potholed, gravel. There was a knack in avoiding the dusty shoulder of the narrow tar-strip until the last second, then both vehicles swinging left to pass wing mirror to wing mirror with two wheels on the gravel and two on the tar. The instant that we were relieved to have survived we were blanketed in thick dust. Prayers then followed that there was not another truck ahead in the dust cloud. Understandably the truck drivers were reluctant to give way to cars coming from any direction. Highway Code? *Hakuna* = Swahili for 'there isn't any such thing'.

I felt tic fever coming on at about 9:00 p.m. so we decided to seek a farm gate and drive off the road to rest up. Cicely donned her nurse's mantle and I climbed into our bivouac to rest as my temperature rocketed. The boys slept in the car. At 2:00 a.m. Land Rover headlamps illuminated the bivouac. I felt as though I had arrived at the Pearly Gates until we heard a gruff yarpy voice with a South African accent that I knew was not St Peter's voice. Blaspheming followed about trespassing, cattle rustling and tourists. Cicely pleaded for clemency for her sick patient, all to no avail, this was not England. We were forced to strike camp and move off his land. What kind of people were these?

We pressed on hoping to reach a pharmacy in Lusaka by dawn. The pharmacist diagnosed tic-fever and gave me antibiotics. We had 900 miles or more to go so we found a car park and I slept awhile. Later Cicely took over the one hundred mile drive to Broken Hill, now renamed Kabwe, on a good road.

Broken Hill was a modern town, busy with white folks; so unlike Tanzania towns, even the shop assistants were white. We were shocked to find the butchers shop did not permit Africans to enter but they were obliged to shop through a hole in the wall. We checked the car over at the garage and found all 'white' Afrikaner mechanics, who seemed to spend my paid-for time, goading and taunting the African "spanner boys" accompanied by peals of taunting laughter. The Africans took it stalwartly in their stride. We were confounded. Why was this country so different from its neighbours in East Africa? We were accustomed to Africans playing key roles in the motor trade, schools, sport, administration and even piloting planes. We learned that Northern Rhodesian Africans were also very bitter against Welensky and "the Federation" of the three States, N.Rhodesia, S.Rhodesia and Malawi. The independence struggle was 'in the air'.

We headed out to the edge of town in the dark to seek a camping spot for the night. We found a pleasant short grassy area and set up the bivouac then returned to the city lights to glory in fish and chips! We agreed that Northern Rhodesia wasn't such a bad place after all.

The dawn rush for the bushes was thwarted by the absence of bushes as far as we could see into the mist. We took turns to look away, lit a cooking fire with a bundle of dry twigs from our boot, and cooked breakfast with eggs and bacon, purchased from the town. As the sun rose and burnt off the mist we were stunned to find ourselves on the Broken Hill Girls Secondary School hockey pitch! We did not fancy the prospect of being accosted by hockey stick waving girls shouting at us in a South African dialect and we were on the road by 8:00 a.m., heading for Mpika some 350 miles north albeit on a corrugated murram road surface, but happily, departing from three very disagreeable countries.

We stopped for a snack at midday and discovered that we had a slight brake fluid leak. We decided that since there was no traffic we would leave it until Mbeya, not that we had much choice. We hammered on along the straight featureless murram road for hour after hour of "mindless monotony". Then suddenly it wasn't. Cicely was driving while I dozed. We were doing about sixty-five mph, brakeless, down-hill, when I sensed danger. The road was narrowing towards a single track wooden bridge. Cicely's nodding navigator stirred, and thought, *we mustn't miss that bridge; no swerving, or skidding, or we'll hit the side rails.*

With only 100 yards to go, and panic mounting, I was suddenly alert and calculating, "Steer ... Steer". I needed to pressurise her not to be distracted by trying to change-down, grab the hand brake or otherwise lose concentration. "Steer ... Steer".

We plummeted onto the decking, springs sagging under the load, and then rocketed out onto the welcome up-slope the other side. Huge sigh of relief all round. For years after that whenever I was, habitually, a bit slow in answering a question, "Do you want tea or coffee Brian?" "Er..." the boys would murmur, "Steer... Steer."

Petrol was a problem over such long distances. Our petrol became low and unfortunately we hadn't found a store that sold jerry cans. We hoped to reach Mpika to refuel, but the car was doing only about twenty miles to the gallon. We then, luckily, met a road grader with a white driver! He was levelling the corrugations. Levelling the road was a necessary activity otherwise vehicles would be shaken to bits. He generously supplied us with a lifesaving gallon of petrol for £2.00 to get us to Mpika. We found a hand pump there owned by an Indian and filled our tank to the cap. We stayed at the Crested Crane overnight. The hotel was 'crawling' with white Northern Rhodesian Police carrying Sten guns. They advised us "don't hang about, leave promptly in the morning and stop for nothing until Isoka." They said the Lumpa Sect uprising was in full swing in the miombo forests.

9th September 1964: After some two weeks and thousands of miles including six hundred miles of monotonous miombo woodland and dust, we crossed the Tanzania border at Tunduma and waved an emotional goodbye to the Union Jack fluttering over the office. It was easy to see why there was a complete separation of culture, trade and language between these two countries, added to which Tippu Tip and his slave traders had cleared the Northern Province of Northern Rhodesia of people. A trail of mango trees follow the route south from Tanzania, said to have been brought there by Arab slavers from the East African coast, spitting out the stones en-route.

We emerged into bright sunshine, and the glorious scenery of the Songwe Valley approaching Mbeya. The roads over the remaining sixty miles or so were very rough, maintained by labourers with shovels and farm tractors trailing brushes, but the welcome air of happy people made up for that. We had covered 3,600 miles since disembarkation from RMS Windsor Castle. Apart from the brake fluid leakage possibly precipitated by the vibration of travelling fast over corrugations in the road surface, the car had done well.

Back at our quarters in Mbeya we felt a sense of achievement, and escape from the troubled south. Cliff Richards was all the rage singing a song about Going on a Summer Holiday; well we felt like that, once we arrived. Since then we have always been emotionally transported back to Mbeya when hearing that sunny song.

The drive up to Mbeya had cost me only £28 in petrol, plus Tanzania Import Duty.

Chapter Three

In The Mountains with Elephants, and Wool Sheep

9th September 1964: Back again in the coolness of Mbeya, in the Southern Highlands, we had been allocated a beautiful government house on the slopes of Loleza Mountain with a fabulous balcony view of 'old Africa'; *Wasafwa* villages and cultivated gardens with a distant backdrop of Mporoto volcanic mountains. There were lovely flowering trees below us and a garden water furrow to grow strawberries and roses. The servants' quarters were good by African standards. Expatriates were expected to provide domestic employment, and Samson Emele, whom we continued to employ from our previous tour, was a talented cook of the Mt Kilimanjaro *Wachagga* tribe. He had his wife with him, but his children remained behind. Tribal languages were still the lingua franca amongst the female gender and their children, hence the desire for them to remain at school in their homelands under the care of their grandparents. My surveyors were from all over Tanzania as per the presidential ethos, hence many tribal languages, but they all were fluent in English and Kiswahili from their Primary School education.

Our 'Tanganyika boiler' was separate structure in the garden utilising a 45 gallon oil drum, bricked round to allow the burning of eucalyptus wood beneath the drum. Eucalyptus burns green and the Forest Department planted extensive woodlands in colonial times for the township's fuel supplies for cooking. Our electricity came from a hydro-electric scheme, as is the case all over Africa, so no carbon-emissions problems in Africa. Township Africans preferred cooking with charcoal using the 'barola' which is a simple metal container with holes in the bottom and a long wire sling with which to swing the device to create draught for the charcoal. This produces more heat than wood.

Unlike the tropical coastal region with its palm, mango, and avocado trees, and its stiflingly high humidity, Mbeya town was beautified by streets of purple flowering Jacaranda trees, and its temperate climate allowing us to grow strawberries, potatoes and roses in the garden. The High Street was dominated by the beautiful Anglican Church. The pervasive influence of Arab/Islamic culture of the coastal regions was completely absent from Mbeya. The upper levels of the town carried the government offices, the Golf Club, the Courthouse, hospital and school, whilst Indian *dukas,* or shops, and the market, occupied the middle strata. The throbbing African township, spread across the lower levels with many streets of concrete block built houses slowly replacing the temporary dwellings of immigrants as they gained employment. Sultry evenings on our balcony imbibing a cool bottle of locally brewed Tusker Lager, which sported on its label an elephant's head to signify its power-giving qualities, was always accompanied by distant rhythmic drumming from the African township. It has to be said, quite a romantic setting for our two soul-mates Cicely and Brian to enjoy.

We were so happy to be back in Tanzania. Mbeya is the capital of the Southern Region, unique in the world for its magnificent, dynamic landscapes and wildnesses, its vast inland lakes, rift valley plains, towering mountains and volcanoes. Mbeya was created in the year that I was born, 1928, to service the Chunya Gold Rush economy, and to support local coffee farmers. Mbeya at 5,576 feet altitude (Mt Snowdon in Wales is 3,560 ft) is sited at the junction of two rift valleys, the Western and the Central, which are low lying at about 2,500 feet altitude, flanked by mountain peaks reaching 9,709 feet on Kitulo Plateau. The volcanoes also carry lakes, Masoko is said to be two kilometres deep, and Rungwe one kilometre wide, contrasting with the shallow soda lake in Rukwa rift valley which dries up at seven year intervals in accordance with the rainfall cycle. Rukwa Lake supports a prosperous Tilapia fishing industry, and is famous for its bird life, its crocodiles and hippos, and the fact that David Livingstone's body was carried across it "on foot" en route for Zanzibar in 1873. The Central Rift Valley, called Usangu is hot and rainless but carries the Ruaha River springing from the high rainfall mountain regions nearby. There is therefore a great diversity of climate within a short distance of Mbeya and hence also in vegetation complexes; from the dry plains of Usangu to the dense rain forest of Rungwe volcano, where can be seen the rarest monkey in Africa, locally named *Kipunji*. This strange monkey has long hair and lives in the tree tops like Sykes Blue, feeding on fruit and vegetable matter. Strangely its DNA has been found by researchers recently to be closer to baboon than monkey.

We enjoyed the Golf Club, the Caledonian Society Scottish dancing every Thursday, swimming in the lakes, trout fishing in mountain streams like Kiwire, and of course the endless attraction of flower bedecked mountain walking. To get into the teaming game and wildfowl shooting on Usangu, one had to make a weekend of it with tent and water carriers. The town is now sustained by African local farming, Arabica coffee and tea plantations, which all profitably utilise the volcanic fertile soils surrounding its location and by some mining activity for gold, niobium and travertine.

Cicely soon had her domestic staff working "no harder than farm workers do in England," she said. She did not subscribe to the gossip about Africans being 'an idle lot', "They are no different to the rest of the human race, and they will follow by example and respond to incentive. If the boss is an idle lay-about they'll sit under the tree in the shade when he's not around."

Since in 1963 Mbeya School was closed down in favour of creating an Agricultural Research Station, financed by the Swedish Government apparently, our boys had been transferred to Arusha School. The British Government's assurances, that we would have no problems with education, were certainly called to question. The Tanzania Government could only afford one national school accommodating European children to the required standard and employing British teachers, so the time had come for our two boys to again face the three-day bus journey to the boarding school at Arusha on the Kenya border in the north. Cicely and I now had to accustomise ourselves to a semi-childless life at the age of 36, in the name of Overseas Aid. Cicely's tears were assuaged by the departing Richard, aged 12, saying, "You are the best Mum in the world," as he waved goodbye and boarded the local bus, with Philip and half a dozen other children, for the 240 miles journey to Iringa, where they would meet the Arusha school bus which would then take them the remaining 450 miles of their journey. We sat together, holding hands, on our balcony, gazing silently at the distant Mporoto Mountains shimmering in the warm sun, listening to distant voices of people going about their businesses in crowded fields below. A gentle refreshing breeze curled the leaves on the tall eucalyptus trees. "My three children are what my life is all about, Brian. Please remind me why are we here?"

The British Government had allocated eleven million pounds to Tanzania in an Aid Package for developing African agriculture as opposed to the European farming of the colonial times. In 'today's money' this is about £190−£200 million of taxpayers money, a very significant sum. A body named the Rural Settlement Commission was to control the disbursement of this money, using private sector staff where necessary and avoiding the 'red tape' hindrances of the Civil Service. Its executive agency was called the Village Settlement Agency, the VSA. I very much approved of this means of bringing about realistic development. This was "why we are here, Cicely." She was not enamoured with my explanation.

The VSA was now my employer and the Matwiga Settlement Scheme that I had set up for the *Wanyakusa* people, who had been recalled from the gold mines of the Republic of South Africa, under President Nyerere's anti-Apartheid sanctions policy, during my previous tour was now under the VSA and enjoying OXFAM aid and World Food Programme, WFP, free food in year one. As an ex-farmer I well understood why any government department such as Agriculture, could not provide the hands-on drive so necessary for setting up and managing the establishment of land development schemes, designed to increase food production.

There was a small private commercial Virginia tobacco farm near Matwiga which was also to be taken over by VSA, enlarged, and to be settled with African family farmers; by me! This farm was called Lupa Tinga Tinga. It was situated in total isolation in the miombo forests using the Lupa River for irrigation. The Kiswahili Tinga Tinga was derived from the sound of the farm tractor; as they used to sound.

I had already secured local political support for a school, health centre, water wells and transport. The reliable rainfall and sandy granitic soils were ideal for quality Virginia tobacco, a valuable export crop at that time. Instead of a colonial style expatriate farmer with hundreds of acres of tobacco, my plan was for hundreds of farmers with one acre each, plus social services and marketing. This was in line with the new government's socialist strategy.

It was now my much relished task to get these two schemes firmly established together with the Wool Sheep Scheme plan for the uninhabited Kitulo Plateau, situated at 8–9,000 ft altitude, which was to be financed by the United Nations Development Programme, UNDP, all up and running by New Year 1965, then to await my further orders.

We noticed a significant increase in the prevalence of Peace Corps girls in Mbeya "and more to come" it was said at the Golf Club "up to 49" in total. Africans in Mbeya market began shouting at Cicely and me "Go home Yankee". This phrase was also heard on the radio. We felt that Peace Corps days were numbered. To us, these girls, mostly teachers, seemed slovenly, dressing like Africans and trying to carry their shopping on their heads. Africans had no respect for people who pretended to affiliate themselves with the same tribe as they were; African aspirations were to elevate their culture to a modern, united, educated, nation, and to escape from their primitive past; not to cultivate it. It was said at the Golf Club, "These girls, between bites of US Aid free food and handfuls of medication tablets, preach democracy and sleep with the *Wanyeje*." The latter refers to an element of the loose living, sexually rampant, young African male, prevalent in the townships.

Before they left for Arusha School, our two boys had collected our black Cocker Spaniel, Sally, from the Reverend Canon Wooley. Despite our efforts to impress upon him the facts of life when we left, Sally appeared with nine puppies! Our boys, being sons of a farmer, expressed no sentiment when I explained that I was too busy to set up a kennels business and eight would have to be 'put down'. "You can choose which one to keep," I had said. The remaining puppy was duly named Totty after its woolly resemblance to its poodle father. When our American anthropologist friends Dr Bill and Barbara Garland came down for the weekend from Matamba, near the Kitulo plateau, Barbara went barmy over Totty's sweet nature, "She's so cute I could die, just die."

The Reverend was also captivated. He announced his impending marriage and return to England, so we gave them Totty for a wedding present. Taking Totty to England, with quarantine regulations would be very costly, so the Parishioners campaigned to raise money for the Vicar. Totty must have been popular with the Vicar's flock, since £200 was raised.

Route Map, Mbeya Region and Oxfam Safari

Cicely was now busying herself unpacking our many crates from the government store, albeit solemnly grief-stricken at the temporary loss of her children – "Not long until Christmas, I suppose," she plaintively said. Nothing seemed to stand still, however, in our lives. Sure enough, a rather ancient Land Rover Station Wagon clattered into our drive one evening. A short stocky, affable gentleman, hair bleached and face tanned by the sun, emerged with a grin, and a curly pipe in the corner of his mouth, which conveyed an image of contemplative comfort. He had piercing blue eyes which took in every detail – a man of the bush.

"I'm Steve Stephenson. I was directed here by the members at the Golf Club. They told me that a certain Brian Dawtrey was out in the bush a lot and might know where to find elephants. Do I have the right person?" he enquired with a knowing grin.

"Yes, indeed," I said. "You are welcome. Fancy a Tusker?"

We occupied the veranda and watched the sun sinking towards the Rukwa rift valley where elephants roamed. We picked up on Steve's Tukuyu background. "Well, Brian, I had a career as the District Commissioner, but, as expected, am now Africanized, so I need to sell some ivory to tide me over until I can get some other employment, hopefully as a Game Warden. I have no intention of leaving Tanzania."

I should mention here that in 1964 elephants were still a major problem everywhere for village food producers and it was government policy to reduce their numbers wherever possible and especially where they were 'crop raiding'.

Steve entertained us by telling us about the old German 'Boma' in Tukuyu. A Boma is a defensive and administrative HQ. Tanzania was initially a German colony and the country was the setting for a number of little known but bloody battles during the First World War. Steve said that his Great War German opposite number used to listen to plotters in other rooms via the plumbing system which linked up all quarters. When he had a confidential meeting, he put the plug in the bath to avoid secrets being overheard elsewhere in the Boma through the plumbing.

We soon learned that Steve was an experienced bush-wallah, and was fascinated by wild elephants, wild bush country, and wild lovers. He and I were of one accord in that respect. He was obviously a character who preferred the challenge of survival in the bush to the refinements of Mbeya society, a man of few words and firm resolve. Well; me too. His wife had given up on him and returned to England in search of a more civilised culture. How lucky was I that Cicely had not similarly given up on me! So far! I then explained to him that my Njerenje Unemployed Resettlement Scheme; part of government strategy to cope with unemployment in urban townships and to boost food production, was plagued by elephant crop-raiders, from Mbeya Range Mountains. We agreed to spend the coming weekend investigating the situation.

In the early 1960s elephants were in great abundance everywhere; reliable statistics indicate an Africa-wide population of six million, and elephant control was a primary feature of colonial rule. The pre-independence Game Warden in Mbeya, George Rushby, a renowned elephant hunter by profession, was ordered to kill 200 elephants per year as a condition of his civil service appointment. He was told that if he failed to achieve this number, his retirement pension would be in jeopardy. Unfortunately by the Millennium the Africa-wide elephant population had fallen to six hundred thousand and the price of a good-sized tusk had risen from £100 in 1964 to £20,000 in 2000 AD. A TV film was made about George Rushby's exploits with the man-eating lions of Njombe and Usangu Plains, near Mbeya.

The mountains were engulfed in an early rains threat, resulting in an inferno of lightning and cannonading as Steve and I sat by the camp fire in Njerenji considering an early 'attack' on the nearby mountain fortress of *Loxodonta Africana,* on the morrow.

My plan was to get some photographs of elephant in their truly wild habitat, carrying a 9.3 mm Mauser rifle for emergencies, whilst Steve's ambition was to kill a large 'tusker' bull elephant. He aspired to own the 'ultimate weapon', he told me, a Rigby double barrelled .577 inch, or 14.7 mm, calibre rifle, but, he said, was 'making do' with a .475 inch, or 12 mm, Jeffrey, firing steel jacketed, round nosed bullets, a devastatingly powerful hard hitting weapon. We decided to take two porters to carry our rifles. There was considerable African scepticism that evening, that these two diminutive *Wazungu,* = Europeans, had the strength to chase elephant up those steep slopes and survive a downhill attack by three tons of fury. This opinion was orchestrated by more terrifying claps of thunder, from the mountain.

Some of my African surveyors were laughing loudly with a young *Msafwa* girl. Speaking in Kiswahili they were saying that they had surveyed dozens of girls all over the region during their work for the *Bwanapima,* which is Kiswahili for Surveyor, "You are the prettiest we have seen and we want to screw you in the bell tent."

Steve's Kiswahili was better than mine and he filled me in on the finer points of this discourse; "They'll keep on trying to seduce her, but they will not succeed. The *Wasafwa* prevent their girls from running off with men of neighbouring tribes, especially their neighbours the *Wanyakusa,* by circumcising the clitoris. It's a barbaric custom, especially the way they do it. It works though, you will see."

She told them she was betrothed and declined their overtures.

At dawn the sky was blue and we scanned the high ridges for elephant with binoculars. No sign. "I'll take you at your word Bwana, that there are elephants up there," said Steve, "we'll climb up to the right there and head back against the wind. We can chance going up without water, these trackers say there is good water on top and we will need to conserve every ounce of energy for that climb."

We found a shady tree and relaxed with binoculars. Suddenly Timothy, my Assistant, came running in a fervour of excitement, "I've found them, sir! Look at the sky over there, under that big white cloud."

I steadied myself against the tree, and yes; dozens of them, tiny at that distance, moving along the ridge, at 7,500 feet altitude, looking like giant weevils with their long proboscises. Doubtless they felt safe surrounded by seemingly unscalable slopes. Steve felt otherwise. Excitement in the village was immense. The headman offered us help with porters. He said that he thought the elephants did a circuit of some 600 miles during the year, going north through Chunya District, round eastwards to the vast Rungwa Game Reserve (now Ruaha National Park) and down southwards to Usangu Plains. He remarked that they had probably been doing this since before mankind was created. Unfortunately they would deviate during darkness to eat-out on the villager's bananas and maize, and kill any man who interfered with them.

We set off with our *Msafwa* tracker in the lead; he was a tall sinewy character, barefoot and wearing a *kikoy,* a sort of skirt. He carried my camera bag and Steve's canvass bag of ammunition, his pipe tobacco and 'rations'. The porters wore shorts, no shoes and the ubiquitous tatty status *Mzungu* vests. One carried Steve's rifle and an array of charms for protection against his most dreaded enemy, the elephant, the other carried my rifle. We set off, somewhat jauntily led by Steve in baggy trousers, 'tackies', or gym shoes − no socks, a khaki bush shirt, and a berry. Steve's light attire was matched by mine, with the exception of my shorts and long socks and a bush hat. This was how we survived solar and body overheating, but still more clothing that any African considered was necessary. I was well short of Steve in leg muscle and reserve strength as I soon painfully discovered! I had to fall back on my agility and tenacity to keep up with him and the Africans. Those slopes tested my slight stature to the limits of endurance and to a degree beyond my previous experience, even in the infantry.

Elephant hunting is quite different to other forms of hunting, involving a great deal of emotional fortitude, strength, endurance and cool courage. The hunt is always strenuous and hazardous;

trekking long distances from dawn until dusk, pushing through thicket, tall grass, swamp and in this case, up 45 degree slopes. The hunter has to get very close to his quarry for a hard enough hit and if the elephant challenges him, then, only swift and deadly accuracy can save the hunter's life.

We climbed hour after hour, lungs burning with carbon dioxide; there being less oxygen at seven thousand feet, as the sun rose and bounced its heat against us from the surrounding yellow grass. "They know the easiest way up don't they; see how their trails rise zig-zag, at a gentle angle to the contour," I said to Steve hoping to halt him for a minute's breather. "Presumably, if they had sensed us they would have gone straight up? Or maybe big tuskers couldn't do that without getting their tusks stuck in the bank?"

"Trouble is with following these zig-zag tracks, it will take too long – we had better cut straight up." insisted Steve.

We continued at a cracking pace up to a narrow, rocky ridge. We found spoor and looked across. Not a sign of elephant as far as we could see, in any direction. We took advantage of the shade of a small tree. I found myself trembling with fatigue, my lungs felt like bursting.

"It looks as though we shall have to cross the next valley, nothing this side. How do you feel, Brian? It means going down about 2000 ft and up again. We can probably get a drink down there though; see those fig trees? There'll be water there."

"Oh!" I said cheerlessly, "no problem." My heart sank. We sat for a full three minutes! A gentle breeze drifted up the slopes lifting a pair of buzzards up to about 10,000 ft. Pointing upwards I said, "I wish we could use their technique to spot the herd."

Steve lit his pipe. "We had better move on."

We scrambled easily down to the valley bottom and sat on the green grass in the coolness of the shady fig trees, consuming Steve's patent for relief of fatigue, a tin of green peas, and one tin each! Never tasted such delicious green peas! The two African porters declined a taste. As we ascended the next murderous slope, the heat added enormously to the stress of the climb. I could understand why we needed porters to carry our rifles and my camera bag.

As we dragged ourselves onto the second narrow ridge we were enthralled to see beyond and below a great herd. They were spread out amidst broken trees, rocks and scattered shrubs; the vegetation was devastated; reminding me of those First World War pictures from Flanders. Grass fires had made the area black. The herd were all ages, but no big tuskers. I had been right about that. We counted 45 elephants before spotting another group right beneath us; just one family of graduated sizes; ideal for a photograph as they came up from the water hole. From our vantage point, we were immune from any attacking matriarch, so we settled down to some fascinating viewing of the day-to-day affairs of elephant family life; teasing, playing, mock charging, gambolling in the muddy patch at the spring, breaking branches and swishing them about like fly whisks.

A wind shift later alerted them to our presence and producing an electrifying turbulence. They took up defensive battle stations, with perimeter guards, scouts and children centred. We left them to settle and headed back to camp. Steve wanted to try again next weekend! "There'll probably be other herds further along."

Next Saturday: "I have no idea what time we'll get back on Sunday night, Cicely, don't worry." I shouted as we pulled out of the driveway in Steve's old Land Rover. We had our cook Samson in the back this time; he had pestered me all week to join the elephant safari; he was fascinated by giants, he being so very small himself.

By the camp fire with my African surveyors that evening, I pulled Samson's leg, "*Samson, Huko ju,*" I pointed to the mountain top, "*tembo ni kubwa sana! Wewe ni fupi sana. Labda tembo kanyaga wewe. Halafu nini! Bwana nja ...*" Swahili phrases can be fun to bandy about. "Samson, up there, the elephants are very big. You are only a very small. Perhaps an elephant might tread on you. Then what! Bwana starves ..." This was the lead up to telling him that he must remain behind and prepare food for our return.

Sunday: At dawn, we began the slog up to that same high ridge and then turned left, this time, towards Rukwa Valley and the lower end of the range. We trekked miles through golden grass with a sheer drop either side.

We spotted another herd below to the right, across a valley, and studied them with binoculars. Yes, there was the white glint of bull ivory. Down and down we slid, then across and up, then down again. We came to a long gentler slope of unburnt 4 ft high grass, with scattered trees. After 300 yards uphill trek we paused and distinctly heard rumblings over the ridge ahead. Pulses raced. "That's them!" whispered Steve, shaking his stocking of wood ash to test the wind, to make sure we remained downwind of our prey. "See that shady tree just below the ridge? Let's make a dash for it. Ready?"

We crouched beneath the tree gasping for oxygen and signalled our two porters to pass the rifles. We loaded and handed them back. I set my camera and telephoto lens ready for use, expecting that we would have to pursue the herd beyond the ridge some way yet. Steve hissed in my ear, "Look! They are coming this way!" Several elephants were browsing on the skyline, oblivious of our presence. Steve shook his wood ash stocking again. "There's the bull! It looks about 70 to 80 pounds a side. He hasn't scented us. We've got a chance. These eddies are tricky. He won't see us – poor eyesight – fantastic sense of smell though." He shook his stocking again nervously.

"I will need to get much closer for a good picture, Steve."

"Oh he's too far for a shot anyway. You ready? Right, let's go!"

We walked silently forward for about 100 yards, shaking the stocking. The herd were no longer visible to us. I whispered, "They've gone back over the top." We neared the top of the ridge with nerves tingling and hearts pounding as though facing a German Panzer Division on foot. The falling sun sat on the ridge now, a giant orange ball about 50 yards ahead. Suddenly, the bull loomed up above us with outspread ears, the red sun flooding his back and head with an alarming fiery glow. A high-pitched scream filled our consciousness, as he tucked his ears tight into his neck and with his trunk between his legs, "He's coming!" My heart began pounding heavily. I turned to reach for my rifle. The porters had bolted; rifles and all!

The bull came upon us with terrifying velocity, gleaming tusks foremost. Our life-time expectancy suddenly fell to a few seconds. We turned and raced after our porters then swung left into the longer grass. As luck would have it, the porters did the same thing and we all stumbled into a heap, grabbing the rifles. The bull swung in our direction, dust and fury pouring out of him, range; 45 yards; 40 yards; 35 yards. He silently concentrated his killing power, at a trot now; 30 yards; 25 yards; 20 yards; 15. Steve seemed to be right underneath him from where I stood. At 40 yards, my finger had frozen on the camera button, but now the camera was in the grass and my Mauser foresight somewhere on the crinkly grey skin. I hardly dared close one eye. A shot rang out echoing across the hills, the bull's head jolted upwards, he hesitated, turned and ran back towards the ridge, with Steve in hot pursuit. He fired again. The bull was gone. Neither shot seemed effective, beyond quelling murderous intent.

Steve's face was ashen. "My God! Two bloody awful shots. The first one lodged in skull tissue, nowhere near the brain, my second shot; probably the kidney. We can't leave the poor sod like that. We'll have to trail him. Did you get your picture?"

"Picture? You kidding? He was too close for a telephoto shot. I grabbed the Mauser. Reminded me of a Spitfire attacking out of the sun."

"We had better find our two 'aides' – it's getting late."

We pressed on for half an hour in failing light, before spotting the herd in the distance. The bull was there amongst them, but trailing behind and looking weak. We pursued what was now an 'errand of mercy' with the utmost speed. We got to within 75 yards before the sun disappeared.

"It's now or never. A side shot to the heart, carefully aimed."

A single shot echoed away to the mountain peaks and the bull collapsed. Several females gathered around and struggled to lift him, then bolted.

The porters burst into frenzied dancing on top of the corpse. In contrasting silence, Steve and I stood either side of the giant corpse and scrutinised each other's expression. There was an unspoken regret. We knew then, that neither of us would ever kill another elephant.

Note: In 1962, the elephant population of Tanzania was estimated to be 360,000. The Game Department killed 3,000 shamba-raiding elephants that year and there was as yet no need for anxiety over declining populations. However, in 1986 the Tanzania Government confiscated 3,283 tusks from poachers and by 1989 the elephant population was thought to be little over 100,000 with a projected extinction by 1996. In 2014 the figures reported for the two biggest Reserves, were 12,000 for the vast Selous Game Reserve and 4,000 for the Ruaha N.P. The market price for raw ivory in 1964 was £1 per pound, only double that of 1864, but in 2015 the price has reached £400 per pound and climbing. Sadly, despite the worldwide ban on the ivory trade, poaching remains a huge threat to the future of the elephant; one tusk providing an income to the poacher equal to anything he can earn in a lifetime in any other trade.

Brian later became a Chairman of the Wildlife Conservation Society of Zambia and Steve became the first National Park Warden of Ruaha N.P and then Mikumi N.P.

Monday: We staggered into Njerenji camp at 3:45 a.m. Did Samson have a welcoming pot on the boil for tea? *Hakuna! "Wapi Samson?"* There was a Samsonite snore from the bell tent. I felt dehydrated and exhausted, then annoyed. I fired a shot over the bell tent, which brought a dramatic response, not only from the incumbent snorer but from the whole village. We were suddenly the centre of a crowd of babbling *Wasafwa*, elated by our porters' dialogue of events in the mountains. Buckets of *pombe,* home brewed beer, appeared and were placed before us. We expressed a dislike for the cardboard flavour and someone produced mead, which was nectar to us thirsty souls. Mead is made from honey which is more pleasant but however much more alcoholic. Soon traditional dancing, *ngoma,* began and lasted all night.

With empty stomachs, the alcohol quickly reached our deprived blood cells. With the throb of drums and the inaudible bell of time passing, the night ended with the sun rising out of the distant Rungwe volcano in the East towards Mbeya. It suddenly dawned on me that Cicely was expecting us back yesterday. We hurriedly arranged for the *Jumbe* to organise his people to climb up to the bull and cut out his tusks in exchange for the meat. Would they go so far, we wondered. My surveyors agreed to bring down the tusks and feet to my house.

The Hunters' Return: As we swung the Land Rover into our driveway and pulled up at the house, Cicely came down the veranda steps above us like that bull elephant, furious, head down and scolding finger to the fore. She lived up to her reputation, 'a ball of fire'. We rather fell-out of the Land Rover. Samson slipped quietly out of the back and disappeared to the *shamba* house. Cicely had spent a sleepless night convinced that we had come to grief, instead, here we were reeking of *pombe*, entranced by African drums and not too steady on our feet either. Furthermore we possessed no tangible evidence that we had been elephant hunting at all. Steve had the brilliant idea to resolve all injustices, "Brian, get her to sniff the smoky barrels." We were treated to a delicious breakfast. Steve muttered to me before leaving, "Quite a weekend!"

On Tuesday a message came from my survey staff at Njerenji that scores of *Wasafwa* men, women and children had climbed the mountain and apparently, battled their way into the inside of the beast with *pangas*, the African machete. In their frenzy to get at the meat some injuries were incurred. They brought the meat down to the village – no tusks.

On Wednesday the tusks arrived in our garden, 98 lbs each. Everyone wanted their photographs taken with this ancient symbol of Africa. Cicely and I admired nature's bounty but we found the four feet that arrived with them rather sinister. Elephant foot coffee tables were popular at the time, though not with Brian and Cicely.

"I'll get them scraped out for curing in case anyone wants them. I think it's undignified for such a king of the beasts – a bit like John the Baptist!" Cicely recoiled and went indoors. Samson and his wife Magdalena ate the scrapings.

The Kitulo Plateau, 8-9,000 ft. altitude: Soil pit descriptions were required by Tengeru Agricultural Research Station as a routine procedure for all development projects. The pits, dug by my staff were 6 ft. deep, grave size. I jumped in with tape measure and sample bags whilst Cicely sat above me, doing her 'heavenly scribe' bit. Kitulo soil profiles are unique, being colourful layers of yellow pumicious wind-blown ash between layers of dark top soil, registering intervals between Rungwe's volcanic eruptions. The profile is like a giant marzipan cake and highly water absorbent, like a sponge in the sky. Below it I found peridotite rock which is bright green and crystalline, said to be from sixty kilometres below. This fascinating vast plateau is the source of the mighty Ruaha and Rufiji Rivers that feed half of Tanzania and in my humble opinion was that this sponge in the sky, should not be 'meddled with' by politicians seeking to plough up this fertile soil for wheat production to 'feed the nation'. This was done successfully at Upper Kitete in the northern mountains near Ngorogoro, but the geomorphology and the geographical situation there is completely different.

The following day Cicely and I drove across unknown Downs-like landscape, far to the west side of the plateau. There were no motor tracks and surprisingly, no cattle either. We were told it was called Sinyangama and proved to be totally unutilised for crops or grazing. We turned back and soon afterwards noticed a small tent in a valley plus a Land Rover. It was most unusual to see anyone camping in this area. As we approached a young, stocky, man appeared. He introduced himself very formally, "I'm Massey, Hides and Skins, Mbeya."

"Pleased to meet you, Massey. Brian and Cicely, Land Planning Officer." We felt like Livingstone and Stanley in that desolate place. "Oh, is this your wife?" I asked on noticing a female companion emerging from the tent.

"Er, no, Ruth's a friend; Peace Corps. She has been off wandering this last four hours. I've been dead worried. I found her on the southern escarpment above Lake Malawi. She's exhausted."

"It can be very tiring at this altitude and very cold at night too. I'm surprised you survived in that little tent. How did you keep warm?"

"We both slept in the same bag," said Massey with a grin.

"That rifle in your Land Rover looks like a .375. Are you looking for buffalo?"

"Hopefully. I didn't want to leave it in Mbeya though in case of theft."

"You are new here, Massey, I would mention that the law says you must not shoot within 15 yards of your vehicle. There are some sharp Game Wardens about. Anyway you won't find buffalo in these mountains. If you come to my office in Mbeya, I will tell you where you can find them."

As an Honorary Game Warden, with full government gazetted executive powers over 'game' hunters, I liked to keep tracks of where they were operating so that I could ensure their legality, and that the calibre of their weapons is appropriate to the size of their quarry. This is something that the authorities in Britain have yet to catch up on, and seem to be quite happy to permit the extreme cruelty of shooting foxes and badgers with shot guns.

Kitulo plateau landscape is a treeless pasture, akin to the English South Downs but with more herbs than grass. The dynamic show of native flora in the rainy season hails from Adam and Eve, since the area has never been disturbed by the African hoe. I was concerned that it should remain so for posterity and intended to recommend National Park status in my report. However, my instructions from the Ministry of Rural Development were to plan for economic development using wool sheep and wheat. African sheep have no fleece for obvious reasons and would not survive the cold wet weather of Kitulo Plateau with night temperatures below zero Centigrade for 95 nights in the dry season, which of course would be no problem for wool sheep from temperate climates like Australia or Wales. Commercial mutton production would find a prosperous market and a boost to the economy. Dairy cattle would obviously do well and supply the townships for a cash return.

However, the agriculture department had instructed me to do wheat growing trials. These had been going on for some time managed by Field Officer Tim Harvard and VSO Dick Brown. The 6 ft of annual rainfall on the Kitulo plateau would certainly cause soil erosion under wheat cultivation, hence the need for contour bunding, in other words banking soil up into ridges along the contour to trap the run-off. My surveyors were there to peg the contours with their Dumpy-levels whilst Dick Brown used the disc plough to set them up. Periodically, I jumped on our farm tractor and took a turn at this job. My African senior surveyor, Brown Mwabulambo, was astonished that I could turn my hand to so many skills and muttered something about the *Bwanapima,* being an *mganga* – witch doctor. One of my ambitions in life had always been to train young people to be competent performers, not simply academics. Over the ensuing days I instructed the surveyors in how to drive the tractor and set up a disc plough.

Ultimately the wheat trials thankfully, from my perspective, proved a failure. Something we hadn't thought of; frosty nights at flowering time meant no grain in the ears. Trials with grass and legumes, however, went well.

Cicely was a person capable of turning her hand to anything from farming to teaching, and survival in wild places. She became handy with a wet fly in the Ndumbi stream that flowed past our workers' log cabin in the valley, as well as in the use of the Primus stove to cook the trout she caught. She was able to swim in the cold stream in her underwear in the evenings after our African staff, who would never stay overnight on the Kitulo for fear of ancestral spirits possessing their brains, had gone back down to Matamba. The *mganga;* decreed that "A land without spirits is no mans' land.". As Europeans, the *Wawanji* people declared us to be immune to their spiritual influences, but I have to say, we all suffered terrible nightmares and became very light-headed, tending to do crazy things such as, when Cicely and I were up there alone, we had climbed Mtorwi Peak 9709 feet, by the cabin, naked.

There were a few leopards in the mountains. Jumbe Solomon, the new political title replacing Chief, by order of the President, told us about the murderous *Wambuda* sect on the lower plateau who posed as leopards. They dressed in leopard skins and, claiming possession by Kitulo ancestral spirits, killed people in the villages who had committed social misdemeanours, especially of an extra-marital nature! When visiting our American anthropologist friends in Matamba on the way down from Kitulo, Dr Bill and Barbara Garland, we learned that an American nurse at Mpangala Medical Mission had been killed by an *Mbuda* leopard. The Chief's son apparently knew her, possibly too well.

Bill had arranged some *Wawanji* tribal dancing for us and we made recordings of their performance. I am not sure whether the word music is quite the right term for the accompaniment to the dancing. The ensemble comprised five men dressed in tatty trousers and holey vests, generating a somewhat plaintive sound by blowing over the tops of bamboo pipes, the sound, rather like blowing across the tops of bottles of various sizes. This sound was accompanied by beating out a rhythm on a corpulent drum, and a whining sonorous note emitted from a one-string fiddle made from a tea chest, the 'stem' being strung with a bicycle cable. These see-sawing, haunting, sounds somehow seemed to complement the backdrop of eerie mountains and cool breezes.

In Norfolk dreaming of Africa

RMS Windsor Castle arriving in Cape Town

Cicely riding nature's Corsair GT

In the Transkei

Forgot to pack our fishing rods!

Heading north east

Heading north

Stop-over in Wankie Game Reserve, Rhodesia

Surplus Maize in N. Rhodesia

The Great North Road, N.Rhodesia to Tanzania

640 miles to go

Our lovely government house in Mbeya, Tanzania

The people are free this side of the border

Hello we're back

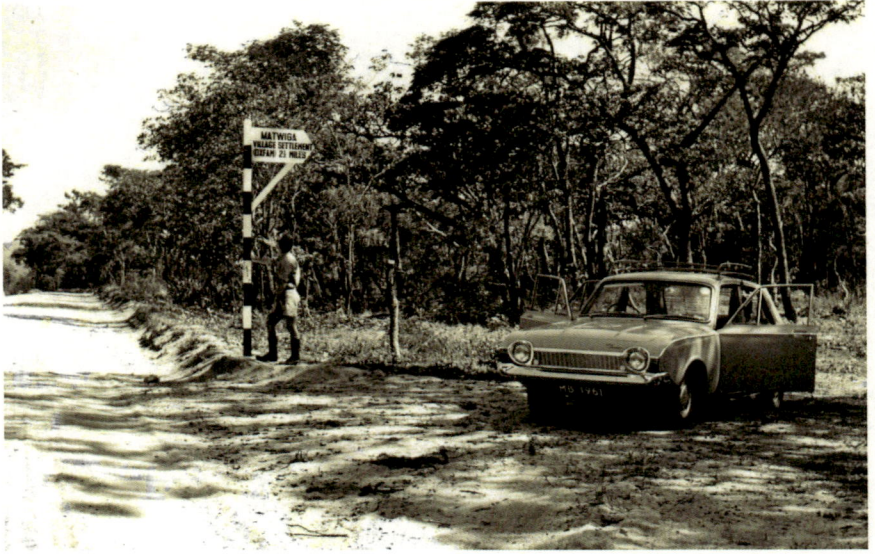

The road to Kipembawe, turn off to Matwiga

Matwiga new family settled in self-help house

Matwiga new farmer with his Turkish tobacco

Virginia tobacco growers at Lupa Tinga Tinga

Matwiga Tobacco nursery plots, with Jan Dreisson, Thomas Athumani, & Frank Rawe

Looking for elephants on top of Mbeya Range

Group alert

Up on top

65

Son Richard's anti-poaching poster

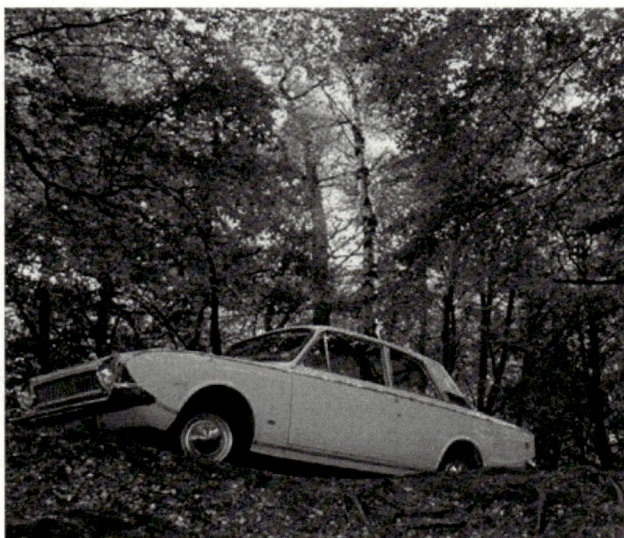

Climbing up to Kitulo Plateau

Cicely's self-help bridge on the Plateau

Crop trials at 9,000 ft

Frosty nights

Rungwe volcanic ash, geomorphic clock, soil pit profile

Wild clematopsis sp. At 9,000 ft alt.

Tim Harvard; "my garden" Kitulo

Cicely and Mike Pash 'under the influence' at 9,000 ft altitude

Wawanji dancers, Dr Bill Garland and Brian

Chapter Four

Usangu: Teeming With Wildlife

October 1964: We received a message to say our two boys had arrived safely at Arusha School, a 38-hour bus journey from Mbeya, a month ago! Two teenagers remained in Mbeya, Peter and Betty MacDougall. They pleaded with us to take them on safari at the weekend. Betty promised to do the cooking and Peter dubiously declared himself to be a crack shot with a .22 rifle and would get us a Guinea Fowl for Betty to cook. We fell for it, after all who would want to spend the weekend socialising at the golf club? Cicely would.

"Now, you two," quoth I, the *Bwanamkubwa*, 'Mr Big', "there is always a measure of risk associated with trekking in the wilderness. Usangu Plains are uninhabited. I've got a Royal Geographical Society report in my drawer, telling us what to expect, I'll just fetch it."

"Here we are. It's by an adventurer named H.L. Pritchard describing Tanganyika for intrepid explorers, like you two. It dates back to 1918, but things haven't changed that much really on Usangu Plains; no AA Rescue, no telephones, no ambulance service, no roads, no petrol, and there ARE lions and elephants." I proceeded to read my authentic copy:

'Imagine a country three times the size of Germany, mostly covered by dense bush with no roads, only two railways and either sweltering under a tropical sun or swept by torrential rain that makes the friable soil impassable to wheeled traffic, a country with wide and swampy areas interspersed with arid areas where water is often more precious than gold, in which man rots with malaria and suffers torments from insect pests; in which animals die wholesale from the ravages of the tsetse fly; where crocodiles and lions seize unwary porters; giraffes destroy telegraph lines; elephants damage tracks; hippopotami attack boats; rhinoceros charge troops on the march and even put whole battalions to flight.'

"There you have it. We've got one advantage; we've got a Ford Corsair GT. So, are you up for it?"

Two fists were raised in the air – "Yes!"

The following weekend we set off with one jerry can of petrol and one of water duly strapped to the Corsair roof rack. At 9:00 a.m. we arriving at the turn off from the main Iringa road for Usangu and headed for the mud-brick house which I knew was owned by a hermit type of character known as Japanese de Villiers. He had slant eyes, shiny black straight hair and olive brown skin, in other, African, words, he was a Coloured, being mixed race. Because of this he was ostracised by black society, and lived alone. His genetic origins were a total mystery to everyone, including himself. We stopped and awaited his appearance. Did the Japanese or Chinese ever inhabit East Africa in the past, as they do today? Some historians think so.

Cicely turned to the children and asked, "That name de Villiers … do you do English history at your Nairobi school? What do you know about King Charles II in about 1660?" Cicely enlightened them, "He was a notorious womaniser, it is said that he had seventeen illegitimate children. Well, his favourite mistress was a woman named Barbara de Villiers. She must have been really good at her trade because she became a millionaire and the King made her the Duchess of Castlemaine, with vast estates." Concluding her story she added, "Not that I am advocating extra-marital sex, but it certainly worked with Royalty in the time of the Tudors and Stuarts. In contrast; all Japanese de Villiers has got is his mud-brick house and the plot it stands on. He might have a black mistress, I suppose."

I tapped into this story, "Japanese does have a substantial estate you know; about 20,000 square miles! It's called Usangu Plains, and it provides him with free meat. He doesn't own it as such, of course; according to Japanese "it's God's country.""

At which point the man himself appeared, the 'Lord of Usangu', carrying a bush buck across his shoulders. As an Honorary Game Warden I had many times needed to get his response to some searching questions. He was always convincing as to the legality of his hunting activities and in any case he was no threat to conservation, in fact his knowledge about poaching was always useful, as for example when we apprehended two Texan Mission youths riding 'shot-gun' on a motorcycle, shooting at lions. Japanese told us where to find hundreds of zebra, so we set off with great enthusiasm trailing clouds of grey dust.

We reached Mkowiji River at mile 120 from Mbeya. It was deep enough to stall my car engine as we waded across; leaving us afloat, like a boat, something the Corsair was not designed for. We pushed it over to the far bank by which time the boot had filled with water and soaked everything including our bread. We made camp to let the engine dry out but no hope for the bread.

The darkness was noisy with animal calls, including the yawing of a male lion. We would have slept better if we had had the bell tent which we usually carried in the department Land Rover rather than just our mosquito nets slung in a tree. At dawn, we were embarrassed to find we were under observation, from on high. A troop of giraffes stared curiously down at us. Peter requested me to let him drive the car and chase off the intruders.

"Well there's not much traffic about these parts. Don't get too close though. It's happened before that a giraffe stepped on a car bonnet. It'd be a long walk home!"

We later found our zebras, looking fat as butter despite being on a grassless plain. We counted 175 reedbuck and 35 *Twiga,* Swa. Giraffe. Looking for elephants we found only a footprint in baked wet clay, deep as a garbage bin.

"We're a long way out, Brian," Cicely cautioned, "better look for elephants another time. I remember you said, rather rashly I thought, you would like to drive to Iringa, via the Usangu plains. Now THAT 250 mile trip would be a challenge for our Corsair! Us too." Looking at Peter and Betty she added, "Pity you two have got to go back to school!"

The prompt response was, "One day there will be a Game Warden named Peter MacDougall, you'll see!"

I said to the children, "We are not the first to contemplate crossing the Usangu Plains. There was an explorer named Captain J F Elton who in 1877 trekked his arduous way on foot, from Nyasaland, now Malawi, over the mountains of Kitulo, across Usangu on his way to Dodoma, and then Bagamoyo on the coast. He didn't make it. He is buried over that way, under a big baobab tree."

"I hope we don't run out of petrol, Mr Dawtrey, there are a lot of Baobabs round here!"

The Yugoslavs: Upon arrival back in Mbeya, our sojourn was short-lived. I received a message from the African Regional Commissioner Waziri Juma to say Yugoslavian Aid bulldozers had arrived at Lupa Tinga Tinga tobacco farm and I should go and show them what to do.

Cicely and I dashed off to the site, 185 miles away and beheld a giant steel ball taller than my hat, designed apparently to hold the huge anchor chain down when being hauled by two bulldozers, one each end, through the woodland thus felling the trees. The purpose of the giant ball was to keep the chain down from over-riding the trees before they are flat. My mind boggled at the thought of how on earth they had got that huge ball up to Lupa Tinga Tinga, 730 miles from Dar es Salaam? The Yugoslav 'boss' jabbered on at length about how they did it but I couldn't understand a word of it.

The burly Yugoslavs listened to me in glum silence. One spoke broken English and another broken Swahili, like me. This was their first experience with miombo woodland trees which have a 30 ft deep tap root to survive the mid-year drought. "It's like drawing wisdom teeth," one said. A big question mark loomed – did they have enough power?

Brian: The 'Battle of Lupa Tinga Tinga' commenced on the 21st October, my birthday, Trafalgar Day, it was not the British against the French this time it was the obdurate Yugoslavs versus the tenacious miombo woodland. I tried to explain to them some key principles to which they needed to adhere, including the basics of soil conservation, preserving the top soil, the need to windrow the fallen trees on the contour, following my surveyors' pegs and leaving tree belts to supply fuel for the tobacco curing barns. Cicely did her usual charismatic laughter raising routine, pretending to push the ball, placing my hat on the top of it and pretending the ball was like the '*Bwanapima*', aka me, unmovable at times. After some months the 'Battle' ended in a draw. The bulldozers proved unreliable and the ball too heavy, but they did half a job quite extensively. I suspected that the Yugoslavs enjoyed the wild 'bush' and some 'Red' game meat but, given the language barrier, I could not prove it.

The Germans: We made another attempt at enjoying our lovely home in Mbeya, hoping for a jolly weekend with Dr Bill and Barbara Garland the American anthropologists, down from

Matamba, in the mountains. The Public Works Department, better known as the PWD, had freshly decorated our house whilst we'd been away. We lounged on the veranda feeling good about the view of the Mporoto volcanoes and the stream tinkling below us watering the roses. The rainy season was approaching; the Eucalyptus trees below were raging and rolling menacingly against a background of black clouds and lightning flashes. It may not rain for a week or two yet but the mood was gloomy. This seemed to set the slightly built, usually chirpy Barbara into a reflective mood. She began to tell us about her background. She declared that she was really one of the hated "Deutsch" as the Africans still called the Germans.

The German East Africa Company began the process of colonising Tanzania in 1887 a process that ended when the Germans were dispossessed by a British invasion of the country in 1916. The three decades of German rule were notable for their brutality, disease epidemics and natural disasters. The catalogue of incidents included the introduction in 1891 of Indian cows, infected with rinderpest, a virulent killer disease, which spread and killed some 95% of the colony's cattle, causing huge hardship most notably to the Maasai tribe over half of whom died. Some years later, in 1905, the German mistreatment of plantation labourers, provoked what became to be known as the 'Maji Maji' rebellion. 'Maji' is the Swahili word for water, and the popular misconception amongst the tribe was that a certain magic potion could turn German bullets into water. Whilst for many rebels that unfortunately did not prove to be the case, it was the German 'scorched earth' policy, which led to the starvation of an estimated 250,000 'natives' that ended the rebellion. The Germans ruled this nation with the "kiboko", a hippo hide whip, as an effective persuader to recognise the benefits of hard work, the benefits to the Deutsch that is. Barbara likened the Germans to the *Wambuda* leopard killers of Kitulo. "The evil lies deep and the leopard cannot change its spots," she declared.

Barbara had been a child under the Nazi regime. "I used to see the Jews being beaten in the streets and their shops being ransacked. My teacher used to ask me how my parents reacted to the frequent scenes of violence and what they thought of the Jews. The Ruskies over-ran us eventually and put us into prison camps." Barbara elaborated on the horrors of the camps. Her mother died and her sister and her father disappeared. She fled across the Soviet border and took refuge in the Untied States Embassy, which was where she met Bill. She became a stenographer at the Embassy. When she was older, she spent ten years searching for her relatives without success and finally decided to give up the search. She had now been married to Bill for ten years. No children. Barbara was now thoroughly Americanized even to the daily use of six battery operated toothbrushes of various 'calibres'.

The new Tanzania Government was imposing its authority in a typically African way, for example; minimum prison sentences were enacted for theft of two years imprisonment plus 24 lashes administered quarterly, whilst for cattle theft, more serious, attracted a minimum sentence of three years prison with 24 lashes per year. So fear, in a sense was restored, by lashes, akin to the Deutsch *kiboko*

We never formally invited people to visit us, as one does in England; they just seemed to turn up. We had a house full one Saturday. I had been out with my driver, Okera Mwakajinga, in the government Land RoverGT 4715, chasing poachers. The chase over very rough terrain took its toll on the vehicle and our track-rod fell out. However, we still managed to apprehend the poacher and commandeered his short wheel base Land Rover DSR 921 which was loaded with poached elephant tusks and a dead young leopard. The ivory was also from young elephants which of course spurred my anger. My frame of mind was further frustrated when I drove up to our house to be greeted by a host of unhappy, accusative faces, obviously stunned by my arrival in a strange Land Rover loaded with 'booty'. They all thought that I'd "been up to no good", until I produced a chastened African, in handcuffs.

Having sorted things out with the Provincial Game Warden, Eric Bolsom, I returned to enjoy our guests. There were two Peace Corps girls and two new English Voluntary Service Overseas, VSO, lads posted to the Department of Agriculture, also Barbara and Bill Garland and Eric Wrintmore the Magistrate. With such an audience, the word spread of my zeal as an Honorary Game Warden and whisperings were heard at the monthly Regional Development Committee meeting, amongst senior African civil servants, "You need to watch out for that Brian Dawtrey, he's dangerous!" It came to my mind that I might be getting to the root of the increasing poaching problem.

North to Matwiga the following week: Cicely and I loaded our camping gear and headed north. It was 140 miles to Lindi, our Matwiga tobacco nursery, to check progress prior to the RDC, Regional Development Committee, monthly meeting. We reached our surveyors' camp after dark and enjoyed a camp fire-side chat with our four surveyors: Alexander Maki, "the black one" his colleagues always said, referring to his tribe the *Wasukuma,* the prosperous cotton growers of the Lake Victoria region; Thomas Athumani of the fine featured, paler-skinned, Mbulu tribe of the Central Highlands; Thomas Ngunwa; and Michael Zuberi from the coast.

The tents were steaming after heavy rain. "The Turkish tobacco plants look magnificent." Thomas told me, "Mr Dreisson the Tobacco Officer has been here and was well pleased, also the District Agricultural Officer from Chunya, Frank Rawe."

Three survey teams were preparing a topographical map for me to plan for an increase in the number of family farms. It was heavy work cutting traces on a 600 x 300 ft grid in 16 square miles of miombo woodland and taking thousands of Dumpy-level readings for interpolation into the topographical map. Understandably, the surveyors did make mistakes and these compounded themselves into the mapping process on their plane-tables; these were tripods with a flat drawing table on top for field use; causing Cicely and me to make many a fruitless journey in the vast woodlands, looking for non-existent ridges and gullies.

My staff raised no objection to the fact that they only saw their wives back in Mbeya once a month. They were supporters of the new 'Build the Nation' political ethic and, more to the point; they were getting extra income from the VSA Camping Allowance. They had a different style of marital relationship to Cicely and me as they saw nothing wrong with enjoying the favours of the local village girls.

Monday: Back in Mbeya the RDC meeting followed the usual African formula, the few expatriates seated at 9:00 a.m., Africans trickling in at 10:00 a.m. and the Chairman at 10:30 a.m., full of *bon homme*. It was reported: "No money to pay the teachers." despite education being top priority for the Government. "200 teachers have been dismissed nation-wide." However, there was full support for Matwiga Scheme and its expansion into Lupa Tinga Tinga. It was reported by the Chairman, Waziri Juma that, "Yugoslavian Aid bulldozers are here clearing miombo woodland at Lupa Tinga Tinga." Loud cheers of support.

I ventured to express a contrary view of this Aid. "I wish to point out to members that we need to be cautious. Yugoslavians know nothing about bush-clearing in the tropics. Careless work could remove the two inches of top soil and produce a desert of sand. Lupa Tinga Tinga soils are basically sand. What we might end up with is a FREE desert!" I was out-voted thirty to one!

Usangu Rift Valley: 6th November 1964. This was the day we decided to recreate that challenge that faced explorer Captain J.F. Elton to cross Usangu Plain; the last chance before the flooding. I had a small Unemployed Resettlement Scheme near Iringa and the Surveyors' labourers needed paying, so that part was legitimate duty. How I got to Iringa was up to me entirely. So we loaded up the Corsair with a small tent, cooking pots, my point 22 rifle – for guinea fowl suppers, and two Jerry cans of petrol which is about ten and half gallons. This should, at 20 miles to the gallon, give us two hundred and ten miles, plus a tank full to the cap. With two hundred and forty miles to Iringa by road, we will make it easily; the hazard being that by travelling slowly in low gear fuel consumption might be doubled. No helicopter rescue service.

We rose with the sun and hit Usangu at 9:00 a.m. The Mkowiji River was lower than our last visit and we easily waded across it and pressed on to find that dried-out *mbuga* swamp area where we had previously found elephant tracks in the solid grey clay bed. We knew that we had to cross this vast dried-out clay bed area. Winding our way around those deep concrete-like footprints took us two and half hours for six miles. One wheel in one of those holes could have done us serious damage. No sign of elephants thank goodness. We had been advised by Japanese de Villiers to follow the fishermen's' track to a place known as Nyakapemba by the river Ruaha. We didn't realise how far it was and after thirty four miles we reached the beautiful wide River Ruaha in the twilight. We set up our tent under the stars and pumped up the Primus – our source of heat for cooking. We had a pressure paraffin lamp for light but that does attract sausage flies and mosquitoes. Sausage flies are fat termites, swarming when the rains are scented. They are, however, quite good eating, roasted.

The name Nyakapembe seems to say in Kiswahili, a place to catch horns? There were some buffalo skulls around. In the morning the yodelling Fish Eagles awoke us to the wonderful sight of a vast flood plain swarming with birds; ugly Marabu storks, beautiful European Storks, colourful Egyptian geese, "Gypies", reminding us of their images in the tombs of Egypt, Spurwing geese with chicks, and white herons. Huge flocks of Sandgrouse filled the sky at dawn, croaking their way in from probably forty miles away, for water. They live on open waterless plains and need daily refreshment and to carry water in their belly feathers back for their chicks. Those hundreds of grouse with that comforting croaking voice, makes one feel 'comfortable' in a sense, but to the European weekender with a shot gun they are a mesmerising, blood racing challenge.

There was the rare Secretary Bird, which stands some three to four feet tall on very long legs. They sport a flash of feathers across their 'ears' giving them their name, from the days when secretaries used a quill pen to do their writing. This Secretary does not have humble characteristics however, it kills its 'clients', by thrashing them on the ground most violently. You've guessed it, snakes. It has to be extremely vigorous in its whirling and thrashing to avoid the bite of the poisonous version; quite a contortionist in fact.

We spotted four elephants, then a colourful topi male, quite blue across the shoulders with yellow legs, the size of a heifer. The Eland antelope is a bit larger than the Topi; Africans should have domesticated the Eland, this herd were so plump and the size of cattle, with short twisting straight up horns to fend off lions. They are not prone to tsetse flies and *trypsomoniasis* as cattle are.

Before leaving we swam in the river, taking turns whilst the other kept watch for crocodiles. Swarms of Red-billed Quelea, Lat.*Qelia quelia,* filled the sky as we left. Surely the most populous bird on the planet. There seemed to be millions of these tiny finches swarming like locusts, darkening the sky. When they descend upon a farmer's garden they did as much damage as a herd of elephants.

We followed the river and then turned up-hill towards *Acacia/Combretum* semi-wooded country. We came upon a hot spring, most unexpected. The site of the hot springs of the Songwe valley west of Mbeya where I found the fossilised dinosaur eggs two years ago, seemed to be related to the metamorphosis of sedimentary rocks and rift valley faulting. Next time we meet up with a geologist, we'd mention it. There was a big black buffalo bull nearby, perhaps elderly, enjoying the hot-spring Turkish bath, obviously an outcast from the herd. Impala were everywhere, leaping ten feet in the air as they bounded away from our car. There were the comical wart hogs with their vertical aerial tails trotting purposefully for cover, Water Buck with beautiful long curving horns, zebra snorting objections to our presence and the ubiquitous baboons, looking for woodland fruits and not caring over much about our presence.

We came across a poacher's camp site. There were Impala horns and discarded tins with Russian labels. Russian tins? It was reasonable to assume that the perpetrators were those Yugoslavians! They were obviously a bit smarter at hunting than they were at bush-clearing. We later reached the upper levels of the valley, inside the old Rungwa Game Reserve, now Ruaha National Park, and made camp for a rest. The heat was oppressive, especially with the car windows closed against the dreaded tsetse flies. Tsetse flies follow moving vehicles like they follow herds of game, but when we are stationary they are no problem. Cooking the guinea fowl I shot earlier, occupied our evening. The following morning we were surprised to find two fishermen wanting to chat. Where ever did they come from? *"Huko Ju."* They pointed to the distant mountains, "Up there." Can't say we were any the wiser, which was their intention I am sure. They told us how to find the track to Ndonya which turned out to be 40 miles, and then a 'cross roads'. Which way to go? I climbed a hillock and saw vast herds of elephant and buffalo. That decided us to take another route. After another 20 miles of hazardous driving, trying to avoid getting our beloved car scratched, we came upon a sign with a large arrow! Did somebody know we were coming? →**Mbage.** That was where our old elephant hunting friend, Steve's, HQ camp was. We arrived in the dark at 7:45 p.m. Steve was astonished, "Where have you come from!"

"Mbeya. We're heading for Iringa. Took the short cut, across Usangu."

"Brian! I sometimes wonder about you. In a car!"

"Lot more comfortable that a Land Rover. Cicely doesn't like Land Rovers."

"Don't blame Cicely for your eccentricities. And don't ask me for petrol either. It's 70 miles to Iringa!"

"I've got five gallons left. Should do it."

After we'd pitched our tent and killed a scorpion, we were fascinated by Steve's tiny pet Dik-dik, a small antelope that is only about 12 to 16 inches tall, running about his aluminium rondavel. Those huge black eyes; that little tuft on top of its head, and pencil thin legs; as Barbara Garland would have said of its charm; "I could just die, just die."

After a supper talking about elephants, we listened to The Ride of the Valkyries on Steve's tape player. He told us that it was about the Norwegian King Rollo and his ten women who had the power to dictate who should die in the next battle. "Well, he got part of the story right." I responded; "Actually, Steve, I descend from the Norman Vikings and my woman definitely determines my destiny. I'm obviously in her favour, thank goodness, having survived a battle these last three days, with the elements that is."

"Oh very good. Here, have some more wine!"

The following day we just lounged about in the shade of the huge *Acacia albida* tree over hanging the site, not only talking about elephants but watching, the now quite tame, bull elephant that come here to collect the delicious seed pods of this tree and to shake the tall palm trees by the river for fruit. They sometimes tore at the grass thatch during the night and one morning I was awaked at dawn by being hauled away in my sleeping bag, not by Cicely but by an elephant trunk. It slid into our tent like a giant python and gripped my bag alarmingly. Fortunately my bag proved *tembo* tasteless, and a bit heavy with me in it. *Tembo* is the African, appropriately heavy sounding name, for elephant.

We crossed on the chain ferry at 9:00 a.m. and reached Iringa at 1:00 p.m. The very sandy soft road had damp spots in the hollows that attracted millions of gorgeous butterflies, supping the moisture with their long proboscises. Wish we'd had a photo of the Corsair driving through clouds of butterflies. In town I met with the Provincial Agricultural Officer Don Muir and the Tobacco Officer Jim Moss to talk about Kitulo and Lupa Ting Tinga tobacco schemes before going down to Nduli. We heard on the radio at the White Horse Inn that evening, that Minister Oscar Kambona had uncovered a plot to overthrow the Tanzania Government. Apparently, he implicated the Americans, a popular target these days.

Matwiga: It was great to be back in Mbeya. The sky was now loaded with rain and terrifying lightning storms. Alternate droughts and floods are, of course, a feature of warmer climes. After a couple of days relaxation I once again, had to bundle my ever-supportive wife into my Corsair and head for a muddy 140 mile drag to Matwiga to meet the new manager, Mervyn Hallier and supply him with such life enhancing provisions as bread and butter, cheese and biscuits, tea and dried milk, eggs and bacon, shampoo and potatoes! Such items are not available at the Kipembawe Indian *duka*. I admired his fortitude in that isolated place. He had built himself a mud-brick house and was busy distributing OXFAM tools. The settlers had cleared the village site and access road in exchange for free WFP food, mainly consisting of surplus American maize, dried milk powder, nutrient-boosted biscuits, and cooking oil.

The cleared trees gave us a clear view of the starlit sky that evening in all its tropical brilliance. Look at that," Mervyn said pointing upwards, "it's moving, could it be a satellite?"

A satellite was something new to us in 1964; it was magic in that clear sky and a portent of new technologies that were soon to dispense with our hard labour surveying forest land with compass, cutlass and axe, cutting traces and tramping hundreds of miles. We were soon to have satellite imagery of the landscape.

These Matwiga settlers were mostly *Wanyakusa* people whose overcrowded homeland on Lake Malawi shores was a banana forest, so they were used to good nutrition added to which they had learned to work hard in the gold mines of RSA from whence they had been ordered to come home by Presidential Decree. They were enlightened, enterprising men facing the hardship of survival in native 'bush' woodland without services for the first establishment year with the prospect of learning how to grow tobacco as a cash crop. The granitic sands here were perfect for quality tobacco and the rainfall was reliable. This unutilised miombo woodland of Chunya District covered an area the size of Wales. Historically, it was a starvation area, ridden with tsetse fly which carries the dreaded human, deadly, sleeping sickness disease. Cattle could not be part of the economy either because of *'Ngana'* = *Trypsomaniasis,* a cattle killer disease spread by 'the fly'.

Chemical fertilisers would give the settlers hybrid maize, and one day enough woodland might be cleared to drive out the tsetse fly.

29ᵗʰ November 1964: The President Dr Julius Nyerere had granted the settlers at Matwiga free corrugated iron sheets to roof their homes when he visited the scheme as our guest; he said, "A man and his family that sleeps dry works harder." This visit to 'his' scheme was a huge morale booster for the settlers. It was not a surprise that such an eminent figure should visit this remote settlement because it was his office that appointed me to do this job when I first arrived back in 1962 'to resettle 23,000 Wenela Repatriates' brought home by his Presidential Decree, from the Apartheid regime. Cicely and I only managed to resettle a fraction of that number, but more would come to Lupa Tinga shortly. She was also introduced to this 'great leader' and as ever, made him laugh within 30 seconds. Creating merriment is a good way to get remembered. Peace has prevailed in Tanzania in stark contrast with many decades of strife in some neighbouring states. This was due in large part to the wisdom of His Excellency Julius Nyerere abolishing all chiefdoms, soon after Independence, thus eliminating tribalism and unifying the nation. My own survey staff were in fact, a tribal mix from all over this vast nation.

Kitulo again: Upon our arrival back again in Mbeya we were to receive guests from Kenya, a U.N. Expert on tropical grassland, Mr Morris who needed to "examine the sward". I found him most enjoyable company on our trip to Kitulo Plateau in my Corsair. His fascination with "the sward" led us on an extension of our study further east into the Livingstone Mountains, to a place called Makwale; the land of the Ukinga people. The track was a challenge for the Corsair beginning with deep volcanic Aeolian 'dust' and some steep gradients here and there. I then had to negotiate narrow gulleys, hump-back bridges across lava bed streams. It was a relief from the extreme heat to cross the 'self-help' bridge over the clear cold water of the Lufirio River. The towering hills and green pastures were a picturesque setting for the Lutheran Mission there. It was they who had organised the rarely used bridge across the river. Mr Morris was quite startled to see the scantily dressed tribal Ukinga looking like the proverbial, Golliwogs. This was because they never combed their hair. District records indicate that in the 1930s these people actually lived in holes in the ground. The Mission had changed all that, thank goodness.

Don Muir, the P.A.O from Iringa, later joined us back on Kitulo Plateau. Don's concern was to organise the layout of sheep paddocks and the siting of U.N. housing. Inevitably, more steep ups and downs, 'downland', high altitude walking, which became quite exhausting, added to which the ultra-violet radiation made my eyes burningly sore. I was beginning to conclude that I must be 'earning my keep'.

The *Wawanji* people solemnly believed that humans could not survive sleeping amongst their ancestral spirits on the high plateau. They said that there had been cases of Africans coming down with their brains 'addled'. In the event, the U.N. staff never did live up there, for whatever reason. When two years later I met some of them they seemed normal enough! My assistant, Tim Harvard, on the other hand, who was living up there in the log cabin, grew a beard, which turned black with carboniferous dust from ploughing the trial plots. This, adding to his broad Devonshire brogue and general clowning about comic behaviour, got the *Wawanji* villagers gossiping about the impending demise of *Bwana Tim* under the influence of their ancestors.

We all called on Jumbe Solomon in Matamba on the way down, and learned that the governing Party, Tanganyika African National Union, TANU, had been making radio pronouncements again, that the American Peace Corps were evil neo-colonialists. This resulted in 200 angry *Wawanji* people surrounding the American Medical Mission at Magoye in Ikuwo Basin nearby. Things became very nasty and there was fear for our American friends, Dr Bill and Barbara Garland too. Jumbe Solomon called a meeting of his people in traditional manner and spoke boldly about the Americans in his tribal area as being very good people in his experience. He ended by expressing his view that TANU were talking about those South American footballers in Rio who rioted and killed hundreds of people. He concluded by declaring briskly that, "The rains are beginning and many *shambas* are not yet planted. I wish to see everyone in the fields within the hour." The American fraternity could now breathe a sigh of relief.

I explained to my UN guest that there was a success story in Uwanji; Pyrethrum; a plant that produces insecticide from the dried flowers. The credit for that goes to Sammy Clerk, the colonial days District Agricultural Officer, who had introduced Pyrethrum as a cash crop that can only grow at high altitude. After initial resistance to growing flowers that they couldn't eat, a co-operative was formed with Jumbe Solomon as the salaried Chairman. He became the driving force, and hence the *Wawanji* people joined the 'cash economy' and prospered. They bought vests, radios, lamps and had money to pay a Land Rover taxi fare down the escarpment "to civilisation". Jumbe Solomon owned the taxi! An undesirable side-effect was that the bride price went through the roof. Overall, Mr Morris was quite impressed!

Tim Harvard explained to me how he had been vainly trying to get the *Wawanji* people to plant wattle tree seed on the plateau to grow timber for *kuni* = firewood, for future generations. Culturally Tanzanians are not generally disposed to plan for the future but rather they prefer to live for today in an uncertain world. However, Tim's trips to the wattle estates in Njombe, over in the Livingstone Mountains, in search of seed, bore fruit in the form of the manager's beautiful daughter.

November, the 'suicide month', was upon us, extremely oppressive heat, sleepless nights, kept awake by terrifying thunderstorms and roaring in the trees surrounding our lovely house. *Wasafwa* women, who did not comprehend privacy, often walked through our garden carrying their head-loads of vegetables to Mbeya market. Their farms were fertile with volcanic ash soils and they quickly learned how to grow the type of vegetables and fruit that the Europeans would pay good money for. One of their tribe took up commercial poultry farming and eggs were now abundantly available in town. He, unfortunately, became ostracised from his community as a tribal-culture non-conformist. African villagers always keep chickens but they never ate eggs, the eggs were for producing the next generation of edible birds. Cicely befriended the *Wasafwa* women and though they did not speak Swahili they loved Cicely's animated humour and giggled happily. They were fascinated by her white toenails and her long hair. Despite their dearth of belongings and arduous life the *Wasafwa* were a happy community. What is it that the Bible says … 'It is harder for a rich man to get to heaven than for a camel to pass through the eye of a needle?'

Cicely joined a multi-racial group called the Mbeya Cultural Society through which she was able to renew her talents as an Eileen Fowler keep fit teacher for the Norfolk County Council in England. She set up a class and the African townswomen attended topless. Most were somewhat beyond the M & S brassiere size range. Great hilarity resulted amongst themselves from the rhythmic gyrations of their black bouncing breasts. How do I know that? Put it down to my egalitarian outlook on life and keen interest in all my wife's activities!

December 1964: We were once again hosting what seemed to be an incessant stream of visitors to Kitulo Plateau, commonly spoken of by Africans as the Garden of God, *Bustani ya Mungu,* by now with early rains, a "Serengeti of Flowers" Cicely called it. Our guests were Don Muir, the Iringa PAO and Glynn Platt the HQ Livestock Officer from Dar es Salaam, with his sexy wife Marie – of whom more later. Back down from several exhausting days on the plateau we enjoyed a joyous reunion with our two boys, **Richard aged 12 and Philip aged 9, home from Arusha School.** After three days on the buses we expected they would be totally exhausted, but no! "Dad, can we go up to Kitulo for trout fishing?"

"Oh, no!" came a motherly voice from the kitchen, "Not again!"

I tried to express some enthusiasm, blinking through bloodshot eyelids from the ultraviolet light of the high plateau. Soon we were on the top again with Richard posing for his mother's camera, proudly holding a four and a half pound rainbow trout. Richard was not an academic at school but he was to become an achiever in the things that really mattered in life. When he was living on the farm in Norfolk at the age of six, he would rise early and ensure that all the calves were fed the correct amount of food before setting out for school to "while away the day, wasting time" as he succinctly described academic life.

Back down again, I was summoned to meet our Regional Commissioner, Waziri Juma at my Matwiga Settlement Scheme. "Once more unto the breach dear friends," I complained to Cicely. She replied, "You'd better go on your own, Brian, I've got a keep fit class tomorrow."

In fact this Oxfam family farming scheme was now well-established with thousands of *Wanyakusa* people having moved from Tukuyu District. It was largely due to the support of Waziri Juma that this scheme got off the ground in 1962/3 in the face of the disinterest of the Department of Agriculture in Dar es Salaam. Our safaris were so much more rewarding when we took our boys along, so I took them with me and stayed at Kipembawe Rest House where the village boys showed Richard how to make catapults, out of old bicycle tyre inner tubes, and how to kill small birds "for supper". He has retained that 'primitive' enthusiasm, and always carries a catapult when out walking his dog in Penine Rise, West Yorkshire, 2015.

Christmas Day became a riot with the arrival of VSO Dick Brown and Farm Mechanisation Officer Tim Harvard, from Kitulo Plateau. They had both grown beards and were tanned as black as Africans. Cicely had a great rapport with Dick, while Tim was a born clown. Add in "that crazy pop group" The Beatles, plus two wild children and a somnolent bwana who declared the Beatles to be "rubbish" and that conjured up the recipe for a good Christmas. Who needed Santa Clause when we had The Beatles?

Boxing Day in England, for ex-farmers like us, was the grand pheasant shooting day of the year, or if you were a horse lover, it was either the Point to Point Chase or The Meet, or if a city dweller, it was football. For us, in Tanzania the challenge was to explore further, the wild little-known Rift Valley landscape of the Songwe River. Shooting? Yes, guinea fowl, for a tasty supper; Point to Point? Yes, in a government Land Rover; killing a fox? Yes, a jackal maybe; football? Well, those fossilised dinosaur eggs I have previously mentioned, perhaps better suited to Rugby Union than football. We needed the Land Rover to carry all of us.

We called in at the ever mysterious Mbozi meteorite, half buried, said to be the second biggest in the world next to a specimen in Namibia. This meteoric iron specimen has been estimated to weigh sixteen tons. Typical composition would be 95% iron, nickel and cobalt, nickel being a high 8%. Because the carbon content had been burnt off by intense heat it shone like chrome when a piece was sawn off with a hack saw. There was evidence of previous 'sawings', I wonder where those precious pieces are today. We were scared off by a single bull elephant, as though he was the guardian of this primordial extra-terrestrial seeming 'Godly idol'. Maybe the elephants know something from way back in their 20 million year evolutionary span, compared to the trifling three million years for *Homo spp.*

After a long drive we reached the old abandoned Galula Mission Station where we were to cross the Songwe River into the Game Reserve in search of Japanese de Villier's spotted zebra, albino buffalo and albino giraffe. We later learned that the albino giraffe had been captured and shipped to Europe as a curiosity. The old bridge was decayed too much and the risk factor kicked in. There were flamingos in the almost dried up salt pan so we made camp there under a tarpaulin slung against the side of the Land Rover.

In the morning, we were awakened by the eerie deep booming call of the Ground Hornbill. This turkey-sized bird with red wattles and a gigantic beak; is a ventriloquist that throws its deep voice this way and that such that one cannot determine its exact location, a good defence mechanism against predators including hooligans with a .22 rifle.

Our boys identified 40 of the recorded 400 species of birds of the Songwe Valley. We turned homeward, reluctantly and came upon a vast flock of guinea fowl. Our Annie Oakley aspirant, who famously sang *You Can't Get a Man with a Gun*, on stage back in our home village in England when we were teenagers, turned her zeal on the guinea fowl flock and winged one with my .22 calibre rifle. She took off after it with Dick Brown in tow, sporting his large Australian Cobber hat. They both soon disappeared from view into the thick thorn bush.

Four anxious hours later, we came across an African wayfarer on a bicycle. He had a little Swahili and pointing, said he had seen "*Mzungu* that way*, mba -a-a-li sana'*, which meant Europeans a very lo-o-o-ng way away. *Mbali* turned out to be about six miles. Two pallid faces hopped up onto the back of the Land Rover as we headed home. Dick Brown was bleeding profusely from deep scratches where he had climbed thorn trees to unsuccessfully navigate. "So how many did you get then?" I enquired knowingly. "Sorry, it'll be a tin of corned beef for your supper tonight Bwana."

During the long drag back to the main Mbeya road my passengers finally broke into song. Darkness fell and we were blessed to find Pennant-winged Nightjars in our headlights, flapping ahead of us, looking for all-the-world like giant ghostly butterflies with their long white wing pennants, waving on the air. Males no doubt!

Chapter Five

The Oxfam Run Around

4th January 1965: The East African Airways Dakota, also known as the DC4, spilled out yet more official guests requiring to be transported to Kitulo Plateau. This was to be our last trip to the mountains since my future was now determined by the Village Settlement Agency, and Kitulo was under the Rural Development Department. My guests this time were Dr Strong, Chief Projects Officer of the United Nations/Food and Agriculture Organisation, which we hoped would fund the Wool Sheep Farm plan for the plateau, accompanied by Livestock Officer Glynn Platt, Don Muir and Brad Houston from Tengeru Research Station, a plant pathologist, whom I had met in 1962 when I was briefly stationed there. We were a merry band of expatriates, with pockets, metaphorically speaking, full of money, for Tanzania.

It was quite a challenging load for our Ford Corsair GT faced with that 3,500 foot escarpment climb of 56 hair-pin bends on loose gravel. Africa does nothing by halves. There is an extravaganza in every aspect of Africa, never a hill but a mountain, never a lake but an inland sea, not just a cat but a cheetah, which I oft-times proclaim can beat the Corsair GT, with an acceleration of three seconds to reach sixty mph.

After three days' trekking across the 159 square miles of the plateau's moorland style floriferous landscape, Dr Strong presented a departing accolade for the two young men Dick Brown and Tim

Harvard, for their hard work on the crop trials under very arduous conditions and to me for the wool sheep farm plan, which meant that international money would flow.

I can say in retrospect that the wool sheep scheme was firmly established by 1967 and my suggestion that this unique floral landscape should be preserved as a National Park, was 'on the cards'.

It transpired that VSO Dick Brown was declared in need of a mental respite, whether from the *Wawanji* ancestral spiritual influences or simply the altitude, which had affected him as a result of him spending such a long period of time up on the high plateau, was not clear, probably both. We would carry him down to Morogoro on the lowland coastal plain, on our impending next safari.

8th January 1965: Cicely and I were now busily packing for an eight weeks' cross country safari in order to compile official reports on the first three Oxfam schemes in East Africa. Matwiga report was already drafted of course. We would carry our two boys to Iringa to catch the school bus to Arusha and take Dick Brown along with us, en route for Morogoro. The boys declared their "hols" to have been "fabulous". This proved to be their last trip to the Kitulo 'rainbow trout paradise', a schoolboys dream holiday that they will never forget.

After the 250-mile muddy, pot holed, drive to Iringa, we sadly off-loaded our 'green shirts', the Arusha School uniform, to the charge of Mr Rushbrook the escort for the long drag, south/north to Arusha School, 450 miles of very rough roads. Cicely and I booked into the White Horse Inn and spent an evening chatting with Greek Manager, Socrates.

"Iringa is much quieter than it was a year ago," he declared, "Africanization of colonial posts is having an impact on my business." Later we learned from the Tobacco Officer's wife Jean Moss that Socrates emmigrated to Australia.

The long drive in our Corsair GT through the River Ruaha Gorges down to Morogoro, lying at only 1500 ft altitude, ended up with us booking into the dreaded Acropol Hotel. It was pretty *shenzi*. This lovely Swahili word admirably described its run-down, scruffy condition. It was also expensive. VSO Dick Brown and Cicely dodged the evening meal by going to the cinema to see a Hindi-Western.

The following morning, I sat in the backseat typing my Matwiga Oxfam Report while Cicely drove in the absolute luxury of a tarred road, to Dar es Salaam. She declared herself to be "in heaven". The last time we had been, in heaven, on tarred main road was in Central Northern Rhodesia on the way up from Cape Town last year.

Our next hotel was the New Africa in Dar es Salaam. The coastal atmosphere was so different to the Southern Highlands. We gorged ourselves on fish and chips on the Oyster Bay beach. Home from home? Well, not exactly, and, it was not oysters either, more like fine bones in squidgy cotton wool.

The next day the Land Use Planners from all over the country gathered at the VSA headquarters, in an excitement of optimism of hoped-for progress. The *bonhomie* amongst us created a merry social gathering, together with wives, on the rooftop restaurant of the Twiga Hotel overlooking the blue tropical bay, drinking iced coffee after Chinese food until 12:45 a.m. – luxury indeed for bush-wallahs like us lot.

"But, ah, next day ..." as that Edwardian Boy Scout camp-fire song that I used to sing, about the African cannibal Chief Adibigudai, went; "... the Chief was ill, and none could tell him why." It was the chief's wife in this case. "... It wasn't his hat, it wasn't his book, nor his toothpick, don't you see: but when they came to the white man's skull, they found it had no teeth! For Adibigudai had swallowed the lot and so had come to grief."

We could guess why Cicely was ill, and it was not the "teeth from the white man's skull" that we didn't have for the hotel supper last night; it was SALAD. "Never eat salad on the coast." the old sages always told us. We received advice from the BBC World Service also, regularly; "Sugar makes you fat." "Avoid fatty foods." "Prawns and lobsters will give you gout." We needed to eat something! What of bread? That was a non-starter as well; African bread had saccharine sweeteners in it. No wonder Cicely was slim and me as thin as a rake! We had the day off to celebrate the massacre of Arabs and Asians on Zanzibar beaches on 12th January 1964, by the Afro-Shirazi Party, thus ending 200 years of Arab dominance under the Sultan; – it was called the Zanzibar Revolution Holiday. This gave Cicely a chance to recover.

13th January 1965: There was still no news of the safe arrival our two boys at school. Oh well, we thought, *no news is good news.* It was time to return for the second scheme of my Oxfam settlement scheme survey. These schemes in 1964 were a new concept for Oxfam support in East Africa. Food supplies are essential for people settling in new areas because of the time required to clear the land, cultivate and plant crops prior to harvest. Settlers could not just pop down to the supermarket for food. Growing one's own food can take up to a year, and there being no other source of food available, non-government organisations, known as NGO's, are often willing to step in. These three such schemes in Tanzania attracted free food from USA, especially surplus maize stocks, known as the World Food Programme, or WFP, sponsored by the United Nations, whilst Oxfam provided transport for the food, plus tools, seeds and other essentials for the settlers.

It took us one and three quarter hours of "heavenly tarmac" driving to get back to Morogoro. The government rest house was filthy but luck came our way and Dick Brown's new colleague, an artist, was off on safari and gave us his house. His name was Paul McCullough and his brush and ink pictures of African scenes enthralled us, especially of the nearby Uluguru Mountains.

Mkata Oxfam Scheme:

This scheme was not as isolated as Matwiga Oxfam Scheme in Chunya District, which I have already described. Mkata Scheme was in fact thirty-five miles out of town, and about twenty miles off the main Iringa road. My initial observations were:

Problem No. 1: Each weekend when free food was distributed to settlers, the local bus did big business rushing townspeople out to Mkata for the pickings.

Problem No. 2: There was no evidence of any work being done. When we arrived, we were told that it was Friday and most of the farmers were Muslims.

Problem No. 3: Two employee tractor drivers were busy ploughing but their ploughs were set up wrongly and weeds were only half covered. I decided to get Dick Brown down there as I knew he would love getting the ploughs set properly. There was no ox ploughing either, the oxen were in the kraal. I was told that some of the plough parts were lost.

"Why is there no food for the oxen in the kraal?" I asked.

"The cowman went to the Office in Morogoro, yesterday, to collect his wages Sir."

Problem No. 4: The village houses were poorly built and the new school had not yet been allocated a teacher, despite much aid having been given. The building of a school and a Health Centre sounds great politically but why no staff?

"Budgeting for staff is a different department Sir." said the Settlement Assistant.

Back in town; Cicely and I relaxed on the veranda admiring the backdrop of the Uluguru Mountains. Morogoro is a beautiful location but extremely hot at that 1,500 ft low altitude, hence the colourful shade trees along the township streets. Speckle-breasted Swallows zipped in and out of the veranda; a train lazily hooted on the balmy air. With a glass of cool Tusker and with my beloved Cicely by my side, I said to her wistfully, "We could live here forever. Would you like that?"

"So how would you make a living, Bwana?"

"We could become farmers again. The economy here is supported by privately owned sisal and sugar cane estates and coconut palm groves."

The next day I received help and advice from the very affable Regional Agricultural Officer, Vincent Allen and also Bob Watts, the Provincial Water Engineer whom we knew from Mbeya. The District Agricultural Officer was an African named Calamira. He understood very well the concept for progress, he said, "Native African cultivation is confined to the mountain's lower slopes and the scattered nature of their shifting cultivation makes it uneconomic to provide services; hence, the Mkata model of concentrated settlement using modern chemical fertilisers to maintain fertility, enables the provision of school, Mkata Health Centre and clean water supply."

When I returned again to the house, Dick Brown and his colleague had returned together with a posse of Peace Corps girls. They were a dirty ragged lot. One girl said, "It's sure nice to live rough – I suppose most people do in this country."

Cicely said thoughtfully, "I can't say I've met anyone who lives rough. I suppose you are contrasting life in the concrete jungles of America with your automated kitchens and lavish furnishing, with African mud-brick houses and cooking pots. But, you know, Africans don't 'live rough' like you Peace Corps girls are doing. In

fact they would feel insulted if you said that, within their ear-shot."
A look of dismay and disbelief emerged.

Our poor impression of the latest Peace Corps contrasts with the two "Peace Corpers" who were in fact the first two to come out to Africa, whom we had met in Mbeya during our last tour of duty. Rodgers Stewart and Griff Griffiths were from Washington DC and Alabama, a civil engineer and a forester. They subsequently became lifelong friends whom we later visited in USA. However, the hordes of Peace Corps teachers now pouring into Tanzania were viewed with increasing mistrust by the African community as well as by their politicians. Hence the phrase 'neo-colonialists' emerged into common parlance. President J. F. Kennedy, who initiated the Peace Corps concept, was so labelled, also. Hence it was not that much of a surprise to many people in Africa, when he was so tragically assassinated, by unknown persons.

Meeting these numerous young teachers, with their tin cabin trunks full of books on the subject of American culture, history and politics, for distribution to school children, together with their attitude "look at us, we're all like you, come and join with us" made us realise that they had been seriously misguided in their orientation training. They did not conceive that Tanzanians had recently escaped from domination by another nation, and aspired to become a stand-alone nation, proud of their own culture and ability, and intensely sensitive to another world power trying to reimpose its influence upon them. In the ensuing years the Peace Corps were evicted from all the African nations south of the Sahara. For the time being, however, Cicely and I blissfully accepted these well intentioned 'girls', as part of the scene.

Saturday: Whilst I spent the day in discussions with a host of African politicians and expatriate administrative staff, Cicely procured a three months' supply of a new German contraceptive pill by Schering, not yet widely approved in the UK. She was still mindful of increasing our family size to the six that we had aspired to and agreed upon when we married in 1948. We became family farmers and abundant family labour would have been an obvious asset. These days there was a problem; the "Bwana" was condemned, as ever, to be over parsimonious; "can't afford it, Cicely." The contraception initiative was to become, for the first time in history, an elevation for the wife to rein supreme over matters of family size. Could this be the beginning of a new socially liberating epoch for the female world?

Sunday: Bob Watts took us to the Morogoro Club. Cicely played snooker. We enjoyed the company of friendly people with Cicely injecting endless double talk. An evening of laughter culminated with a potentially painful rejoinder from a 'comic film' entitled 'The Dentist in the Chair'. As previously observed, dentistry was pretty much unknown in Tanzania at the time, so we thought it would add some pathos to the evening, however, it turned out to be somewhat horrific.

Monday: This week was to be spent on the Scheme at Mkata and writing a detailed report for the VSA and Oxfam. In summary: The scheme was disappointing; built on benevolence but with the wrong premises and a basic lack of grass roots co-ordination. After two years' expenditure, too few settlers were committed. On paper, huge numbers appeared but in reality they lived in Morogoro. I was required to suggest, with reference to local official opinions whether this scheme should be rejuvenated or abandoned.

I measured approximately 207 acres of cultivated land out of the approximately 8000 acres of fertile alluvial soil available. Prior to the scheme the nearest school was eighteen miles away, the nearest health clinic was 35 miles away and the water supply was a hippo-fouled river. Management was provided by a young African Settlement Assistant. A new primary school had been built on the project but was unused.

The Mkata Scheme had indicated that stand-alone charity could be a sad failure. The tractor work was provided by the Department of Agriculture; the storage barn was provided by the Sisal Estates; the 16 oxen were also a gift and in danger of being eaten; the tools and a spraying machine were gifts from the Oxfam UK − all charity with no settler input.

There were beneficiaries of the WFP/Oxfam free food ethic; elephants, hippos and baboons; so that was a plus!

There was another worry in my mind springing from 1873. The explorer Cotterill, left a diary which I had obtained from the Royal Geographical Society.

'When crossing Mkata plain,' he wrote, 'on our way to Morogoro, we had to wade all day, chest deep in floodwater.'

"Who selected this site?" "Why was this fertile land unused?" I enquired at the District Office. "Ah! Too many elephants," the District Agricultural Officer ventured. No one mentioned flooding.

Cicely talked to the 20 settlers living there, and they told her that they had been paid 80 shillings each for the whole of their last year's cotton crop from the communal-block. The Settlement Assistant said he had budgeted for 500 shillings.

Oxfam allocation of funds in addition to free food were recorded by the R.A.O., up to 31st December 1964 as follows:

Road Construction £1,200

Water Supplies £2,000

Buildings £1,000

Transport of Food £1,150

The conclusion of my report was not optimistic but was sincere.

Before Cicely and I drove on to our third Oxfam Scheme, near the distant Lake Victoria, we felt the need to pick up where we left off in our last tour and dig up my elephant hunting pal Steve Stephenson, who was sure to cheer us up, with his tape player; he did, most appropriately with **Bert Kaempfert Swinging Safari, and African Beat**. He was now the Park Warden at the new National Park near Morogoro called Mikumi, 60 miles out of Morogoro. We always enjoyed Steve's hospitality. He took us on a tour of the Park before dusk. The density of animals was astonishing and easy to locate, unlike Ruaha National Park where we had to fly to view the vast herds of buffalo and elephant. It was a wonderful impression of what wild Africa was like before colonialism and firearms.

We conveniently ran out of petrol, so were obliged to stay overnight and enjoy the warm night air laden with the night calls of the wild. As Cicely had said before, she loved people but even more where there weren't any! The next day we were able to enjoy the unique experience of trekking on foot in a wild habitat, as our ancestors would have done – a very different experience to driving. The intense excitement of being on foot close to elephant and lion led to a most conversationally stimulating evening with Steve, not to mention an equally stimulating sojourn with Cicely, under the engulfing tropical star canopy. There was no chance of love-making getting tedious in wild Africa; it was always wild in the wild! Cicely enslaved me with her bare mid-rift, hot climate outfit, as we eventually took to the road in our beloved Ford Corsair GT following the route that the Arab slavers took.

We reached Kongwa and stopped for a picnic and to enjoy a very different vista of baobab trees and acacia thorn bush, indicative of low semi-desert rainfall. Such a landscape carried no farmers but only Maasai cattle herders; and rhinos.

The Groundnut Scheme: In 1947 the Labour Government Minister of Food, Mr Stacey, sent 'ministry men' to find unused land to grow ground nuts for margarine to feed starving Britain.

There is no record of who these ministry men were, but they omitted to check with the local village headmen or even the colonial agricultural officers as to why the land was uncultivated. If they had done that, the UK taxpayer would have ended up £3.6 billion, in today's money, better off. This confrontation with nature lasted six years, produced 600,000 tons of ground nuts from 5,210,000 acres, employing 2,000 British expatriate staff and 30,000 Africans. The financial loss was immense, and entirely due to a total absence of common sense. The Overseas Food Corporation, a kind of Quango, took over in 1953, spent another £40 million and went bust. It was finally decided to hand over to private enterprise and in 1955 the Tanzania Agricultural Corporation took over. They adopted the Maasai idea and created a huge cattle ranch in Kongwa which is still operational today.

I would simply add that the staff employed on the groundnut project did very well out of it and a great deal was learned about the mechanisation of land clearing and large scale ploughing in the tropics. One or two veterans set up in business with 'heavy plant'; in other words bulldozers, tree-pushers, mighty rakes, heavy duty disc ploughs; doing contractual land development work in Rhodesia, Zambia and Brazil. In my own experience I have subsequently witnessed some such mighty land development projects, financed by governments, World Bank and the United Nations that have been declared, 'an economic failure'; but that, in the outcome, have precipitated a 'side-effect' of substantial benefits to the local people and to staff, before they finally became redundant.

One can conclude that meeting the 'challenge of nature', whether at Kongwa or Mkata, is not just to throw money at it. Understanding and inspiring the human resource is always the key to success with rural development projects. Personal incentives, not communal responsibility, are equally essential to inspire the **very hard work** that clearing the land and growing food crops requires.

The fundamentals of increasing food production in Africa demand an over-riding dose of common sense, as well as underlying scientific and economic studies. In the case of the VSA there was an awareness of these criteria, plus the need for competent follow-up field management. Hence; Kongwa scheme was a failure, and Mkata scheme was a failure.

Buyombe Oxfam Scheme: Our next stop for Cicely and I was far away Mwanza on the shores of Lake Victoria, famous in recent history for that connection with Sir Henry Morton Stanley. This Welsh explorer met Dr David Livingstone in 1872 not at Mwanza but on the shores of Lake Tanganyika 300 miles inland at, what was then a village, named Ujiji. Livingstone gave his name in perpetuity to the magnificent mountain ranges flanking Lake Malawi, and of which Kitulo Plateau forms a part. This came about as a result his relentless campaign, which began in Nyasaland, now Malawi, to abolish slavery, earlier in his career. The records show that he was in a very poor physical condition by the time he reached Ujiji, due to persistent dysentery. He remained with Stanley convalescing for three months before trekking south, the route that we had driven up, over 500 miles, to die of malaria in Ilala, in what is now northern Zambia, in 1873. As a result of the immense respect that Africans had for his campaign against slavery, his servants undertook to carry his body over that huge distance back to reach Bagamoyo/Zanzibar, Tanzania, and hence Westminster Abbey.

The seemingly endless muddy murram road drive of over 500 miles had been, in our hearts, an award winner for our Ford Corsair GT. Its bucket leather seats, comfortable suspension on the gravel road, which made for a, thankfully happy, arrival at Mwanza, and not a single puncture on her new radial ply tyres! We had averaged twenty miles per gallon. We headed for the lakeside, blue refreshing water and naked African boys diving and gambolling joyfully near the shore. It was Sunday, so we later relaxed at the local hotel with colleagues; John Luscombe, Chris and Ann Bowden and a new officer, ex Harper Adams Agricultural University, named Hassell. Ann was friendly and unpretentiously beautiful, and hence we were two beautiful women and four old rustics, heading for a lively evening.

Our energetic, vivacious group proved a marked contrast to the neighbouring crowded table. There sat an unusually ugly African woman burdened with five children, the little girls being as pretty as blossom, sitting quietly until the chauvinistic African husband loudly ordered his wife and the children in truly Edwardian style, "Be gone. I wish to sit and smoke."

I puzzled over what the two Americans, man and wife seemingly, were doing there in Mwanza. They spoke loudly as though everyone else was dying to hear what they had to say. By way of contrast in the other corner sat an Englishman in white shorts, long white socks, shoes and shirt, reading The Times, his spectacles on a long lace, the epitome of a colonial senior government officer. Another conceited image prevailed by the window of a more intellectual air. A bespectacled British youth with bristly hair and untidy apparel, was lecturing a grubby square shouldered, square-faced brunette. She had a slim waist, her only saving grace. She listened intently to a discourse on how to treat Africans. "I know what I am talking about." he said condescendingly. "What say we meet again tomorrow for lunch then?"

The girl sluggishly agreed. A second girl at that table had not spoken a word or looked at anyone. I thought; *not a happy lady.* She rose and stood over six feet tall looking huge in her voluminous dress. Her face was bright red from solar exposure indicating a new arrival; perhaps a VSO?

By the door stood a slim black girl obviously doting on a Scandinavian type fellow, blonde and with a threatening Viking countenance. Could they be married? Her hair was fine plaited and stood up in spikes like a sea urchin. She had one central tooth removed to beautify her smile or at least to catch the eye, or perhaps to distract the attention from her massive breasts urging to break out from her brown sweater. This heavy-duty top contrasted with her skin-tight yellow slacks around her small bottom. I turned to John Luscombe who was also a skilled surveyor of landscape features, "They couldn't look less compatible even if he grew a beard and horns!"

The two continued to amuse us by turning the toast over thoughtfully. She held out the palm of her hand, flat, upon which he placed the toast and proceeded to ladle butter upon it thickly like a bricklayer. Was she contemplating flattening it on his face?

Suddenly the drama was interrupted by the arrival of the Greek manager of the hotel loudly demanding that we all vacate the dining room at once, on pain of surcharge. It was 9:00 p.m. He demanded cash-on-the-nail, in view of the fact that we were not having breakfast. A small black-haired man in the corner just sat and grinned with the look of an assassin. We learned that he was Japanese, selling fishing nets. He certainly had the air about him of a Samurai.

Cicely and I left the hotel the next day at 6:00 a.m. in order to catch the 7:00 a.m. ferry across the estuary to the Geita road. At Geita we met the manager of Buyombe Oxfam Scheme, a Polish man named Mr Marcizewski. We jumped into his Land Rover and endured half an hour of incessant one-way discourse. I thought, *do all Poles suffer from the need to talk non-stop? Maybe it's just because he's living alone in isolation.* I was actually feeling only half present myself by the time we reached Buyombe, uncertain whether it was the effects of the previous evening, or the interminable monologue with horror stories, of Mr Marcicewski's time in Russian concentration camps in Siberia, reminiscent of Barbara Garland's Jewish concentration camp trauma. He said that people died in thousands at the hands of callous camp guards. Oh dear! We wished that we could find the means to help this gentleman in his valiant endeavours to raise the standard of living of the local people, in this remote region.

Mr Marciszewski continued, "Joseph Stalin is a murderer. I can never understand why Roosevelt was pro-Stalin; but then, he was an American; what do they know!"

Cicely dragged my feeble, feverish frame to the local government rest house to recuperate. I was thankful Cicely was with me to take it all in. With Cicely's help my final draft report was deep and revealing despite my rising feverish temperature.

This is an extract from my **Buyombe Settlement Scheme Report:** '... set up three years ago in a miombo woodland area of hungry sandy soils, altitude of 3,800 ft. The Scheme was intended to accommodate the unemployed from Mwanza town. The cash crop is cotton, grown communally in a block for 200 farmers. Incentive to work: free food. The 'unemployed' are, sad to say, quite unemployable and have deserted the scheme. The land is now taken over by 50 local villagers whom my wife and I interviewed. They are cheerful and optimistic, and request more help, mainly mechanical. I am convinced that they could, as it was said, "Do something with the place." and they certainly have a chance with a diligent manager.

Agricultural Department Advisors and the Manager are paid by the Tanzanian Government. Oxfam has contributed £15,410 for transport of food from Dar es Salaam, storage facilities and tools. Local charities have contributed £6,820. The World Food Programme, WFP, are supplying maize meal, dried milk, cooking oil etc. The USA has proved especially benevolent in also supplying clothing and tools. The list of practical Oxfam and private assistance looks like this: chain saw, clothing, tools, seeds, soap, paraffin, bicycles, water containers and thirty shillings per month for each working settler. Total crop sales for the scheme are £386 only, over three years. The site was heavy native woodland at the start now partially cleared, by hand.

Contributing to this failure is communal farming, paternalism, minimal community services and maximum baboons, which were now the only permanent settlers and looking particularly fat and confident, and multiplying. How did the *Hominids* loose that spirit of primate enterprise exhibited by the baboons?

After two days' drive we arrived back at the Morogoro government rest house on the hillside, sharing with other government officials on tour. At this point my diary is blank for six days. I had contracted Cerebral Malaria, a life and death event, requiring full-time nursing by a beautiful charismatic woman; "Don't you dare die." I didn't dare; due largely to my luck in benefitting from the wisdom of an elderly ex-colonial doctor at Morogoro hospital. He recognised the protozoa as the deadly version of malaria and treated me accordingly. For recovery, he recommended champagne and rest, in bed, which was back at the friend's house.

5th February 1965: My first recollection of being back in the world was a very active brain – probably the champagne. I read a book, vividly written, about the D-Day landings, how difficulties with navigation caused by rough seas, strong tides, high winds, smoke and mist obscuring landmarks, which resulted in the Americans landing on the wrong points on Omaha beach, with 2,000 casualties. The Americans on Utah beach did better and lost only 197 men. Montgomery's men were slightly more fortunate landing at Gold and Sword Beaches with 1,000 casualties on each beach, whilst the Canadians on Juno beach also suffered 1,000 casualties. Total beach casualties = 5,197. The number of British troops was greater than the Americans. The British were described as storming up their beaches to the swirl of Highland pipes "like tigers". The numbers are now listed as USA 57,000, British 61,000, and Commonwealth Canadian 22,000. The author of my book described some failures, such as poorly designed barges, amphibious tanks that sank and about some airborne landings with gliders and paratroopers going astray of their target points due to high winds. German casualties overall were stated to be between 4000–9000 men. After reading this harrowing book, I felt, appropriately to my condition, as though I had been there and survived.

Cicely had a party organised with old companions from Tengeru Research Station, Mbeya and R.A.O. Vincent Allen, who asked if the three women who were staying with him could come too. Obviously a popular fellow! The Beatles added heat to the humidity. Cicely and her convalescent Brian practised a rather slow jive, to the phrases, "I Know a Love like Ours Can Never Die" and "As I Have You, Near Me" from the Beatles tracks of 'And I Love Her'.

I was quite weak for a while. Cicely built up her agility playing squash, swimming, coffee mornings and British Council film shows with Dick. Later, our daughter Caroline said in her letter from England that her Iringa school friend's dad had died of the same bug in Modui Diamond Mine in Tanzania. I felt lucky to have survived my D-Day.

Morogoro had proved to be a lively sojourn! I was always happy that Cicely took the stage socially. Whenever she entered the room, conversation paused to hear what she would say; a kind of 'stage entrance' was what she always made of it. I only worried that I might be a constraint to her happy, vivacious personality. I loved her intractably, and had no doubt about her fidelity, as did everyone else who knew her.

9th February 1965: I had to report my survey to the VSA in Dar es Salaam. It was considered that the reason why only Matwiga was successful was fundamentally due to the higher element of self-help amongst the settlers, engendered by avoiding the 'something for nothing' syndrome, as well as their background of hard work in the gold mines of South Africa. The applicants were screened by local authorities. Capable field management provided at the outset was also vital. So often with 'charitable' aid schemes the fund-raising agency is lacking responsibility for the implementation.

In retrospect I understand that Oxfam later in 1965 changed its Constitution to lay more emphasis upon agricultural development, as opposed to 'relief', with more dependence upon dedicated professional staff instead of enthusiastic volunteers. They appointed a Field Officer for Tanzania named Jimmy Betts, who was the brother of the Minister for Overseas Development Barbara Castle. This gentleman served closely with the Tanzania Government for some years thereafter in the field of village regrouping.

Having forwarded the reports to Oxfam via my Dar es Salaam office, I was advised that I was posted to Tanga on the steaming coast, some 120 miles north of Dar es Salaam and that I must visit there and secure a government house. In the meantime, we had a few days to 'enjoy' Dar. Riddoch Motors advised another new set of radial ply tyres. My mileage was only 18,000.

Cicely went down with dysentery, yet again. Dicky's beautiful brunette wife from the West Indies, Nibbs Briggs, looked after her. Our stay with them was a happy one. They took Cicely out in their boat to help her recovery. The hot and humid climate on the coast was very exhausting, even swimming and beach walking for us mountain-folk was tiring. The streets of Dar es Salaam were deserted at midday; siesta time.

Stella and Dimitri Mantheakis, the couple we met in Mbeya, had invited us to visit them on their farm near Dar. We took up their invitation. The intelligent and beautiful Stella showed us around their farm, 2,500 acres of coast line. We yet again, tiresomely, heard the phrases "lack of moral fibre" and "pride in their juvenile attitudes" and "neo-colonialism" about the Peace Corps. Provoking this prevailing scepticism was the news that the American Ambassador had been obliged to depart Dar es Salaam after a heated confrontation with the Tanzanian Government. It was said officially that it arose because of USA planes flying from the Congo, bombed neighbouring Uganda. This somewhat logically incomprehensible report, doubtless arose from a general mistrust of USA long-time involvement in the Congo mining sector in their search for uranium; the recent assassination of the first elected Congolese President Lumumba "who had done it?" and a general leaning towards Chinese communism at that time, aggravated the anti-Americanism mood. Unfortunately the Cold War of conflict between 'world powers', United States, China and Russia, was often to be played out on the continent of Africa.

18ᵗʰ February 1965: En route to Tanga via Handeni, we called in to see Chris Rodgers, a fellow VSA Officer who was striving to create a scheme for local villagers to learn the skills of commercial sisal growing as 'Out-growers' to the local sisal estate. This project would soon fall within my jurisdiction and I was confident it could be a winner. Pioneer Chris, was living in a caravan and had a guest, a Swiss lady named Lilian Bond, wife of the sisal estate manager John Bond, whom we knew from Mbeya Forestry Department. She said, "Brian, why are you in the red? What on earth have you been up to?"

I was soaked and muddied in red soil from the waist down, originally white shorts and long white socks of the coastal rig. "My Corsair slid off the red muddy road; got caught in a heavy storm near Handeni. Cicely drove whilst I pushed; often the way in our relationship, usually gets me out of 'the red' but today the spinning wheels got me into it."

I never did get rid of that colour from my socks, it served to remind me of this great concept of 'Out-growers' to a commercial sisal estate. Chris proceeded to relate an unfortunate experience he had had, resulting from an increasingly common problem in Tanzania, illegal TANU Youth League road blocks. After finding a South African Beitbridge rubber stamp in his passport, he was arrested on suspicion of being a spy. Beitbridge is the border post between R.S.A. and N. Rhodesia, now Zimbabwe, the stamp of which also existed in our passports, from our drive up from Cape Town to Mbeya.

The rain cleared and we spent a hilarious evening, chewing on biltong, under a grass shelter, followed by a cuddle under a sheet for Cicely and I, hoping it wouldn't rain heavily again.

Chris was renowned as a tough 'bush wallah' character, indeed he needed to be, to live in that place. I think the new breed of Brits on Overseas Aid were a seriously self-reliant lot, working without the cosy protection of the defunct Colonial Civil Service, determined to give the 'common people' a leg-up to economic stability.

We secured an old German house overlooking Tanga Bay, Number 46 Raskazone. The Power and Works Department, PWD, undertook to do minimal redecorating. They were short of funds like every department of government. The location could only be described as utterly wonderful, so close to the sea and coral beaches and with a house enclosed in overgrown Bougainvillea and exotic scented Frangipani. We were heading for an environmental transformation, from the cool Southern Highlands to the steaming tropical coast.

The next day we were off again for a very long drive back to Morogoro in our Ford Corsair GT. We were over taken by a "fat

Asian driver, in a fat Mercedes limousine, with fat tyres". Cicely declared to the folks at the Club in Morogoro. "He sprayed us with stones and smashed our windscreen. Brian blew his horn furiously but in vain; and then it rained! We got soaked." Cicely played Bingo and won! That boosted our morale for the next 200 mile journey to Iringa; without a windscreen!

21st February 1965: En route to Iringa we popped in to see our elephant lover friend Steve Stevenson, in Mikumi National Park, just in time for lunch. He had guests from Greece, Cyprus and Holland. There is something about Africa that elevates the sense of humour of Europeans. An hour of mirth revived our morale for the windscreen-less journey onwards. We were now dying to get back home. We duly ordered a windscreen with Riddoch Motors, the Ford Agent in Iringa, but were told that there were no windscreens for Corsairs in Tanzania. "The Ford Agent in Nairobi might oblige."

There were rumours that the government were planning to revoke the land titles of the many Iringa tobacco and maize farmers, mainly Greeks. The Tobacco Officer, Jim Moss confirmed our fears. The pendulum was swinging away from European commercial farmers in general in Tanzania, as well as in Rhodesia, towards more involvement by African farmers. In Zambia, in due course, the pendulum also swung towards African tobacco farmers, with the creation of the Tobacco Board of Zambia which recruited and trained local people to become tenant tobacco farmers on State Land. Later when President K. Kaunda took over, he was wise enough not to expel the expatriate farmers in the independence process, realising that they were earning foreign exchange as well as feeding the nation. Mr Jim Moss ended up in Zambia eventually. An air of gloom prevailed in Iringa, but not amongst the Africans. In 1965, Tanzanians were a happy race with a new world opening up to them, as it did to us after World War Two.

It took two days by air freight to get our windscreen. We enjoyed the refreshing atmosphere of Iringa's 5,363 ft altitude after or long coastal sweat. We found an amusing book in our hotel bedroom, subject; 'How to …' Hindu style:

(i) Hot milk and sugar every morning.

(ii) Massage oil daily to increase penile elasticity.

(iii) Choose the time of peak sensitivity, i.e. 7:00 p.m. This would be about 5:00 p.m. Iringa time; we decided 'cup of tea time' was more appropriate.

We left Iringa at 2:45 p.m. The 245 mile trip in the rainy season was a challenge for our Corsair with the road more like a tank testing range. I lost my exhaust pipe on some mud covered rock. We arrived in Mbeya noisily at 10:00 p.m. The coolness of Mbeya at 5,575 ft altitude impressed us. We had been away from our lovely house from 6th January to 24th February. The water and electricity had been cut off. We checked into the Railway Hotel. Our house was full of fleas. We procured insecticide powder and cleared a track to the bedroom. We collected water from the water furrow to flush the toilet, lit the pressure lamp from my safari kit, threw out the stinking python skin from the store room and collected Sally Spaniel from our neighbour, looking very much plumper than when we left.

At last we could relax, until the following morning that is! I received a phone call from my boss, the Commissioner for Rural Settlement. He was at Mbeya airport, accompanied by Mr Short of UN. Food and Agriculture Organisation and a Mr Mbelwa, the Deputy Head of VSA. They wanted to visit my Kipembawe tobacco schemes, and, you've guessed it, Kitulo Plateau. It was going to be a noisy trip in my Corsair! I managed to persuade them to enjoy a Tusker on our balcony whilst I got the electric power back on. Why were H.Q. people always in such a hurry?

Cicely packed lunch boxes and we set off for the 185 miles of muddy road to the Kipembawe area, at 8:00 a.m., arriving at 12:45 p.m. quite a good time under such sticky conditions. In the UK, of course that distance would take about three hours in this car. The tobacco crop looked marvellous. It was worth the effort. At 4:00 p.m. at Lupa Tinga Tinga farm, we met with the African Area Commissioner and the new Manager Mr Gondwe who was keen to host his guests right-royally. We finally jumped into my Corsair at 8:00 p.m. Surprise, surprise, I had the inevitable; flat tyre. My spare was also flat from coming over the Chunya mountains on the way up. I managed to repair the puncture. I had installed inner tubes and was therefore able to repair punctures, with my Australian hot-patch kit. We left in cloudy darkness at 9:45 p.m.

The rainstorms were horrendous. It was an epic journey over the mountains. My sump shield was buckled by rocks in muddy holes. Hairpin bends on slippery mud meant that I needed to keep the revs up for the continuing climb. This made the drive a hair-raising experience for my guests. We arrived home at 12:45 a.m. I was overwhelmed with gratitude "for saving their lives" they said. I simply felt grateful to Ford that my car didn't disintegrate. This car was designed for luxury high speed travel on tarmac roads; if Mr Ford could have seen us then, maybe he would have gifted us a 'free copy'.

After a fleeting, very noisy trip to Kitulo Plateau and back, my guests were more than ready for an escape back to their steamy offices in Dar es Salaam. We chatted at Mbeya airport whilst the Dakota spiralled down from crossing Kitulo Mountains and landed on the grass with a 'feathered' engine. My guests were determined to get away however and so they ordered a charter plane. On the way home I picked up the local paper in town. A flying disaster; a Game Warden known to me, plus his child and five others were all killed due to overloading his Piper Apache. He hit a tree. I was put off the flying lessons that had been offered to me, for aerial survey and poacher spotting.

Later that week Mervyn and Mrs Hallyer came to tea. They were doing a wonderful job of organising Matwiga Scheme to the benefit of hundreds of escapees from the Apartheid regime. Somebody should recommend them for the M.B.E. for pioneering this re-settlement scheme. Together with Lupa Tinga Tinga the whole area became known as Kipembawe Tobacco Scheme. I met the High Commissioner for Tanzania, ten years later, in Zambia. He told me that Kipembawe had become the principle tobacco growing region of Tanzania.

Cicely seemed to have gained four inches in bust measurement since we began our Oxfam safari – side-effects? Anyway, looking even better at 36, 25, 36 inches.

8th March 1965: Mike Pash, my replacement in the Department of Agriculture arrived in Mbeya. That meant more safaris to familiarise him with the area. Coincidentally, Glynn Platt arrived on a tractor much to Mike's dismay. There would be more surprises for single Mike! Glynn, the Livestock Officer, declared that his Land Rover was stuck up at Kitulo. Probably the low air pressure at that altitude killing the engine; or was it those ancestral spirits again? He had left his wife Marie up there, "Could you please rescue her, as I have to fly to Tabora this morning."

"Okay. Mike; a maiden in distress; you're in charge now." Maiden was a misnomer as it turned out. Mike found his bath and his pillow decorated with rose petals by Marie. This new experience of life in Mbeya, at high altitude, with its heavenly surprises, made Mike quickly realise that it might be unwise to explore Marie too closely.

On Sunday, everyone proclaimed a day of rest. Marie was full of somewhat irreverent, but funny, stories such as about "Asian queers climbing over the seats" to join their pals, in the Dar es Salaam cinema; subsequently referring to them as the "jumping queers". There were tales about crawling through "dark tunnels with strange men" under the Pyramids in Egypt, and "meeting mummies", all of which sent Cicely into one of her giggling fits. Cicely's giggling fits at the age of 17 years always filled her suitor, me, with foreboding, with the prospect of possibly spending a life-time with a giggling wife. I chanced it; I always say it pays to take chances in life; we'd been married sixteen years by this time and rarely a giggle. Its takes two to giggle and my sense of humour is somewhat different!

Everyone enjoyed Marie's vivid imagination and her good will towards all the many races one meets in Tanzania. She was pretty good at jiving too as it turned out when Mike produced his new Pye Black Box record player. Cicely's dancing was renowned from the 1940's American G.I's and Glen Millar jitterbugging days. She soon had Mike, plus the Beatles, doing the 'Kitulo Jive' to exhibition standards.

Mike's old Land Rover had brought him down from Arusha so we thought it should take us all up to Kitulo, 9,000 ft. He said he would need to load it carefully as the springs were weak. It developed a serious list to starboard when the driver got in. The night before we left, Glynn arrived back. "I am pleased to find my wife is not still in the clouds, at least not more than usual!"

10th March 1965: Marie and Glenn finally set off home in his rescued Land Rover, only to be replaced as our guest by mountain-crazy Tim "Yogi Bear" Harvard, his black face hidden in an ever-expanding beard. He was alone at work now on the trial plots at Kitulo Plateau with only the *Wawanji* ancestral spirits for company. Some said that he had become obsessed with strange, unbelievable stories about events on the plateau, that he now called 'the lost world'. He enquired about a Peace Corps girl in Mbeya. "Sorry, old chap, she left. Kirk Douglas is on at 'the fleapit' though."

We did the cinema, followed by the Black Box. Cicely plus three attentive men gave Cicely one heck of an evening of laughter, jiving and repartee. We turned in at 2:00 a.m.

The Ford Corsair GT in Matamba, at 7,000 ft alt.

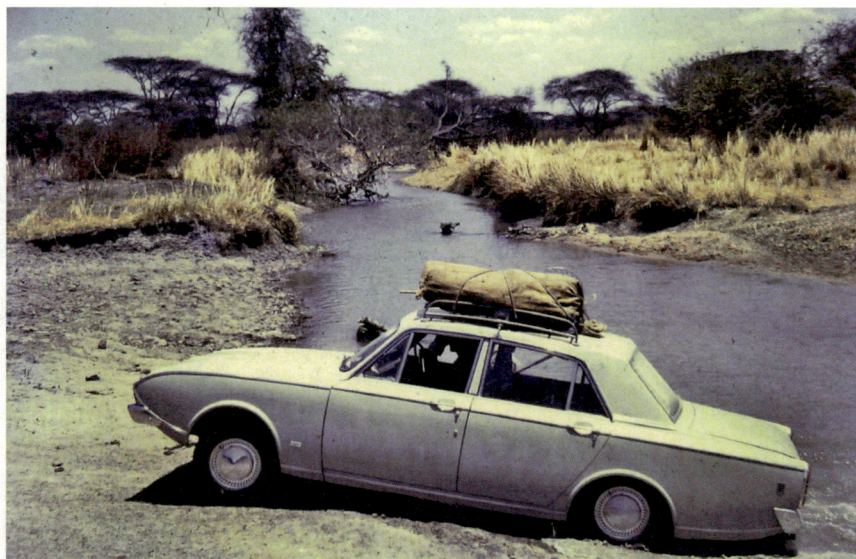

Wading across Mkowiji River on Usangu Plains

"Nice car"

Overnight stop by the Ruaha River swamps Usangu, 2,500 ft.

Fish eagle on Ruaha River

'Chocolate Elephants' in Rungwa Game Reserve (Ruaha Nat.Pk.)

Son Richard's painting of Kudu

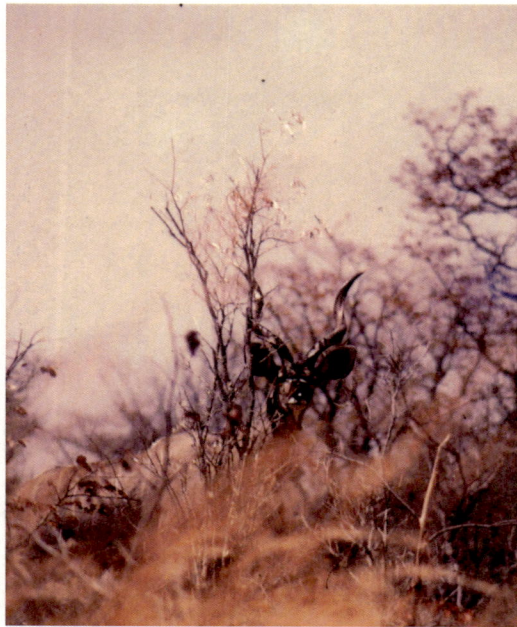

Kudu near Steve's camp (in Ruaha Nat Pk.)

Simba in posing mood near Steve's camp

'Keep it under your hat', the Yugoslavian ball at Lupa Tinga Tinga.

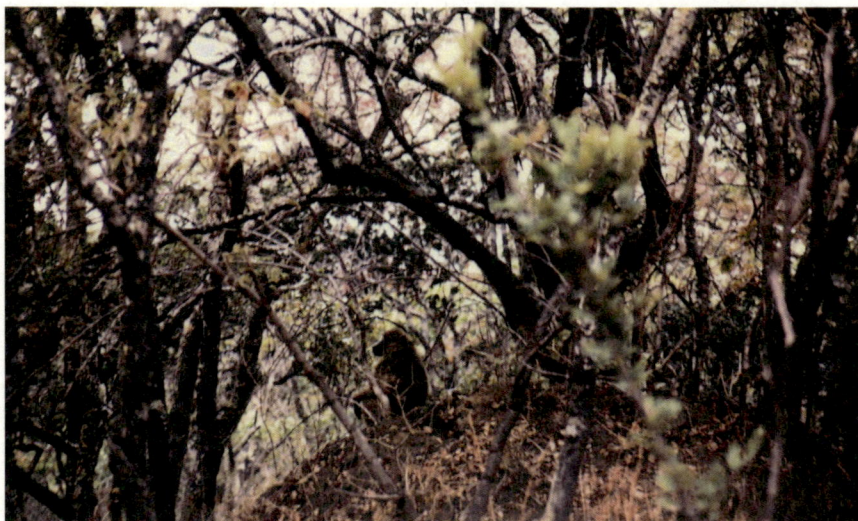

Thinker. "Should be some nice maize here soon"

Miombo woodland

Mbozi meteorite is now on display for tourists

Coffee plantation

'The Ventriloquist' = Ground Hornbill

We met a man on a bike who said he'd seen two Wazungu very far away, in the 'bush'.
Must have been Cicely and Dick Brown.

Our balcony view towards Mporoto Mountains

Kitulo   Trout

Kitulo trout

How to kill a bird for supper

In Morogoro. Uluguru Mountains backdrop

Next stop Mikumi Game Reserve

Brian at Mikumi; herds of buffalo

Cicely enjoying Lake Victoria at Mwanza

On the way back to Morogoro; service station

Returning home with a smashed windscreen.
In Ruaha River Gorges

Back in the Southern Highlands, 7000 ft.alt.

Our next home No 46 Raskazone, Tanga:
No windows? 50 ft. alt.

Brian in Tanga – losing weight

Agave sisalana; sisal at Mlingano Research Station

Bleaching the fibre in the sun

Victorian Magila Mission Station with ship's bells

Mlinga 'sacrificial' Mountain with Richard

East African Safari Rally Amani check point 1965

WINNERS OF EAST AFRICAN SAFARI, 1965

Mr. Jaswant Singh, Mr. Joginder Singh.

The 'local' winners with their Volvo: News clip

Chapter Six

Up-Sticks for a New Life

17th March 1965: We had been transferred to Tanga and were saying our farewells at Kitulo Plateau. We left Tim Harvard in his lair in the mists of Kitulo, alone now. We called upon our anthropologist friends Dr Bill and Barbara Garland in Matamba – two very sad farewells.

"Do come and stay with us at Minnesota University Campus." The world grows smaller.

Bill gave us some startling news. Jumbe Solomon and most of the Pyrethrum Co-operative Committee were in jail for embezzlement. Growing pains of the new 'cash economy' I supposed. It was not that the growers were unhappy with their quite good profits or that they minded their Jumbe getting his substantial illegal cut but that the laws were made elsewhere, "These are not our laws," they said. The *Wawanji* tribe had always lived by their own rules and customs but now it was President Nyerere's edict that all tribes be unified into "One Nation". This was logical. Tanzania, did not exist as a geographical or political entity until it came under colonial rule. The Germans and British partitioned continental East Africa between them in 1886 and the formal boundaries of Tanganyika were only established when it became a British Protectorate in 1920. President Nyerere recognised the threat that tribal customs and loyalties represented to the prospects of peace and unity. Following independence in December 1961, he put in place a whole series of measures including the creation of a one party state with Kiswahili the official language for all tribes, and the abolition of Chiefdoms.

We pulled into my surveyors' camp for farewells. Faces were long and feelings of sadness genuine. *"Kwa heri Bwana, nafika salama,"* said Brown Mwabulambo, "Goodbye and arrive in peace."

"Kama gari yetu hapana kufa!" responded Cicely, raising a smile, "If our car doesn't die!"

The 'Swinging Sixties' certainly hit the Southern Highlands for our send-off party. The mixture of all the leftover alcohol, the Beatles, Bill Haley and the Comets and Rock and Roll made for a merry gathering. Our guests included; the Magistrate, two doctors, foresters, the Vicar, Land-use Planning staff, Asian Indians, local farmers, old-timer Nessy Stead, the Vet, the Game Warden, the White Fathers from Chunya, our Italian motor mechanic friend Mr Sossi, plus various children and dogs. The party reached dawn and some guests stayed on for breakfast and helped us pack our fifteen large crates to be transported to Tanga by East African Railways and Harbours lorry.

We checked in to the White Horse Inn, Iringa, at 9:45 p.m. the next day, feeling only marginally alive after eight hours of noise, swerving round potholes and ploughing through shallow tomato-soup-coloured lakes. Riddoch Motors spent the day on my Corsair GT fitting a new exhaust system, replacement of the bent sump guard, removal of some dents, and once again, fitting four new tyres. They only had tubeless tyres, "All the vogue," they said. I was not impressed. Trouble was; puncture repairs which I was accustomed to having to do frequently en route, required the use of rubber plugs and notwithstanding the considerable difficulty in inserting them, rubber plugs are prone to blowing out on rough roads. Moreover, one cannot inflate a plugged tyre with a foot pump without strapping the casing like a tourniquet with a rope to get the tyre casing in place against the rim of the wheel. I needed to carry a stock of inner tubes, which had become an expensive and rare commodity. Four new tyres cost 2,000 shillings, which would be about £200 in Millennia money.

Annoyingly we had two punctures going down through the Ruaha Gorges and so did not reach Morogoro until 6:45 p.m. for our 'lunch stop' at 'The Planters Hotel'. I discovered that most Brits, had left the Department of Agriculture, and Tanzanian Ramus Lyatu, now had the top job in Morogoro. I knew him well from his position as District Agricultural Officer in remote Chunya District, of Lupa Tinga Tinga fame. I was to meet him again in 1967 when he was the Chairman of the Moshi Coffee Growers Association. There were good career opportunities for educated Africans. It would be some time before our boxes reached Tanga so we decided to accept the invitation of Jeff Jefferies, the ex-farm manager of Lupa Tinga Tinga Virginia Tobacco farm, to visit him in the steamy **Kilombero Valley**.

Jeff was a jovial Rhodesian, married to a Welsh wife with two small daughters. They knew how to enjoy the pleasures in life, in a way that had sustained them when living in isolated, wild places before and now again. I gather he was employed by a company, possibly the TAC, to create a farming enterprise based upon sugar cane, rice and beans. The country was short of rice. The low altitude meant it was hot and steamy. The house he built was set back on a rise and shaded by dense escarpment forest. The Rufiji River sprawled out across the plains below feeding the whole of South West Tanzania, its source in remote Kitulo Plateau.

Jeff jovially invited us to "Come down to our new pool for a swim, the servants will see to your suitcases. Swimwear is optional."

The pool was in a natural rock basin below us, deeply forested and invitingly secluded for aspirant nude bathers, as Jeff had suggested. It was not to be however. The water was deliciously cool, supplied by a cascading mountain stream. To our surprise we were greeted by other guests; two Peace Corps girls mewing priggishly about how they understood the African mentality and, worse still, there was a German family who were vigorously throwing their six-year-old son into the middle of the pool, shouting wildly, "Svim! Svim!" The boy was struggling to avoid drowning. Barbara Garland, our German refugee anthropologist friend from Kitulo, would have had something to say about that!

The subsequent supper table gave us the pleasure of conversation with a cultured couple of French speaking African doctors from Abidjan, on the Ivory Coast. They suggested that African culture in their country was much deeper rooted and devoid of European influence as is the case in East Africa. They had imported the know-how of growing pineapples at low altitude and had set up an estate nearby.

Cicely went down with dysentery yet again the next day. It was the eternal menace of low altitude living, caused by bacteria, usually found in foul water and hence salads or fruit washed in it. Why Cicely seemed to be more prone than me was a mystery. Time, painkillers, and boiled water were the only treatment we knew of.

After several days Cicely was better and we were able to set off for Mikumi National Park to stay with Steve and enjoin with his life and share his love of the wild. We were fascinated by the great herds of elephant in Mikumi, so greatly feared by village people; they have held mastery of the landscape for millennia. The invention of firearms has changed all that. Native hunting with poisoned arrows was never a real threat to the survival of *Loxodonta africana.* Steve said, "The elephants are a problem in as much as the bulls fancy the challenge of the steam trains. There is the occasional derailment, but the metal brainless giants win the day most of the time."

After a rough drive of 300 of miles of rutted Murram road we arrived in Tanga on:

26th March 1965: Our German 1905 built house, No. 46, was situated in a part of the town called Raskazone the Arabic name of the peninsula where the house overlooked the bay with its constant flow of ships coming in to collect sisal bales, craned on board from 'lighters'.

A famous battle took place here in World War I in 1914 when the British troops, mostly the Kashmir Rifles, mounted an amphibious invasion. One force landed at the 'lookout tower', still there today, whilst the main force landed on the inviting beach where the Yacht Club is today. Their defeat was described as a debacle of bad planning and their Major General Aitken was later sacked. The German force was a smaller brigade of African and German troops. According to the records, the British attack was characterised by a catalogue of misfortunes, including carnage by superior German machine guns, with losses of 800 troops compared to the German loss of 145. The Kashmir troops actually reached Tanga railway station, which was the machine gun post, only to be ordered to withdraw by the, offshore, General Aitken, 'fearful of the mounting casualties'.

The engagement is also recorded as 'The Battle of the Bees' as swarms of angry bees, infuriated by bullets, attacked both sides. It is known that sisal blooms attract great numbers of bees even today. The British troops subsequently left behind nearly all their weapons and ammunition thus greatly benefitting their adversaries! Unbeknown to General Aitken the German forces had surrendered simultaneously, leaving Tanga completely undefended overnight. However, the German Commander, Lieutenant Colonel Paul von Lettow-Vorbeck, countermanded the withdrawal and re-occupied the town the following day. All I can say is; typical military blunder.

Military commanders need to be on the battlefield, like Rommel and Montgomery famously were in WWII, in the desert.

These details come from the *Official History of the War* and also by a log of the diaries of the men of the Jammu and Kashmir Rifles by Andrew Kerr entitled *I Can Never Say Enough About the Men* who stated that this event was 'one of the most notable failures in British military history'. It was two years later that the British eventually pushed the German forces out of Tanga. Anyway, the Germans left us a super house, designed in 1905 with no windows and overhanging eaves to shade the mosquito netting. The sea breeze blew steadily through the whole house, laden with scent from the frangipani bushes in the garden.

"Come on Cicely, let's move in, boxes or no boxes, – it will be better than the Planters Hotel."

The house servants' quarters were enveloped in creepers; in fact, the major domestic work was going to be the battle against encroaching verdure, so we decided to employ a 'garden boy' named Ali instead of a cook. The humidity and heat in this lovely place was a challenge for us after life in the Southern Highlands. We were advised to take a cold shower twice a day and to always walk in the shade of the Flamboyant trees that lined the streets of Raskazone.

Our new neighbours of the Survey Department, Peter and Emma Endean, supported us, pending the arrival of our boxes. Cicely made me porridge daily "to make me a big, strong, boy". I always suspected that she dreamt of marriage to an overwhelmingly big strong man. I was not quite sure what she had in mind, but she was now in charge of family size with the advent of the German pill. The Deutsche influence had returned to Tanga.

We explored the beaches on our first Sunday. It seemed to us like an initiation into paradise. The whispering Cassuarina Pines, the coconut and kapok trees, the brightly-coloured lizards basking in the sun on every rock and wall and the centuries-old baobab trees above the cliff. There was one very big old baobab, hollow in the middle, which we learned was used to hold prisoners in remand, pending a decision as to their destiny. Still today, one's destiny in Africa can be uncertain.

A lady popped up over her garden hedge along the beach and happily invited us in for drinks, not the usual English reserve. Her name was Mrs Payne. Her friend, Miss Robinson, knew our Mbeya friend, Dr Don Curry. Africa can be a small place in the social sense. We began to feel at home. As the sun fell at 6:00 p.m., we felt the need of sustenance and hit the Twiga rooftop restaurant. "This is really civilised." Cicely smiled, after downing steak and a pint of Pimms.

Tanga: The reason for Tanga's existence is sisal. It was introduced by the Germans in 1893, possibly from South America. They invented the essential processing machine, the decorticator. There are mini railways across the fields to haul the loads of heavy leaves to the decorticator. Vast plantations are like 'deserts' of sisal plants, growing in Germanic regimental lines across the landscape. The long leathery leaves have a razor sharp murderous point that makes hand cutting a very hard job. There is a research centre that is constantly seeking higher yielding varieties of, botanical name, *Agave sisalana.*

Tanga eventually became the largest producer and exporter of sisal in the world. The significance of sisal is that it has the longest, strongest natural plant fibres. These can be made into the largest, strongest ropes, as well as into binder twine. Sisal was at one point so lucrative it was described as 'the white gold of Tanzania'. Nationalisation and the development of synthetics have almost destroyed the sisal industry which at the Millennium is only about 10% of its late 1950s peak. Sisal had an interesting by-product; in so much as it attracted a diverse labour force. Thus Tanga became a uniquely cosmopolitan African and European community.

The next day: I had been told to visit Amani Rest House in the Usambara Mountains and study the area for a potential tea growing settlement scheme. As we drove higher and higher, the trees became taller and taller, and the views became more and more spectacular. The government rest house was at 3,500 ft. altitude in tropical rain forest. It was an old German research station. We learned that the Germans had a monorail carriageway up the mountain, powered by *Wasamba* tribal muscle, energised by the *kiboko*. The old *mzee* caretaker showed us the German library, now converted by the World Health Organisation, W.H.O., into a malarial research station. The botanical garden was devoted to propagating, for export, the native flowering plant, Saintpaulia, commonly known as the African Violet, which grew everywhere on the humid forest floor.

We met the African Area Commissioner and enquired whether the local villagers would be amenable to a scheme as out-growers of tea for the commercial tea estate. "I will talk to them," he replied. "In the meantime, I have recruited the TANU Youth League to come up here and plant tea bushes on the open land at Dereme. That will encourage the villagers to join."

We trekked across to the tea estate the next day to look at the soils. The existing tea estate, on very steep slopes, alternated with native tree belts for soil conservation. The soils were dark red. We were impressed with vista of the landscape of flat topped tea bushes, stretching away into the distance in such, civilised, orderliness. Despite the 45-degree slopes, there was no sign of soil erosion. "This is not exactly in accordance with the book, Cicely, especially in a high rainfall zone. Be OK, I suppose, as long as the settlers don't start planting maize."

Troops of the beautiful Sykes Blue monkeys barked at us from the rainforest canopy. "I doubt they will take to tea bushes Brian.

Wild nature is a structure, I think, that falls apart if you remove one strut of the eco-system. Sykes Blue monkeys are fruit eaters, not tea drinkers."

We drove across to nearby Dereme. The TANU Youth League knew of our impending arrival and had dug us a 6 ft. deep soil inspection pit. We watched them in their camp, from our soil pit site, parading in the chill mountain air, in green uniforms with wooden rifles. They looked most incongruous in the agricultural setting. "What has this got to do with planting tea?" Cicely questioned. Boys and girls were dressed alike. Teenagers enjoy uniforms, of course, as well as the mixed sex company in camp. They said they were here to 'build the nation' and intended to have a good time doing it.

I jumped into the soil pit with my beautiful scribe in her broad brimmed sun hat, sitting above me, pen poised to record my revelations of the millennia about the result of weathering from the pre-dinosaur native rock. The soil profile was dark red, deep, stone-less, free-draining clay with a deep, organic top soil from the forest leaf fall. This is the best type of soil profile that can be found in the tropics. It took two hours in the shade of my London umbrella to describe and sample the pit for Tengeru Research Station.

"Well, Brian, all this scientific technology – is it relevant? What of the human resources, the people that are expected to work this land? Shouldn't we be studying the human profile?" *How wise of her*, I thought.

"We just have to play the game the ministry way if we want government backing."

Cicely continued sarcastically, "I was forgetting, you can't expect the government to listen to the advice of a mere farmer like yourself. You need to have a Ph.D. in something or other."

We were later able to observe the Youth League planting tea bushes supplied free by Karimjee Tea Estate, through my binoculars. We could see the pre-marked rows across the hillside for planting. We could also see that some rows were planted upside down 'for a lark'.

"Imagine what this is costing. It would have been cheaper and more beneficial to employ local village labourers who would also have benefitted educationally." Cicely added, "At this rate of progress, with the whole hillside to plant up, some of these girls will be leaving with a bonus, babes in arms!"

On our third day at Amani, the local headmaster invited us to Amani Primary School dance. It turned out to be a colourful affair with exotic drumming and part-singing. Despite their tender years, the rhythmic style of movement was most suggestive of fertility rites, comparable, we supposed, to UK efforts to introduce sex education into the state schools.

Finally, we ended up at the Karimjee Estate Manager's house, picking his brains over a Scotch or two, on his veranda. He, Walter, invited us to supper which turned out to be very conversational, since we were both ex-farmers from East Anglia in England. He said he had a farm in Saxmundham, Suffolk. *Lucky Devil* we both thought. He said that he needed the work in Tanzania to keep his farm solvent. Well! That said it all.

The mist crept up the valleys as darkness fell. Cicely dug deep into his stolid personality to seek a sense of humour. His laughter finally set off some male monkey barking nearby as though startled at this event. I pursued Walter on the subject of wildlife conservation.

"How many species of monkeys are there in these forests? Any Colobus?"

"I can assure you, Brian, that I have no time for game watching in this job." So that was that. It was close to midnight so we took our leave. Back in steaming Tanga it was the weekend. We strolled along the cliff to the Paynes' house again.

A week after our arrival in Tanga, the Paynes enquired whether we had any news of our boxes, to which we answered "no". We were subsequently invited to stay for supper. We watched the setting sun, the six o'clock red glow creeping across the bay from the high mountains where we had been all week. Looking out across the water the mysterious forested island in the centre of the bay turned yellow in the glow. "That's Toten Island. Nobody goes there," Mrs Payne said, "the Africans say it's haunted. There are lots of graves there of Germans and Arabs. Pirates came centuries ago and they might have buried their treasure there when the Portuguese came after them. In fact the name of the island comes from the German word for killed. It's uninhabited."

"That gives me an idea, why don't I organise a treasure hunt for the children. Our two boys are due home for the Easter hols and its Richard's thirteenth birthday on the 26th. We are hoping to buy a GP 4 sailing dinghy and I can teach Richard to sail it. It's a stable and safe boat to sail in the bay. Wow! I am inspired. Toten Island here we come.

The next day, Cicely and I shot off to Amani Hill Station again to see the Minister Sijaoma and to discuss peasant farmers getting into tea production. Dr Gordon Anderson, the soil scientist from Tengeru Research Station, was also due to meet me there to discuss the soils at Dereme. Everyone had lots to say. We, however, were concerned to get back to Tanga to meet our two boys off the train from Arusha School. This was going to be a major event for them. Gordon talked on until midnight on his beloved topic, tropical soils. He was an internationally renowned expert and he provided me with a whole new discipline over the years, for which I have been extremely grateful. We had to leave at 4:00 a.m. in our Corsair, full speed ahead in order to meet that Arusha train. The train steamed in at 7:45 a.m. The children burst onto the platform, satchels flying. The excitement on that platform was immense. There were so many children in their green shirts and grey hats and so many happy parents, especially Cicely and me. The dawn glow spread its glory across the bay, illuminating the red, flamboyant tree blossoms. The Palm trees silhouetted the shining blue sea and the two black cargo ships flying Chinese flags, awaited their loads of sisal bales, providing a glorious image for the children on their way to their new home in Raskazone.

We were apprehensive that our bare house and overgrown garden would appear unwelcoming but we need not have worried. The seashore proved irresistible and the boys spent their first day immersed in warm saltwater. Philip was now a strong swimmer at ten years old, taking the school swimming colours. Sally Spaniel qualified too as an inseparable companion in all marine expeditions. This was a paradise world for the young. Philip's birthday was nine days' passed with Richard's thirteenth at the month's end. We found Philip a drawing board in town and he set to, creating a picture of the train steaming through the regimental lines of sisal. He was heading for a career in drawing and designing. Philip thoughtfully presented his land resources surveyor Dad a chunk of gemstone that he had found on a school trip to Maasai land. This was a spectacular green stone with huge porphyritic red ruby inserts is known as anyolite, and remains a prized possession in the family archives. Anyolite is unique to Tanzania and derives its name from the Maasai word anyoli meaning green.

A few days later, Richard announced that he had spent his savings, five shillings, at the Indian *duka* on a very large Perspex 'bowl' and wanted to make it into a fish tank. "It is in the bedroom, come and have a look." We all trooped in to discover dozens of hermit crabs clattering about and dragging their variety of seashells all over the floor. "If these are your pets, Richard, I would be glad if you would keep the bedroom door closed!" Cicely responded. The house had come to life.

12th April 1965: It was Cicely's 36th birthday and we had a guest. Whilst shopping for food in town, Richard jumped up and declared, "There's Mr Rushbrook, our School Escort." We stopped and spoke to him. He was entering the Sea View Hotel, in other words, purgatory! We invited him to our Spartan abode. "At least you will not be devoured by mosquitoes!" He was a most pleasant young man who obviously loved children. "By the way," he said, "I am interested in snakes. Do you have any around here?

"Well," Cicely replied, "a cobra came calling, for my birthday. Found it by the front door."

"Oh; it came to say many happy returns. Did you keep it?" he said excitedly.

"Oh, yes. It's dead though. Brian threw a petrol soaked gunny bag over it. That's the way to kill snakes. It's instantaneous."

"Oh … Shame!" he said sadly.

The boys took their teacher rambling around the bay, delightedly expounding their natural history knowledge. New though they were to the tropical coast, they recognised migrant birds they had seen on leave at Blakeney Point in Norfolk. These were sandpiper, ringed plover and terns. Then there were the comic fiddler crabs with their eyes on stalks and the ubiquitous multi-coloured lizards scouting on every rock. They watched the black and white pied kingfisher hovering over the lagoon, like a kestrel over a meadow in England, then closing its wings to drop like a stone to administer death upon some edible fish. Mr Rushbrook told us after supper that Richard was top of the class in Nature Study.

"Oh, thanks for telling us that – he would never have mentioned it."

A chap turned up at the door in the evening. "I am off on leave and I must get rid of my GP14 tomorrow. I heard that you might be interested in buying it. Fifty quid would suit me."

"Done!" said Richard, "Get your cheque on the table, Dad, it's a bargain!"

"It's the one with blue sails. Its name is Aqua Birda. Good family sailor."

Dad as usual thought about the price. What's that Chinese saying? 'He who considers everything makes a good planner? No, 'decides nothing'.

"Steer. Steer," from the two boys.

"OK." A cheer hit the roof, followed by the singing of 'Happy Birthday' Mum.

Kiwanda and Magila Mission: I now had survey staff and transport settled in Tanga from V.S.A. HQ. I was instructed to plan a settlement scheme for an area called Kiwanda for African village people, in those fertile hills and valleys of Usambara Mountains. There was talk of growing cocoa, about which I knew nothing of course. My challenge was to learn what habitat cocoa enjoyed and then check-out whether Kiwanda was suitable.

There were 2,600 acres of mountainous countryside which had been excised by the government. I learned it was originally a goodwill gift by the C.P.E.A., Church Province of East Africa, previously known as the U.M.C.A.; University Mission to Central Africa. This land had never been cultivated since it was acquired as Enemy Property in 1923 from whence it was held by the Bishop of Zanzibar until 1932. It was then developed as a 'retreat' and later a teacher training college by U.M.C.A. The land was steep, low-lying at 600 feet altitude and humid. With 50 inches of rainfall and fertile soil, the prospects were good, especially for hand-hoe cultivation on those steep slopes. The surrounding tribal villagers were designated as being 'in hunger'. The Government insisted on a 'cash crop' for export as well as self-sufficiency food.

"Right, Boys. How do you feel about a safari into the mountains? Not far away, if you look over the bay, you can see the place in the mountains over there."

"Well ... OK. Can we take Sally?"

We called at the Mlingano Sisal Research Station to show the boys that chemistry really did have a practical use in real life. We reached Korogwe and met the Bishop. He told us the history of old Magila Mission on the hill and the old bell that called the converted of the *Wabondei* tribe to prayer. This bell was from the ship that brought the missionaries here even before the Germans came, in 1875.

Looming dramatically above the Mission was a great pinnacle of granite, a monolith not unlike the Matterhorn. The name of this pinnacle was Mlinga. The Bishop explained that Mlinga threw a rain shadow over the *Wabondei* gardens, depending upon the direction of the monsoon. "This is fundamental to the understanding of the *Wabondei* custom of sacrificing a chosen daughter by throwing her off the peak of Mlinga in order to appease the rain God. The missionaries achieved an element of success in preventing this sorry sacrifice. Their bell reminded the people that there was a better route to salvation. Our host told us, "There is still some opposition to this concept by the *mganga*, to this day."

I was also asked to design a small earth dam below Mlinga to be built by the villagers. This was easily done quite soon. The *mganga* was forced by the villagers to camp in the rain shadow, reservoir area, in his shelter to maximise his influence, until the rain came. Presumably, if he drowned, he would be posthumously proclaimed a hero. His services, in any case, would then be dispensable.

The Bishop explained that the custom of sacrifice in times of drought was ceremonial with dancing and beer drinking. The parents of the chosen girl considered themselves to be privileged and would subsequently be provisioned with food by the tribe through the cropping season, so that they had no need to work in the fields. The guiles of human ideology! Scientific knowledge has, thankfully, superseded superstition and educated maidens today attract a premium bride price.

Having located Kiwanda, which lay under heavy forest, we drove down to the lowland plain, to find an abandoned citrus fruit farm at Misovwe near that abandoned Magila Mission used during the war to produce fruit for the troops. The grass grew 5 ft tall, hiding the fruit trees. We drove around in the Land Rover and found loaded grapefruit bushes hidden in the tall *Panicum* grass. The young company present soon worked out that if we removed the canvass canopy from the Land Rover and reversed vigorously into the tree, we would arrive back in Tanga with half a ton of ripe grapefruits. It proved a great way to make ourselves known to the membership of the Yacht Club. Richard and Philip were nicknamed the 'Grapefruit Kids'. We made several trips over that Easter holiday, with accumulated considerable pocket money from the TYC members.

Tanga proved an exciting place, not only for its history, Toten Island and pirates, but also sailing, diving on the coral reef for cowry shells and crayfish, swimming in the warm sea, coral beach barbeques, and of course, the Lowenthal Theatre, of more later. The game, 'Buccaneer', suddenly became popular with the boys, which seemed somehow appropriate to our new life style.

East African Safari Rally: Back in the 1953 Safari Rally that took in Kenya, Uganda and Tanganyika, was held to mark the coronation of Queen Elizabeth II. It had subsequently become an annual event, held over the Easter weekend. By 1965 it had established a reputation as one of the most gruelling motor races in the world. The course itself varied from year to year and ranged from 3500 to 4000 miles in length traversing through the three East African countries predominantly on dirt roads, often rendered barely passable by the rainy season. Wild animals, with little respect for the Highway Code added an extra hazard! The event had proved to be an exceptional testing ground for cars and drivers. To put that in context in 1963 only seven cars of the 84 starters finished the event. If your car could finish the East African Safari Rally it was tough enough to endure anything! So by 1965 the rally was attracting international drivers and factory teams. Typically the event started and finished in Nairobi. This year the event started in Dar es Salaam and followed the old disused coast road up into the Usambara Mountains and across the border into Kenya, ending in Nairobi after trekking through Uganda. This was surely the toughest route in the world.

"Enter the Corsair, Dad."

"Come on, I love my Corsair. That would be cruel."

Since we knew Amani, we were detailed to do the late shift at Amani Checkpoint. The boys were in their element. It was the *Mvuli* rains, torrential now, with deep mud. We had the use of the Government rest house to clean up next day. The boys stood by, armed with pencils and autograph books. 84 cars left Dar es Salaam, only 16 reached Nairobi; none of them British. Peugeot and Saab were the seasoned drivers' favourites. They ploughed in through the mud at Amani over a period of seven hours. Some had lost a door, as well as bumpers and head lamps. The boys procured the signature of Pat Moss, who arrived four and a half hours after the rally leaders, Joginder and Jaswant Singh, in their privately owned Volvo PV544. She was driving the rather egg-shaped small Saab which she said she had rolled over several times. Her brother

Stirling Moss was following her in a back-up car. She sat in our lamp light looking dazed and zombie-like.

Following Pat Moss were two big Citroens, one with flat front tyres and the other without the driver's door. A Peugeot 404 pulled in with no bonnet. The driver said he had had a confrontation with a buffalo. Many drivers were barefoot, having lost their shoes in the mud when pushing their car. The rain crashed down on Amani for 24 hours unceasingly. The torrents turned to showers by Friday.

On Saturday morning, the sun was back to turn everything to steam. The boys, plus Sally Spaniel, disappeared to the beach early leaving Cicely and I dozing in our twin beds. A swarm of those Raskazone bees gathered noisily in the tree by the window, their buzzing filled the house reminding us of that story of the invasion of Tanga in 1914 by the British Indian Army. They were defeated by 'swarms of bees', so it is recorded.

Cicely leapt out of bed naked. "I hope there are no holes in the mosquito screens."

"Hey, there is a buzzing in my bed – come and help me!"

She pulled off my bed sheet. "Where is it then?"

"You mean you can't see it? I am disappointed."

"You sod!" she said, digging her nails into my flesh. "I am going to make tea."

Towards the end of April the rains were abating, a new challenge emerged for us all – sailing out on the Indian Ocean. Well, just the Tanga Bay actually, out as far as the coral reef. Formally we joined the 120 member Tanga Yacht Club, a largely expatriate institution comprising the sisal estates staff, the Judiciary, the Port Authorities, the Railway Engineers and the Banks. There were a few 'upper class' Tanzanian members who joined for social reasons, but did not sail despite the fact that many of the local Africans were extremely competent sailors in their *ngalawas* which they used for fishing. *Ngalawas* were similar to the River Nile version, with a triangular sail and canoe outriggers.

We had also purchased a Dabchick for the boys in addition to our GP14 dinghy Aqua Birda. The Dabchick was a great single sail flat board, ideal for children to learn to sail on. The Yacht Club fraternity assumed that as mature age members we knew what we were about and treated our first sailing expedition with complete indifference, at least for the first hour at which point they noticed that we seemed to be missing from the bay. I remembered my book 'How to Sail for Beginners' and followed the procedure for a gentle breeze; "down rudder, down centre board, watch the burgee at the top of the mast for wind direction and sheet in accordingly. 'Be positive in orders for the crew' i.e. the beautiful Cicely.

The dark blue sails filled and off we went at an exhilarating pace, on a 'broad reach', with Cicely leaning out backwards over the water in an effort to keep the boat upright. The experience filled our souls as well as our sails. I tightened the 'jib sheet', meaning rope and headed seaward as the breeze picked up with the image of a Corsair twin carburettor GT in mind, 0 – 60 mph in 13 seconds. Question for me was, how do we slow down? What did the book say? Something about; going-about. A ship was approaching as we headed towards India. We would definitely need to 'go-about', sooner rather than later. Cicely was striving to keep us in a state of normality, as was her wont.

I firmly ordered "ready about, LEE HO" and swung the tiller to bring the bow into the wind. We stopped dead, sails flapping alarmingly. Aqua Birda exhibited that female gender reluctance to be pushed around, in other words, to port. I was obliged to tighten up the sheet and she returned to the starboard tack and bolted like a rabbit.

We were now miles out from the bay in a strengthening wind and beyond view of the OOD's Box, Officer Of the Day, which was, apparently, against the Rules.

I gave the order again, in the hope that our ancestral spirits were on our side. My trusting crew 'un-cleated' her sheet and down went the tiller, "LEE HO". The wind was so strong that we ended up back on the starboard tack going less like a Corsair GT, more like a charging elephant on a string. We now faced the option of either hitting the coral reef or the cargo ship. The ship was flying a Chinese flag; they might not comprehend our rather British problem. My crew's abundant flowing auburn hair shrouded her face and the wind swept away her loving last few words.

The book word 'jibe' emerged in my brain. Ah yes, I thought, it is possible to turn around another way but I would have to slow down to avoid a knock-out blow to my crew as the boom of the mainsail slammed across from starboard to port. I eased the sheet, "Ready to jibe." She unclipped her sheet and flung herself into the bottom of the boat as the boom slammed across "JIBE OH". We pitched heavily to starboard, almost capsizing the boat. Aqua Birda was transformed into a rolling cork. I tightened up gently as we found ourselves alongside a wall of steel, travelling in the same direction, towards Tanga. Gesticulating Chinese were shouting down at us "Rotten capitalists!"

Trembling limbs carried us at a steady pace past Raskazone Cliffs into the Bay of Tranquillity and past the crowded (!) OODs Box. We gave them a cheery wave so as to infer that we had enjoyed our cruise out to the coral reef and crash-landed on the beach. Cicely fell into the sea prematurely. The Commodore approached. "Are you two OK? You've been away a long time. We thought you'd emigrated; to the Seychelles!"

"We have been out to the reef. Strong wind!"

"My God! We usually make up a fleet to do that. It is safer to go in a group. Nobody wears a lifejacket in this Club. By the way, there are plenty of sharks about out there. They follow the ships in, looking for garbage. It is not a good place to capsize."

After a few Tuskers on the Quarter Deck, Cicely let it slip that we had never helmed a boat before and this had been our first trip out in a dinghy. Gasps of derision were audible as the word spread, followed by a reverend hush. We felt that we had become members of note.

The following afternoon at the Club, news came through of America's first spacewalk. It was an awesome thought, much debated in relation to our lives in Africa. Could being out on that long umbilical cord, travelling at seventeen thousand miles an hour, according to the BBC, be more exciting than being on a trapeze, in the Kaskazi gale, in an Osprey, the top class sailing boat that most members owned, or, come to that, being caught amongst a herd of elephants in six foot tall grass as Cicely and I once were. Who wanted to walk in space for adventure when they had Tanzania as the challenge?

Treasure Island

26th April 1965: It was Richard's 13th birthday party. I had a treasure hunt organised. "Pirates always buried their 'loot' on remote tropical islands to be collected later," I declared to the assembled group of children, "these pirates were caught and killed long ago but I am told they left a Chart."

They found the Chart, as planned, in the hollow tree in our garden, with some help from Sally Spaniel's keen sense of smell. Herewith a copy of the old faded Chart of Toten Island. The excitement grew and it was decided to sail in Aqua Birda, which by then Richard had learned to sail, to Toten Island. With so many children, a back-up boat would be needed also. "I can arrange that." I said. Richard had been congratulated upon his sailing skills by the

Commodore and the older ones felt safe with him. So off they went full of enthusiasm.

By the time they had crossed the bay, their hair and party clothes were dishevelled by the wind and sea spray, but they just did not care about what Mummy would say. They did care about what horrible surprises there might be awaiting them in the forest on Toten Island. The little ones were afraid. Little Minnie asked, "Are dare any cannibals on dat island, Philip?" Philip, was Richard's brother age ten.

"Streuth, I hope not!" Philip began to wonder how it would feel to be cooked in a big black pot, surrounded by German and Arab graves. Then he remembered Richard's words when they had climbed the derelict German tower overlooking the Indian Sea. "Toten Island is uninhabited."

His courage returned. He tapped his pocket and said, "Don't worry, Millie, I am ready for 'em – I have got my catty with me." Catty is short for catapult. Philip had a passion for abbreviations.

As they approached the island, they could see a white sandy beach beneath the coconut palms, but along the water's edge it was all slimy mud and coral boulders. Richard had 14-year-old Gilles Dingwall for crew. The rest of the children were following in a larger boat belonging to Mr Chaple. They watched as Richard headed for shore at full speed. He hit the mud, stopped dead, slewed sideways and Gilles fell out backwards in the sea. He was under for a second then stood up, waist deep in the sea.

"Blimey, Richard!" he said wiping the sea water from his eyes.

"Grab the bow rope, Gilles, and pull us inshore, quick!" Richard ordered as he let go the mainsail to release the wind. He didn't want to listen to any criticism of his sailing skill from Gilles, "The mud'll wash off." he said, glancing down at Gilles's filthy legs and feet.

Richard pulled down the flapping blue sails and the dinghy lay peacefully on the tide line.

The children all gathered on the white sand with coconut palms rattling in the breeze over their heads, all feeling a bit lonely.

Richard restored their confidence by shouting, "Commodore! … Chart!"

Philip pulled the chart out of his canvass bag and spread it out on the hot sand. Everyone crowded around and peered down at it. The hot sun beat down on the back of their necks as Richard read out loud, "Peg Leg's grave. Spade here."

They all looked along the beach. Adventurous Millie was the first to locate the spot. "Dare's da gwave," she said boldly and ran off, followed by everyone else.

Philip was left behind, struggling to fold the chart and stow it away carefully in the canvass bag. "Hey, you guys!" he shouted, "Suppose the tide comes in? Aqua Birda will float away and then what? We will be here until we die!" He grabbed the bow rope and tied it to an old tree root, then ran after the others.

Everyone stood around the grave in silence at first. "Streuth, spade here it said; must be IN the grave Rich … Shall we have to dig it out with our hands?"

"I'm going home," said Molly, the eldest.

Then Little Millie added, "Dare might be spiders in dat gwave."

"Never mind," said Richard, in a tiresome tone of voice, "I'll do it … who cares about a few old dry bones." Everyone shuddered as he began to roll away the stones. Under the stones were bones all right! There were also shells and one big piece of shiny wood, rounded and shaped. Everyone shuddered again, watching silently as it was pulled out of the grave.

Philip broke the silence, "Any skull?"

"I can't see one but I reckon this is Peg Leg's wooden leg and, ah, what's this?" Everyone pulled back in fright. "Give it to Molly."

Nobody moved. Richard grabbed the piece sticking out from under the rock. It looked like an arm and a hand half buried. Molly turned pale and said weakly, "I don't know why we want to go looking for treasure anyway. There won't be any."

"It's only the spade!" declared the Commodore cheerfully.

Molly was shaking, "I'm not going into that dark forest, Richard, amongst all those graves."

Richard began to feel that he was doing everything himself whilst the others just stood and grumbled. He turned to Molly and looked her in the eye, "You are not helping at all. Do you want a share of the treasure? If so, help me pull the spade out of the grave."

Gilles picked up the spade and marched off towards the forest without looking back.

"Chart Commodore," called Richard, "the chart says 200 strides, deep well, nearby is a Baobab tree, march 75 strides on compass bearing 350 degrees to find buried treasure. Hm- mm - not far," said the Captain. Whereupon he and Sally Spaniel marched off or rather Sally raced off and Richard followed with a line of children behind along the muddy track leading into the dark forest. It was as though Sally knew the way.

Soon they began to see ancient gravestones covered in creepers. One bare stone had a large brightly-coloured lizard reclining on top, enjoying a bright patch of sunlight and rolling its eyes in ecstasy. It began bobbing its head up and down in amazement at this intrusion into its otherwise silent world. Suddenly there was an outburst of loud clapping all around the children. Was it spirits of the dead arisen? No, it was a flock of Green Pigeons that had been feeding on figs shaken down to the ground by foraging monkeys.

Nevertheless that sudden clapping of wings in the forests silence left their hearts beating wildly with fright.

Further down the track another patch of sunlight illuminated a patch of Arab graves. They then noticed a man standing there, dressed in rags gathered by a thick leather belt and tucked into that belt a large cutlass. He had a black patch over one eye and a head scarf tightly bound across his forehead with a knot at the back of his head.

Molly hissed, "It's a pirate!"

The pirate grinned slyly and boomed in a deep voice, "Hold it there me hearties! Don't run away, there is no need to be afraid of me, I like children, in fact I think they are DELICIOUS!"

"He sounds hungry to me," whispered Philip, "I bet he has got a big cooking pot back there somewhere."

The pirate spoke again in a friendly but sly manner, grinning a lot and showing gold teeth. He still looked fierce and Sally growled. Everyone knew that Sally was a good judge of character and the children crowded together for comfort. "Ho, Ho, Ho, my fine jolly lads. What have you got in that bag then? Have you by any chance found our chart? I have been looking for it for 290 years. You had better hand it over, it belongs to me! Give it to me and I will lead you to the treasure. What could be fairer than that me hearties?"

The feeling of mistrust grew more than ever as Sally began growling again. Then everyone jumped as Philip blurted out loudly. "I'm not giving you the chart. We found it in the hollow tree in our garden and anyway. You're dead!"

The children all felt like cheering Philip but dare not as the pirate's face changed to menacing. His one eye narrowed, shining with fury and his mouth dropped down at one corner. He placed his hand on the handle of his cutlass and spoke in a low threatening voice. "Tell yer wot, I'll cut the treasure with yer, arf an arf. I'll let yer pass fur a piece a the gold."

The way he said 'gold' made it sound like chocolate cake. They all looked at Captain Richard for a response. He said coldly, "We agree."

They set off again, trailing the pirate at the end of the line where he was able to keep an eye on the Commodore's shoulder bag with the chart inside. The forest closed in all around them again. A flock of Louries about the size of magpies with very loud voices flapped clumsily above the tree tops ahead of them like heralds trumpeting their presence to the spirits of the forest.

"They make enough noise to awaken the dead." said Richard half-jokingly.

The pirate was the only one to laugh. "Ah! Here's the well and there's the baobab tree!" Richard announced triumphantly.

Just as they reached the baobab tree, a figure appeared dressed in a black gown and a mortar board like a high school headmaster. He had a broad moustache like bicycle handlebars and a long whippy cane in his hand.

"Good morning, children," he said cheerfully, but looking slightly threatening as he bent the cane between his hands. "Ah, Richard, I've been waiting for you. You're late! Bend over, boy!"

Richard suddenly recognised the teacher's voice and that smile. "I know you, you are Eddie, Eddie Barry and the pirate is your brother Gerry! Thank goodness for that. Gerry had us all fooled."

There was a sigh of relief all round and everyone laughed as the joke emerged. Even Sally wagged her tail again. Eddie and Gerry were teenagers on holiday from St Mary School, Nairobi.

The children were all very happy now. The teacher showed them how to take a bearing of 350 degrees with the compass. "There, that way!" he pointed.

They carefully measured 75 large strides and began digging madly. Suddenly 'clonk', the spade struck a hard object.

"That's it," shouted Molly, "there IS treasure after all. Hooray!"

Up came a wooden box with handles each end. The lid was duly prized open with a spade to reveal many parcels all wrapped in shiny gold paper. Each parcel bore the name of one of the children and also Eddie and Gerry.

"Isn't that super," said Molly, "a piece of 'gold' for everybody. But what about poor Sally! We wouldn't have even found the treasure without her. She drove back the pirate when we were all threatened. Never mind, Sally," she said stroking her silken black coat and long ears, "I'll get you a bone from Peg Leg's grave. What could be fairer than that me hearty?"

I'll leave my readers to visualise the effort involved in setting up this epic birthday event and especially the fabulous input by Eddie and Gerry Barry.

If my reader has any children around the age of Richard and Philip they would love this true story of what life was, sometimes, like before computer games.

THE CHART

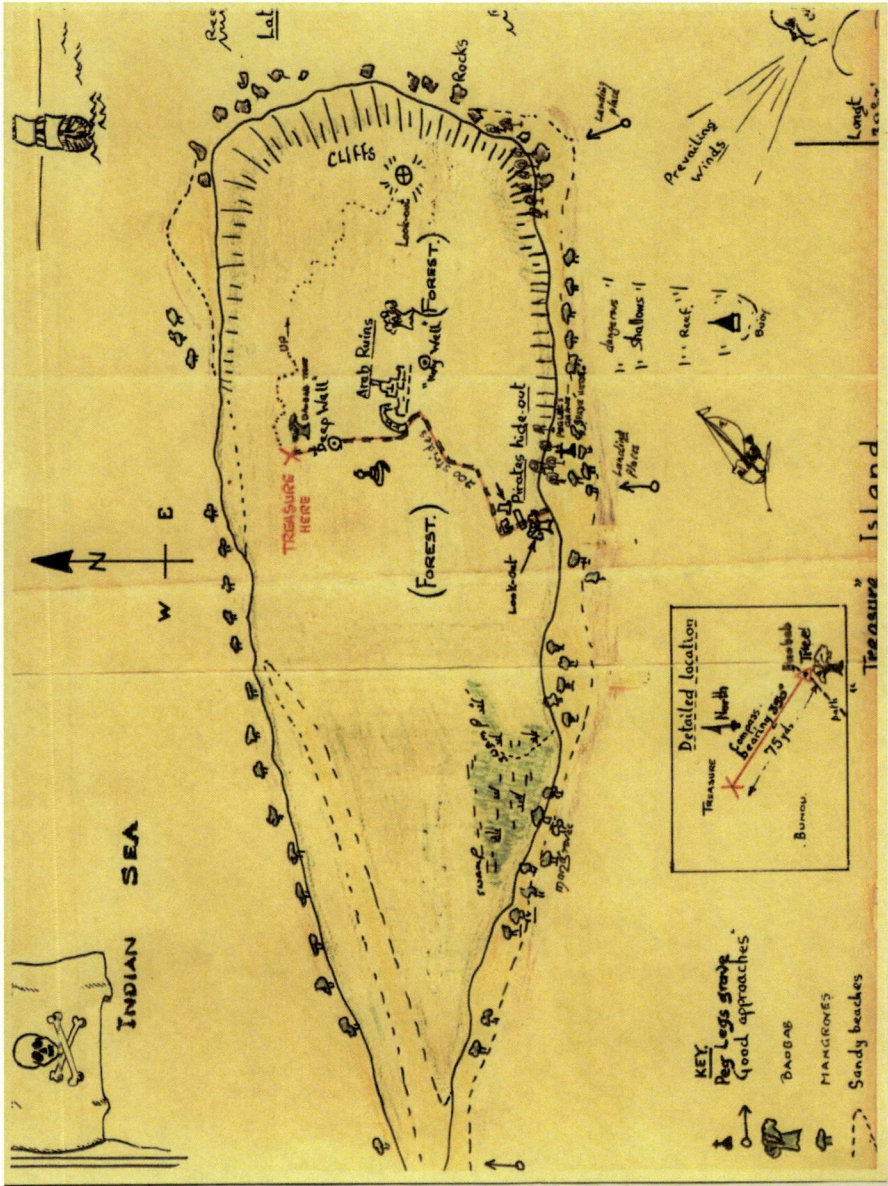

ROUTE MAP
COASTAL AND NORTHERN REGION

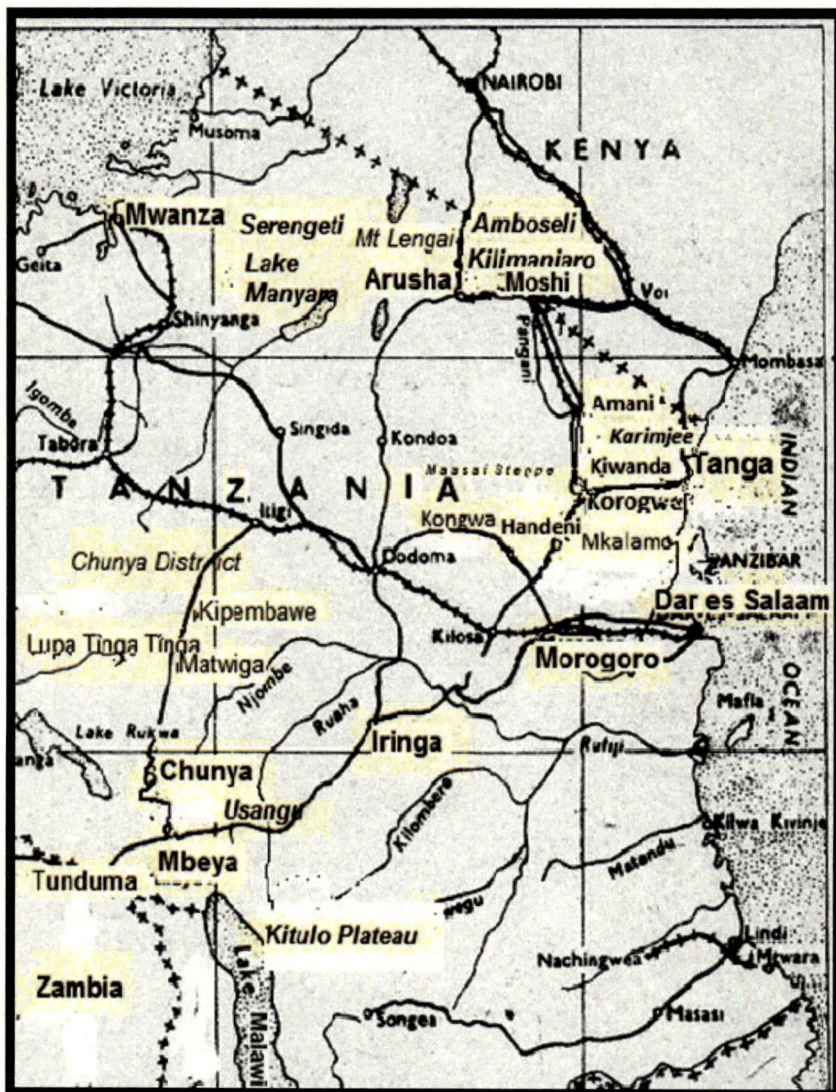

Chapter Seven

Mountains, Beaches, Railways, and Amboseli

Our boxes arrived on 17th April. They had taken from the 20th March to reach us, a three days' drive, the mind boggles? It was raining 'cats and dogs' as we all stood staring at the boxes outside the house. We gave the six smiley Africans two shillings each tip and they removed their shirts and set to work humping the boxes into the house. The biggest crate they called the *toto* which means small child. As they struggled with it on the very large sack barrow belonging to the East African Railway & Harbours, Richard shouted *"Umepata pancture"* You've got a puncture. Cries of *"Al ... La!"* followed by much merriment. Eventually the boys opened their toy box and extracted their favourite toy the powerful polystyrene ball pump shot gun. We now had our *barafu* or fridge and revelled in the prospect of much sought after cool drinks.

We decided upon another adventure. We had heard of a 'heavenly' coral beach 26 miles down the coast called Kigombe, but the road south disappears after a while and becomes no road as such. The thing about the Corsair, it weighed less than half as much as a Land Rover and could be pushed out of a muddy hole whereas with a Land Rover one was faced with a major retrieval operation. The Swahili word *mbuga* is used, amongst other things, to describe a section of topographically low level land, usually water-logged, and prone to mosquitoes – *mbu.* There was a lot of it en-route to Kigombe. We successfully negotiated an *mbuga* crossing built of sticks and planks, sewn together with bark string by the local villagers.

We enjoyed that wonderful Kigombe vista of the Indian Ocean. The cool breeze brushed our faces and whistled through the Casuarinas; a pine common along tropical beaches and known as the 'whispering pines'. Coconut palms promised refreshment and the shells, fuel for our fire. The Indian Ocean crashed into the coral reef throwing up a white spray on the horizon but the blue water was calm for the children and Sally Spaniel to wallow in. All that was missing was the romantic introductory tune to the BBC's Desert Island Discs programme. There was no sign of human activity but the boys did find an old circular table top from somewhere to take home. They later learned to water-ski on it.

Eventually the tide fell and we were able to explore the coral reef with a piece of mosquito net converted for fishing. We caught brilliantly-coloured small fish and wished we had a glass tank. Top of the Pops was squid, which expressed their emotions by changing their body colour. They have very large eyes and travel by jet propulsion which we humans thought we had invented. However, they travel exclusively in reverse gear which might cause insurmountable problems for Corsair drivers.

The boys spent the day in a delirium of happiness, mainly in the warm surf, swimming, diving, tumbling and then chasing along the coral sands after lizards and fiddler crabs. Knocking down coconuts for a drink of 'coconut milk' was a challenge. The old shells gave us fire to boil a kettle for tea, for stick-in-the-mud Mum and Dad.

Back at home in Tanga, the boys dozed at the supper table. They did not ask the interminable question, "When will we be going back to Home Farm, Dad?" but instead "When will we be able to go to Kigombe beach again, Mum?"

That opportunity, arrived sooner than expected. We heard a radio message from Dar es Salaam that 1st May would become a National

Holiday for Labour Day, or as some of our brethren might say "A day of mourning for those who have to work." For us; guess what; a 100% vote for a day at Kigombe beach. The temperature was 33 degrees C.

Down on the beach we listened to the BBC World Service on our portable battery radio whilst reclining on the sand. We were treated to a speech by the Minister of Overseas Development, Barbara Castle. She was talking about Tanzania, "Such a wonderful country," etc. Well she got that right. She had visited a huge wheat growing farm called Upper Kitete, near Ngorogoro Crater, a scheme I had helped set up when I first arrived in the country. She explained that British Aid had set up this "successful scheme" and how she was "very impressed" with how well the local people had responded. She didn't get that quite so right, trying to be a tactful politician. Whilst local people were shareholders in the Co-operative, the scheme's success was actually attributable to the employment of competent farm manager and the use of modern machinery, seed and fertilisers on a large scale. Barbara Castle went on to say, correctly, that she thought tourism should be developed for this very beautiful area and its abundant wildlife. Today this is the well-known area of the National Parks of Lake Manyara and Ngorogoro Crater. She continued to say that, "The new Rural Development Committees are working well." I will rephrase that, speaking as an RDC member for some three years; "RDC's are an entertaining forum, with such charming oratory as Africans are very good at, making a parliament for optimistic debate and aspirations." I might refrain from adding that, "At the conclusion of business for the day that was that; until the next month's meeting. Nothing more of consequence actually happened."

There were two casualties at Kigombe that day. Sally Spaniel caught a conger eel, not her best achievement, which latched onto her long ear causing it to bleed profusely. Then *Bwanamkubwa,* in other words me; was struck by his old enemy lumbago whilst

171

demonstrating his goggling skills on the coral reef. A plaintive cry came ashore on the breeze, "I can't move. Need help!"

Back on the beach, a certain lady was heard to mutter, "Serves him right really. He has been very greedy lately." She raised her voice and waved. "OK, Brian, we're coming." Despite the lack of sympathy I was rescued and, after a brief respite, sufficiently recovered to drive them all home. Fingers crossed for no sudden cloud burst.

The school holidays were drawing to a close. Snorkelling had proved immensely popular with the two boys. They both became obsessed with the quest for a sighting of the elusive black and white banded Lionfish. It is called Lionfish because it has venomous spines I later learned that there were typically three or four Lionfish regularly to be found sheltering under the raft which all the kids used to play on, at the Yacht Club. Philip paddled about for ages in the shallows followed by clouds of tiny fish around his legs, rather like a football crowd heading for an important match. Richard went down into a fish trap without his snorkel and ended up being spat at by a squid. He was really frightened and pale-faced when he came home.

Saturday 8th May 1965 was the day the boys went back to school. This day was 'the end'. This death and rebirth every three months was extremely wearing for all of us. We all sat at the breakfast table in deathly silence, the boys in their grey shorts, dark green shirts and ties, with their green jackets on the chair backs. Soon we were on Tanga Railway Station platform, the E.A.R & H, engine hissing away impatiently. Everything was orderly but tense. Philip just seemed to take the day as it came but by all accounts broke down in tears as the train pulled out. Railway stations are famously places of great joy or can be, conversely, places of utter grief. How well I recall from my Army leave days, the absolute joy of finding the love of my life Cicely, awaiting my arrival on the

Kenilworth station platform, and inevitably the utter grief of our separation upon my return to barracks. Those feelings were back to haunt us.

Back at home the silence was deafening. We pondered, yet again, what we were doing. Sally searched the garden, stood below the limp rope that led up to the hollow tree where they found the chart; she was looking upwards, whimpering. Cicely and I spent the next day, Sunday, together in the garden waiting anxiously for news of the boy's safe arrival in Arusha. Sally was still coursing round the garden for scents of the boys and into the bedroom where a catapult lay 'dead' on the bed. On Friday last, it had been a lethal weapon. The bush babies in the trees made a dense racket at about 10 p.m. They were alarmed about something incomprehensible to us. Did they sense some bad event?

We later learned that the children's heartbreak was shorter lived on the train than with their parents. Stories of great hilarity reached us eventually; the making of water bombs out of paper from their exercise books for the purpose of bombing African boy traders on the numerous railway station halts. We heard how the boys disembarked from the slow-moving train on the climb towards Kilimanjaro to throw gravel and sand under the engine wheels to keep it moving, which caused sparks to fly when the wheels slipped. Also, there was the mad-cap minibus drive for the 50 miles from Moshi to Arusha when drivers competed with each other to get there first. Accidents did happen, but luck prevailed for Richard and Philip.

Since the trains never exceeded 30 mph, the taxi runs were the equivalent of Formula One and must have been exciting. The African train journeys with E.A.R & H. were notoriously romantic for school children, traversing forests, and plains where wildlife of every description was often to be seen from the carriage windows, wide brown sultry rivers, dramatic raging gorges, and mountain ranges, and covering vast distances powered by the burning of hard wood logs to make steam. Roger Whittaker famously sings a memorable ballad about travelling to school by E.A.R & H.

A few days later we found ourselves, drowning our sorrows, after another day of torrential rain, on the Quarter Deck of the Yacht Club watching the red sun sink behind the Usambara Mountains and Mlinga Peak, reminding us of so many sacrificial maidens.

"Cheer up, Cicely. We have got a letter from Caroline."

On the back of her blue airmail form she had written; 'From little me, who is controversial yet taciturn and is very perfunctory. Miss Dawtrey, St Vincents, Warwick.' We pondered upon that momentarily before slitting open her letter, "She takes after you, Brian," whispered Cicely. Caroline had obviously had a great time visiting her 'Home Farm days' horse riding pal Suzanne Parkinson in Norfolk. She said that she will be flying to Tanga at the end of the summer term. We now had a desperate longing for that day to arrive.

On the Quarter Deck a radio was on. It was the BBC Overseas Service and John Arlott's measured tones drifted through the humid air. "That ball lifted a bit on the leg side and it's GONE! COULD BE A SIX." The suspense was killing. Then somebody switched to Voice of America, more volume, more powerful transmitter, endless boring irrelevant news, almost as bad as Moscow. Fortunately soon thereafter it was switched over to music on the BBC – the Swinging Sixties! The Supremes, Three Degrees, The Rolling Stones, Dusty Springfield singing her 'hit' Island of Dreams.

It was the Kiwanda Village Settlement Plan that next demanded my attention and so we set off to the Usambara Mountains again in our Corsair. This time we stayed with Walter Waller on Karimjee tea estate. His log fire up there in the mountains added a glow to his whisky. We were learning how to enjoy the restful atmospheric change from the debilitating heat of the coast. It was actually raining and very chilly.

After picking up some mapping beacons and some more soil samples, we ended up a few days later at Korogwe Mission having lunch with the Bishop. We wanted to discuss the Kiwanda Scheme Plan of Settlement in the light of his knowledge of local people and customs. We met the United Society for the Propagation of the Gospel (U.S.P.G.), staff at the Teacher Training Centre. They were all, may I say, die-hard Anglicans, but well-spoken of by the educated African elite. One of them knew our previous Mbeya Vicar, Canon Woolly. Apparently he had settled in Sussex with his new wife, and Totty. We were told that he had applied to be the Secretary of the Society for the Propagation of the Gospel, a missionary organisation. Like so many overseas good friends, we have never subsequently been able to trace him in that over-crowded island that is Britain.

The Bishop showed us part an old document written by the German explorer Krapf about this area: 'Johann Ludwig Krapf, Second Journey to Usambara 1853'.

Extract: 'Round about Mruka stream is extremely romantic country and reminded me of parts of Switzerland and the Black Forest the river flowing through a deep rocky ravine (this is Kiwanda today), clad on either side by noble woods.'

Extract: 'King Kweri allows the Maasai to pass though his land to raid the cattle of the Wasigua.' (Further south along the railway line to Dar es Salaam today.)

Extract: 'The Wasamba believe that they are all slaves of their King and live in dread of the covetousness and jealousy of the King and his Governors.' 'Disobedient soldiers are sold into slavery. However law and order prevails, unlike elsewhere near the coast where republicans are drunken and quarrelsome.' *Wasamba* '... need only bananas for hill climbing and carrying loads at great speed. They enjoy excellent health, only illness known is rheumatism and 'cutaneous disorders'.

Whilst in Korogwe we met a Food and Agriculture Organisation (F.A.O.) Cocoa Expert named Mr Torto. I was most grateful for the knowledge he imparted. He said Kiwanda was an ideal site for cocoa. This would be a new crop for Tanzania normally associated with Ghana. I later met a village farmer who told me that he had been growing cocoa for four years.

"It flowers well," he said, "sets pods but then dies back. I've yet to harvest a single pod." The trouble with agricultural advisors is that they get paid regardless of the validity of their advice, whereas the farmers' survival depends upon him harvesting a crop. Mr Torto did comment that we might need to grow some farmers as well as doing cocoa-growing trials.

Back in Tanga later that day a less fruitful but more humorous exchange, was our stroll along Tanga beach with the Lord Chief Justice of Tanzania, a West Indian. The Colonial concept of bringing professional magistrates from 'outside' for criminal cases continued to be very successful. He was a comic at impersonating colourful characters that had appeared before him. He chuckled constantly. He asked, "Do you know Brian Nicholson, the New Zealand Magistrate in Tanga? You must meet him. He is the Chairman of the Theatre Group." That last tip transpired to be the beginning of a whole new dynamism in our lives in Tanga, of which more later.

Six days after the boys left for Arusha School, we received their letter of safe arrival, enclosing a school fees bill of £63, net of Government Grant. Philip, whose mind was always on food, wrote, '… we had mincemeat on toast for our evening meal.' Cicely dismally thought, *Oh dear. I hope it was cooked.* Our new young sailing friend, Dr Ian Kennedy said in his Scottish brogue, "They are not being spoilt anyway, of that you can be sure."

Our next visitor was John English, a colleague from Head Office. He introduced his guest, Mr Eccles from **The Ford Foundation**! Apparently it was hoped that I could persuade him to 'cough up' some funds for Kiwanda Village Settlement Scheme. So off I went again to the mountains in my Corsair GT. I felt the need to impress him with my Ford car and reached 100 mph on that tar road out of town. I think my two, by now somewhat pallid, guests were relieved to pull into Magila Mission for lunch with the nuns.

The atmosphere of timeless tranquillity after that 100 mph drive was an anti-climax as we were mentally transposed from a modern, Ford-driven Western world, into the realms of local tribal culture and customs expounded on by the nuns. This particular human resource the *Wasamba* was the only one available to drive our Kiwanda agricultural development plan and we gave it our full attention.

Mr Eccles remarked, "Well, this is back-down-to-earth, as the astronauts might say."

I never did hear whether Mr Eccles was impressed enough to cough up some funds.

Tanga was another world for us hard-working, used to the cooler Southern Highlands, folk. Here, excuses for breaking-off work, and enjoying life, were the hallmark of survival, for both Africans and Europeans, the reason being the oppressive humid heat. The temperature was thirty plus degrees centigrade all year round; quite hot but manageable with practice. Tanga's salvation was its closeness to the warm sea. There is something about the seashore that sparks off the fun and relaxation side of human nature. Scientists have evidence that life was created in the ocean, about three and a half billion years ago, which might explain our obsessions, at all ages, with water.

In Tanga, everyone from the meanest African fisherman to the most prestigious Bank Manager had time for boating. That seemed appropriate as 'Tanga' means 'sail' in Kiswahili. Swimming trunks were *de rigueur* for eleven months of the year. The fact that the seat of Government was in Dar es Salaam, on the coast, produced the decreed office hours, 7:30 a.m. to 2:30 p.m., with no lunch break. This meant that afternoons could be spent on or in the water. A weekly event was the extraordinary venue for the sisal estate Board Meeting which was held offshore of the Quarter Deck, in the sea. Hence, the unique sight of a circle of white-haired men bobbing on the surface of the water with a bikini clad Company Secretary '*in camera*'.

The range of Tanga leisure pursuits was immense; gardening with exotic plants like Bougainvillea, Frangipani, oranges, paw-paw and melons; cowry shell collecting; skin diving on the coral reef; bird watching; fishing; beach parties. The most exciting challenge that a seaside worshipper could have was 'plane-ing' in an Osprey yacht when the powerful monsoon *Kaskazi* wind blew and you felt you were about to take off into the sky like a glider. We decided that we needed to experience that wind power, to supplement our past adventures with elephant power in wild places in 1962–4.

At home, we collected weaver birds in a cage attached to our windowless dining room. They piled in through a funnel in the roof and set about building nests. Their chirping was competitive with the children at the breakfast table in the holidays. The numbers built up to such a degree that we had to allocate Saturday mornings to clear-out time. They were obviously as passionately enamoured with Raskazoni as we were.

The end May 1965 found us back in Kiwanda. It was strenuous work. I must have walked 30 miles of survey traverses in the Kiwanda forest while also teaching my young African staff how to use the three-foot soil auger and how to texture the soil and record correctly. They were very willing, hard workers, while not over-educated they were keen to learn more. Higher level graduates always wanted desk jobs. I shed pounds in the oppressive heat. Cicely complained that she could soon thread me through the eye of her needle and that I should relax at the weekend down at the Yacht Club. I did not take much persuading. It would be a chance to practice our sailing skills, referring to my waterproof hand booklet "How to Sail in 10 Easy Stages", or was it 100?

We relaxed on the beach with our new short wave radio. The BBC Overseas Service was a godsend but the transmitter was weak. We tuned into Voice of America. On that occasion they were broadcasting a discussion between Professor Oscar Leubeck of Manhattan University and Doctor Wally Ackermann Junior, Anthropologist from Minnesota Mining and Exploration Incorporated, on the subject of British Colonial Rule and the break-up of African native culture. That was the one thing the Colonial Service went to great pains to avoid doing. Maybe they were getting confused with Christian Missionaries, many of whom were American and certainly intent upon changing a perceived 'evil' native culture.

We switched stations to the experts on American Culture, Peking Radio. It was hot stuff like the Goon Show, all backwards around and upside down. If you were to take a look at our American friends through a pane of fluted glass, the image would relate to the way the Chinese see the Americans. Peking continued, "Their imperialist schemes, i.e. the Peace Corps in Africa, Vietnam and India, are an example of the evil perpetrated by these dollar-brandishing murderers, who only want their bag of rice. Mr Chou then spoke. The similarly pronounced word 'Choo' means toilet in Kiswahili. "Tanzania, Kenya and Uganda are ripe for revolution." One wonders how that ancient nation, China, then lost the art of diplomacy.

There was no relaxation on radio short wave so we thought to try the short waves of the blue water of Tanga Bay. I hoisted the blue sails of Aqua Birda, sat my gorgeous wife amid ships, clasping the jib sheet and pushed off into the breeze. After ten minutes in this other world, dodging Chinese ships, buoys and Toten Island, we jibed unexpectedly giving Cicely a severe clip around the ear. "That's enough for today!" she shouted.

I headed for the Club beach to recuperate, over-shot, and jammed the centre board in the sand thus causing the dinghy to slew to one side, shooting Cicely onto the beach in a trembling heap. Our 'One for All and All for One' marital relationship was being put to the test. I called for assistance from Lutan Gayla, who was employed as the Beach Boy. His role was to help with the boats rather than, as his title suggests, a songster of one of the popular group of singers, The Beach Boys. Together, we escorted Cicely up the steps to the Quarter Deck for a double brandy. My "relaxing weekend" wasn't going as well as it should. Then, I realised that I had not lowered the main sail and horror of horrors, Aqua Birda had caught the wind and was sailing helmless back towards Toten Island. I dashed into the water up to my chest and managed to reach the tiller, jabbing my toe painfully on the rudder. Under control, I headed back to the beach shouting for Lutan Gayla again, trying to wear the countenance of a person who normally did this sort of thing as a keep-fit routine.

Cicely greeted me with a stony look. "I am not sure which is worse, following you in some remote bush with an air-photo or hanging onto a jib sheet in a gale. At least in miombo woodland I had a vague confidence that we'd arrive somewhere safe, with a compass."

In June it was arranged by the African Area Commissioner for me to meet him and a local village headman near Mkalamo, where it was planned to build a railway station. The location was sixty-five miles down the coast about twenty miles inland from the Indian Ocean bounded on the seaward side by Mkwaja Ranch and on the western side by the new railway to Dar es Salaam. The location was extremely inaccessible by road. I had a plan in my head to settle families on the fertile vacant land, to the east of the railway line, which looked good on the aerial photos. The villagers belonged to that 'inferior' tribe *Wasigua* that we read about in explorer Krapf report on the *Wasambara*. They all lived on the westerly side of the railway line. The only access on the eastern side was the old remnant railway construction track which was rutted and boggy from the recent *Mvuli* rains. The Corsair GT was not the ideal vehicle but it had to stand-in for my Land Rover on this occasion.

Cicely and I motored all day, along bush encroached roadways and tracks, plunging through mud holes, straddling crevices and ruts, which had the potential to tear the bottom out of the car if I had any loss of concentration. The countryside was verdant and enchanting. Nature had much of this Pangani District in its grip, alternatively flooding it and starving it, of rain. The *Wasigua* had a harder time of it that the *Wasambara* mountain tribe. We saw very little Game in these 5,000 square miles of wild country. Having achieved an overview of the area I decided to try and reach the better murram road homewards on the west side of the railway line. The Village Headman told me that everyone travels that way to Tanga. "It's a long way round *Bwana* but *hakuna matata*". This lovely phrase, used for many occasions basically means, 'no problem'.

There was, however, one problem; "But what about the railway line?"

"Velly solly, Bwana."

Cicely agreed that we should try and drive across the railway line. Having scrutinised the air photos with my pocket stereoscope, I found a level spot by the rails. We finally reached it but a train then pulled up right there blocking my route. After a lengthy, tiresome, time-of-day chat with the driver in Kiswahili, I broached the matter of moving the train.

"Bwana! Hakuna nafasi." That isn't possible, (didn't have permission), he said irritably.

"Labda yardy hamsini tu?" Only 50 yards perhaps?

"OK. Upesi." Be quick, he said.

With some high revs and without losing my new exhaust system, we made it over. I blew my horn in thanks and headed for the wooded upland. Finally after meeting up with the African Area Secretary to discuss my impression of this, previous to the railway, isolated region, and what grant aid would be available from the VSA, we relished a smoother journey home. Mkalamo was 65 miles from Tanga by muddy track but by the road it proved to be 210 miles round trip, no less! I suffered two punctures calling for inner tubes and was shattered on reaching home. I had in mind one of those 'relaxing weekends' that Cicely had appealed for. Back at No.46 Raskazone I greedily consumed four grapefruits from the sack-full we had gathered from the abandoned Misovwe Mission farm. Africans do not eat grapefruit except for *"dawa"*, which is Kiswahili for medicine, for malaria. Their word for grapefruit is "fever fruit". Live-and-learn; I suffered a severe stomach problem the next day.

My Land Rover driver, Ali Chande, came back from the Kiwanda Survey and remarked, "Ah, the Chief is ill!" That reminded me again of the song I remembered about Adibigudai who 'was a cannibal chief out there ...' and what did explorer, Krapf say; 'the *Wasigua*' where we'd been that day, 'are cannibals'; 'and when they'd finished their awful feast and scattered the bones afar, the CMS were a Missionary less in Southern Nigeria'. My imagination was running away with me. At least I had refrained from eating any of the nuns at Misovwe Mission near the grapefruit farm, not so much out of commendable restraint however, doubtless due to the hardships of their existence, they were plainly a bunch of tough old birds.

The glorious mix of colourful characters and extraordinary landscapes in Tanzania stimulated my interest in black and white photography. However, the temperatures in Tanga were too high for the developing chemicals, 70 degrees Fahrenheit maximum for developer. To overcome this problem night-time work was essential. We had several rolls of film from the East African Safari Rally, the tea estates, Amani and the sailing. So this was to be our relaxing weekend. It was still oppressively humid and we both laboured stark naked in the infra-red glow. I had some nude photos of us both too but they were somewhat lacking in technical competence. It became an unending 'jibe' at the Yacht Club when the news escaped of our 'dark room' activity, now referred at the club as "canoodling".

On Sunday at the Club, Dick Blakeway leered, "Ah, Brian, get much development last night in the dark room then?" One helmsman, who shall remain nameless, said, "Brian and Cicely have been canoodling in the dark room again!"

Dick was lounging in his chair in a string vest. The girls referred to him as a "hairy monster", in his usual macho pose, skin mahogany brown and tousled black hair. His body hair was so exuberant that putting a shirt on was like dressing a chimpanzee. The hair across his shoulders grew vertically like elephant grass. "Do you need some advice for the improvement of your night life, Brian?" Cicely responded to his cheeky question, "How about some herbicide to get your brushwood under control?"

Dick continued his jibing. "Hey Gorgeous, let the old man do his own fixing and you come and crew for me in a real boat. What do you say? There's a race tomorrow." Dick owned an Osprey called Naiad and was by far the most prolific winner of sailing trophies at the Yacht Club. He also attracted some notoriety as he and his partner, Enid, were not married. This was then considered somewhat scandalous behaviour.

Cicely whispered with her anti-macho brigade of ladies. One of them moved in on Dick, "I like real men, especially the hairy ones. I'll crew for you, Dick, any time." Suddenly his chair flew and he found himself flat on the floor, pinned down by the sheer weight of women bent on his undoing or I should I say, doing. This was achieved by the ladies exercising their skills with crochet, knotting his body hair through his string vest. When he was released, an agonised expression added to his red-faced fury. There were so many knots. He had to spend the rest of his evening with scissors, painfully cutting off his vest. He was never seen again in a string vest nor did he race his Osprey yacht the following day. We did though, and Aqua Birda came in third.

Cicely became adept at starting comical, social bush fires amongst the male members of the Yacht Club. She had that animated leg-pulling persona which she inherited from Arthur Marriott, her father, and which added attraction to her natural beauty. This resulted in her being given a job. She was elected to the Club Management Committee as Lady Member.

Cicely's life style was changing from 'Tarzan's wife', the fictitious man of the wild jungle, to an actress on the Tanga Lowenthal Theatre Club stage. The theatre was a sophisticated modern building on the cliff overlooking the Bay. Known as the Lead Memorial Hall, it was built in the early 1950s, by a wealthy sisal estate magnate named David Lead in honour of his father, Sir William Lead, the founder and President of the Tanzania Sisal Growers Association.

It then occurred to me that Cicely was, by nature, an actress. I began to recall her being in all the 'shows' in the village during the war, and putting on a stage show in Epperstone village in Nottinghamshire when we were farmers, followed by her becoming a keep fit teacher in her spare time. I felt, having been blinded by the pressures of work that I had not realised until then that possibly she had missed her vocation by marrying me. Perhaps I should have married that girl that in 1951, as a student, I had a minor flirtation with. She was then an unknown girl with "magnetic eyes", of my age, when at the Packhorse Inn on the River Dove, I was on a fly fishing weekend. We had both suffered a trauma in the war and chatted a lot, then ended up with my pals having a sing-song evening with my ukulele. I later looked up her name in the Visitors Book with a view to looking her up. Had she become my wife she would certainly have remained unknown, like Cicely, though interestingly enough Audrey did end up doing Aid work in Africa for the United Nations. Here she is:

Cicely was given the lead role, Mrs Puffin, a cockney char lady, in "Goodnight Mrs Puffin". Her comic performance was the talk of the coast from Dar es Salaam to Mombasa. The Club could not believe that she was not a pure blooded cockney. For a while, during rehearsals, I had to address her, at the breakfast table, in a cockney accent to get her attention. The Producer, Brian Nicholson, a New Zealander, decided that the name Cicely Dawtrey did not flow easily off the tongue as a stage name and for the Programme. A selection of first names was banded around to 'match' her surname. Jo was mutually decided upon, with no reference to her husband, and henceforth she has become perennially known worldwide, as **Jo**

Dawtrey. My old school and farming friends whom we didn't meet up with until later, tactfully assumed that I had remarried. Cicely the mother, the farmer's wife and the wild-lifer, became Jo the socialiser, the actress, the sailor, the renowned Yacht Club Hostess. Henceforth in my text I feel I should use her 'nickname' though I prefer Cicely May. Life with Society Jo proved just as rewarding as life with the demur Cicely.

Such changes in habitat and life style can be refreshing in any marital relationship, however, our successful everlasting love affair over the previous seventeen years had resulted from trust, a unity of purpose and hobby interests, shared work challenges and above all, family building ambitions. However, the theatre world was not my scene. I am basically shy of the limelight and I am somewhat taciturn in conversation like my hunting friend Steve Stephenson, a man of few words. To me, the theatre club was a threat, especially as my field work meant nights away. I was so used to having my companion, the new 'Jo', always with me.

"Brian, you are becoming a recluse – what's up?"

"Well … I am your number one admirer. I am so proud of your performance on stage and I don't wish to drag you back into the bush, if you know what I mean."

"I can guess."

"I am not included in your new hobby or your new circle of friends. I did hear that a certain well-known single gentleman had tried to persuade you to marry him. Was this on stage or at the Stage Door?"

"You're right. It was most embarrassing and I was angry and told him to get lost. You know what my temper is like. He's leaving anyway. I'm staying; with my Farmer's Boy."

"Jo; the theatre group are all urban folk. I am an Honorary Game Warden and a Land-use Planner, an outdoor fanatic. I will be away sometimes and it won't fit with rehearsals."

"Listen, my Brian. You were very good at Art at school, our son Philip takes after you too; you got a distinction in Art didn't you, in your School Certificate. The theatre club needs a set painter. What do you say?"

And so it was. The dark room was closed. Additionally; the male fraternity of Tanga learned not to mess around with Jo Dawtrey.

Unexpectedly, a new Land Rover plus two more African Surveyors arrived from Dar es Salaam detailed to work at Kiwanda. As well as acting Jo was also now producing plays. However, one day she said, "Brian; they can await my attention now. I am coming with you for some mountain air."

We soon found ourselves enjoying the mountain air, on the verandah of the old Misovwe Mission station. Although we were only at 600 ft. altitude, the evenings and mornings were a joy of coolness. The rest house cook boiled our eggs for thirty minutes! The idea of eating eggs was completely alien to village people. We were somewhat egg bound in the morning! The morning mists hung around the mountain God Mlinga. As the sun crept up the shiny rock, the mist turned to cloud and gathered at the peak, looking like a smoking chimney. The mountain God had the knack of attracting clouds from the ocean and wringing them out to the benefit of the local *Wabondei* tribe fuelling their superstitions about the need to make human sacrifices in order to attract the favour of Mlinga for the supply of rain for their food crops. In fact the problem was the 'rain shadow'.

My work was about planning settlement schemes of family farmers with a cash crop to sell, and at Kiwanda, probably cocoa, pineapples, citrus fruits, maize, and even spices. The grouping of villages enables the government to provide social services. To make this practical the two local tribes would have to reject their traditional hostility towards each other, under the banner of 'national unity' as preached by the President Nyerere, and learn about modern methods of crop husbandry. This was an area of fertile soils and good rainfall, fifty inches per annum, about equivalent to Somerset in England. Hence, detailed environmental studies, mapping and co-ordination were required, as well as, of course, the good will of Mlinga the mountain God, in addition to, the government.

Jo and I were also concerned with the conservation of soil fertility and wildlife, long term. The *Wabondei* and the *Wasambaa* did not see Kiwanda as a beautiful place in that sense. We were so conscious of the beauty of those mighty ancient evergreen trees, echoing with the bark of *Kima*, the Sykes Blue monkey, the fur-flying black and white Colobus monkey, the predatory tree climbing leopard, the ubiquitous bush pigs and the profusion of colourful birds. The native attitude to such a beautiful habitat tended to be exploitative thus enabling their survival and hopefully a better standard of living. I was, of course, employed to initiate that process.

Traversing survey grids determined from air photos with soil augers, land chains, Dumpy levels and compasses was hard work for all, except perhaps the Land Rover driver, who nevertheless everyone depended upon for their comfortable survival! Ali Chande did in fact perform all sorts of supplementary jobs.

Jo's participation in all this field work, after the previous two days of stage rehearsals at Lead Memorial Hall, illustrated the immense versatility of "that village girl" as my mother disparagingly called her. Her Theatre Club colleagues would have been fascinated by her performance, for example when our surveyors were confronted with a black forest Cobra at Kiwanda. "Stamp the ground. It'll run away!" she shouted. It didn't.

"Stubborn blighter this one!" It stood its ground quite literally, rearing up, flashing a yellow throat. I always carried my light weight .22 calibre rifle, mainly for the cooking pot. I used a hollow nose bullet on this cobra. It measured 5 ft 6 inches, as enthusiastically measured by our Survey Assistant.

The village headman who was working as a labourer with us, cutting traverses through the forest said, "There are many *nyoka* - Kiswahili for snake, around here Bwana. They guard the Mission boundaries. They put the fear of the Mission God into the local people who like to come in here and kill our *nyama.*" This word in Swahili means both wild animals and meat, one and the same word.

"Did we make a mistake?" asked Jo.

June 1965: Back from Kiwanda survey in the mountains, we were greeted with a shock letter from Arusha School. Richard had suffered extensive scalding of his leg from a pan of boiling fat at the weekend Boy Scout camp. They said that a new synthetic skin spray had been applied successfully. It was approaching half-term so we would soon see. The school reported that he came third in his class, surprise-surprise. A new skill has dawned upon him; listening.

At the end of the two hundred and fifty mile drive **to Arusha,** climbing ever upwards into the mountainous plateau region flanked by the 'godly' Kilimanjaro mountain and in the comfort of our Ford Corsair GT bucket leather seats, was a joy. We found Richard hobbling about in the road outside our friends' house, awaiting our arrival. Jean Wrintmore, our charming hostess, and Eric were old friends featured in my previous published book 'Voyage to Wild Africa'. Eric was the Resident Magistrate and told us about a recent murder case he had before him which involved a Maasai warrior who had speared an expatriate Veterinary Field Officer. He declared in Court, through an interpreter; "I caught that man in the act of injecting poison into my cattle." It was, in fact, the vaccination campaign against the deadly rinderpest, a virulent disease of cattle. The warrior's spear and buffalo hide shield were exhibits at his trial for murder and are now part of the domestic décor in my house in England, in other words; enter here with caution. The offender was given three years prison. This sentence for a man who knew only the absolute freedom of the open plains and the vastness of blue skies, would, in the native African context, have been un-survivable.

Richard and Philip and their school friend J. J. Crowder, plus Jane and Peter, Eric's children, packed our cars, not to mention two spaniels, for a day trip to Ngurdoto Volcanic Crater and Momella Lakes. We saw thousands of black buffalo with their tail of predatory lions, picking off the weak stragglers. A lion is no match for a mature buffalo's head of formidable horns, but a concerted group attack on a youngster, despite the mother returning, albeit helplessly, to the foray, provided supper for six.

More ambitious was Eric's plan to drive to **Manyara Hotel** for lunch the next day which would be a one hundred mile journey on dusty roads with two cars. Manyara Hotel is the height of luxury in one of the wildest places on the planet. It is set on the edge of the Rift Valley vertical wall, 3,000 ft. above the alkaline Lake Manyara, streaked red with Flamingos. These beautiful birds gain their red plumage colour from their diet of algae and crustaceans that proliferate in the warm shallow margins of the lake. This Game Reserve below is heavily populated with elephant, zebra, impala antelope, buffalo and lions that famously squat in the trees. A sparkling blue swimming pool is perched on the edge of the escarpment wall so that one can gaze in leisurely cool tranquillity down at the primeval scene below. The animals below were fat as butter, as indeed seems to be the case in all the alkaline sedimentary areas in East Africa, mainly Rift Valleys and Serengeti Plains. In the UK, this alkaline habitat prevails on the Downs of England renowned for their rich sheep grazing, rare plants and butterflies, as compared with the acid conditions of the nearby heather bound New Forest National Park which is relatively poor in wildlife. It would seem that alkaline habitats provide a significantly richer nutrient status.

There were no guests at the hotel so we chatted with the handsome *Wambulu* waiters who professed their tribe to be the most handsome looking in Tanzania. They are a fairly pale upland tribe and uniformly possess very fine features. Inter-tribal mixing was very strongly resisted in the past, hence the phrase 'pureblooded'. They proceeded to tell us about the Singida Lion Cult of witchcraft killings. So many tribes seem to have this traditional way of maintaining social order with which we were so familiar in the *Wawanji* tribe of Kitulo Mountains. In *Uwanji* it was a way of invoking the power of the ancestors, via their spirits, to maintain social order. In West Africa this same concept appears as spiritually possessed masquerades that carry a long stick which gives leprosy to anyone it touches. The *Wazungu* or European, equivalent might be a policeman with a truncheon. However, I am told that in the recent past some African tribal lion and leopard cults became a means of terrorising and murdering significant numbers of people in order to gain power by subjugating the vulnerable.

The next day back in Arusha, the children dragged a tricycle out of the shed, which they said had suffered a mortal blow by the Magistrate's old Land Rover, which had run over a rear wheel. This created a hilarious switch back ride for anyone prepared to chance it. They enjoyed it as much as the Manyara elephants. Children's do-it-yourself creations typically prove their greatest joy. They spent most of the day bucking and gyrating in turns across the tennis court, into bushes, across the strawberry patch which had some unfortunate side-effects and through muddy pools. Arusha has mid dry season rainfall.

Freedom terminated at 5:30 p.m. that day and we accompanied the boys back to school. The children joked about all the things they did at school but there was an air of sombre foreboding about the morrow. We presented them giant-size bags of biscuits and sweets, moistened with tears at the vision of minced meat on toast, which they had previously told us about.

After leaving, Cicely in tears, "No woman should have to suffer her children being dragged away from her like this, Brian. We could have stayed on the farm, couldn't we?"

I had a surprise up my sleeve. It was soon our seventeenth wedding anniversary.

"Well, Bwana mkubwa, surprise me."

"I thought we would spend the weekend in the honeymoon tented hotel in Amboseli Game Park. It is not that far, only about 130 miles, just to the other side of Kili."

"Wow! Great idea, Brian. Can we afford it?"

"Not really, but the VSA have promised to sort out my overdue increment."

We took refuge in the Arusha cinema on our final night. It was hilarious; 'The Pink Panther' with Peter Sellers.

Amboseli Game Reserve is in Kenya, but there were no border post formalities at that time and our Corsair GT loved the drive on good roads to the entrance. The tented hotel was luxury *par excellence* and the Kenyan waiters were warmly welcoming. We were soon relaxing in the heat over outdoor tea and cakes, marvelling at the snow blizzards carpeting the 19,340 ft peak of Mount Kilimanjaro and filling the blue sky above us. Mount Kilimanjaro is the tallest mountain in Africa and the highest freestanding mountain in the world. The name appears to say starving or hungry hill in the Kiswahili language, though in the *Wachagga* language, njaro means whiteness, hence white hill or mountain, and in Maasai language njaro means water. Doubtless the coastal Kiswahili, with the name *kilima* for hill, was readily adopted after nineteenth century explorers, hearing the Kichagga word *kileme*, meaning 'which defeats' the climber, makes sense. It seems to be less snowy today as a result of 'global warming' and there is a fear that it may become snowless in a couple of decades, thus distracting from its striking beauty.

We gathered in the dining tent and were waited on hand and foot for a change and met the other diners; honeymooners from Sweden and USA. Later on in the darkness of the wild, we gathered round a campfire and talked of animals, snakes, mosquitoes and Maasai, who roamed freely in the Game Reserve. We told them about our lives in Tanzania and the Americans told us about Madagascar and the Swedes about Ethiopia.

We were all up and about at 6:00 a.m., cold but raring to go after the lions. Kilimanjaro was hiding in a cloud but the atmosphere was boisterous with birds urging the day on. There was hot water for shaving and tea then away, blissfully, in the Corsair GT. I got an exciting cine film shot of Cicely walking towards me, as I sat in the car, with ten lions in the distance behind her, of which she was unaware until she saw the movie years later, on leave in England. "Brian! Why didn't you tell me?"

"Just wanted to show the folks how brave you are."

The Amboseli plain seemed almost bare of grass in June yet the zebra were fat as butter. The grassland is fed by melting snow, *njaro* in the Maasai language, but if 'global warming' affected 'the hill' what would become of the fat zebra? They congregate in the open plain for safety, dressed in beautiful eye-catching uniforms. Why did nature conjure up that striking eye-catching coat? Not exactly good camouflage. Some researchers suspect that the dreaded tsetse flies go all dizzy when they settle on a zebra and so they avoid them. The gnu or wildebeest in contrast, are evolved to be ugly in the same habitat. The lions do not show any particular preference for their evening meal however – no colour-bar there!

On the way back for breakfast at 10:00 a.m. we spotted a black rhino standing stolidly as though stuffed, or should I say posing. We circled around him for a picture, keeping the Corsair engine running, however, there was a mood change and we departed in a hurry. Our acceleration, whilst not up to the cheetah standard of nought to sixty mph in three seconds, would certainly exceed a rhino in the open plain. In his favoured thorn bush habitat however, we wouldn't stand a chance.

The elephants in the swamp ignored our car, similar colour to them really, but when Cicely did her stepping out on the stage thing, panic set in and they gathered their young and moved away rapidly. Whilst they admired my beautiful Ford Corsair, it seems that they got 'stage fright' when Cicely stepped of the car.

Quite near the tented hotel, a huge 'Umbrella Thorn' Acacia tree shaded a pride of lions in somnolent posture. Cicely wound down her window and poked out the cine camera. They considered metal and four wheels irrelevant garbage, adopting inviting pussycat postures of "How's this for a pose, come and stroke me," style. BUT the whirring sound of the cine camera in a human hand produced a sudden, alarming electrification of feline threatening posture; a sharp move of the head, two large golden burning eyes focused on Cicely; pensive, calculating, warning, accompanied by an almost imperceptible slow rise to the feet. That faintest suggestion of human presence had transformed that dozing, hapless, lovable, cuddly-looking creature into a powerful, aggressive, terrifying, killing machine which, with one swipe of its dinner plate sized paw could take off the side of your face in an instant. Cicely grabbed the window winder and the slim, dusty, glass pane rose up to its full height to a complaining accompaniment of grinding squeaks. Our only air-conditioning in the tropics in the 1960's had been open or closed windows, hence we were soon sweltering.

"Yes. Well, I think we should back off a bit now, and go look for a cool lager."

Breakfast was pineapple, bacon, eggs, toast, marmalade and coffee. Kenya already had its eye on tourism in the 60s.

Chapter Eight

Life in Tanga and on the Serengeti Plains

7th July 1965 – Back to Tanga, 'the place of sail'. It was Saba Saba national holiday. Saba is Arabic/Kiswahili word for 'Seven', so seventh day of the seventh month, which is the founding day of the Tanzania African National Union Party, TANU. No *Mzungu,* = European, "would dare to work on Saba Saba Day" either. Good to take the day off and go sailing. We sailed our recent exciting acquisition, fourteen foot dinghy Aqua Birda, to regain our sea legs after so much Corsair GT motoring.

We received letters from Arusha School. Richard wrote that he and Philip were not happy at school, but that they had plenty of tuck. This emotional seesaw left us clinging to each other for solace. A second letter did not relieve our concern. It was from the Village Settlement Agency (VSA) headquarters, saying they could not find the funds to pay the salary of one of my new surveyors and he would have to be sent back to his previous ministry. Ominous indeed! We realised that we needed to go to DSM and find out what was causing this crisis of funding against what had been a very substantial donation by H M Government only eighteen months before.

We set off by road to Dar-es-Salaam. We stayed with Glynn Platt and his charismatic wife Marie; who persistently sheeted close to the wind in her sexual phraseology, as always, but kept us in fits of laughter all week. On the Friday the commissioner called me into his office and explained that some funds had gone missing in the administrative chain but he was confident that he could sort it out. In the meantime, however, he was able to offer me the promised increase in salary to £1,929 per annum, back-dated to the start of my contract with the VSA. This paradox found Cicely and I elated. At long last we might be able to save something. So what was ominous, was still ominous, but at least we now had butter on our 'burnt' toast.

Cicely was now the Lady Member of the Committee of the Tanga Yacht Club and had acquired the indelible name of Jo. I preferred My Darling Cicely but was obliged to conform to the Establishment. It went deeper than that; this actress/sailor - style nickname has stuck permanently, even within the family. Her parents, unsurprisingly, sternly disapproved, and my old school friends were heard to remark "Who's this Jo? Old Dawtrey must have remarried. Kept that quiet."

Another holiday emerged, Maulid; a celebration of the birth of 'The Prophet'. So it was a case of abandoning the Ford Corsair and adopting Aqua Birda. We were shattered after a hard day beating to windward in the Monthly Mug race, especially Jo. We came in third. Not bad.

It was an achievement for us, more accustomed to wheels. We celebrated Maulid by going to Tanga Stadium to a 'cultural exchange'. It turned out to be a very fine dancing performance by some beautiful Indonesian girls. They even sang the TANU Party song in Kiswahili. They wore colourful silk dresses down to their ankles, tight at the hips, with long flowing hair decorated with scented frangipani flowers. They smiled constantly, taking small steps, rocking their shoulders and bodies and then wiggling when the music wiggled. We were familiar with tribal rhythmic pounding the dust with excited colourful abandonment to a heavy drum beat; by contrast this was charming femininity, making graceful expressive gestures with long curving fingers. The orchestration was by an assortment of steel and brass percussion instruments being struck with mallets. The Harvest Dance was performed with plates in the palm of the hand with a lighted candle in the centre of each.

18th July 1965: We had been praying for this day for a whole year – **Caroline's arrival** from England. She was now sixteen years old. We were aware that our pseudo-African, now cultured English girl, would have been changed by a year at a girls boarding school in England, but when she descended the steps of that East African Airways Fokker Friendship aircraft from Nairobi, we were overwhelmed by her blonde beauty dressed in a creamy white costume; not a school girl but a young lady. We were not the only ones to be overwhelmed; there was a sixteen-year-old young man named Oliver Delany who happened to be on the tarmac. He turned out to be as swift as an Osprey in the wind, when it came to dating our daughter. Caroline was deliriously happy to see her mother, whilst I complimented her on her apparel, to which she proudly announced that she had made the suit herself. She presented me with a new Veteran Driver badge for 19 years accident-free driving, which I proudly mounted on my Ford Corsair GT radiator grill.

Caroline was now travelling in a new-world, modern style. She left London in a Comet, landing at Tripoli, Khartoum and Nairobi, arriving in Tanga 21 hours after take off, a journey that would have taken four weeks by sea and train. Her Student air fare cost three times more than it would today. We were delighted to discover that our daughter had developed a strong personality and was very confident. She laughed a lot and was open and frankly spoken, with firm ideas about personal relationships and people. She had discovered her power over the 'inferior sex' – my phrase – despite having been to a single-sex school.

Caroline certainly had developed the go-getting, entertaining persona of her mother. We took her to the best eat-out restaurant we had in Tanga, The Twiga, with its high up rooftop bar for browsing the tropical scene. Visiting merchant ship sailors hovered around Caroline, attracted by her good looks and sociable manner. We were going to have to keep tags on her wanderings 'about town'. Tanga was suddenly swarming with teenagers. Caroline's first encounter was with no less than Tim Harvard from Kitulo Plateau, who had dropped in for a stay. He was confident that his bearded broad Devonshire brogue and amorous humour would bowl Caroline over, especially as she was so young and impressionable. Caroline enjoyed another evening out at The Twiga.

Upon their return home, Tim's witty banter and teasing had attained vibrant and comic proportions. He found himself, however, struggling to keep top side on the romantic front. This was Jo's daughter, after all.

At breakfast, Tim was subdued. His normal success with his chat-up technique had proved lacking in a way he could not get to grips with. I commented to Jo, "I think Tim is developing a complex. He certainly has an attractive, playful humour, is good-looking; has an eye for a straight furrow behind a plough; a farmer's eye for quality livestock."

"Hmm. And good taste in choice of the opposite sex," was all the response I got from Jo?

In the next seven days Caroline did six teenage parties and a cinema trip. In the day time she could be seen lounging on the beach in her bikini with the new beau of her own age named Oliver. She confided to her Mum that, "He makes my heart beat like a primordial drum." Oliver had to face competition, however, with an older suitor, named Lofty Drews, a rally driver no less, who took Caroline out to the Twiga. In the outcome, on that occasion, it was Oliver that brought Caroline home!

Bikinis were a recent feature of the Tanga scene and confined to teenage girls. Some consternation was registered amongst certain of the more conservative yacht club wives, about "that blonde girl" on the beach "cavorting amorously" with their vulnerable sons, in particular the handsome Oliver. This somewhat embroidered anxiety was reported to the Lady Member who was requested to "speak to" the offending girl. Jo was renowned for her 'short fuse' and Caroline bore the, unjust, brunt of it for some short minutes, long enough for Caroline to suffer corporal punishment with the back of a hairbrush to the upper thigh, leaving this 16-year-old young lady with a red mark embarrassingly just below her bikini. At this juncture the beau Oliver also suffered an embarrassing interview with his father as a result of his amorous behaviour on the beach with Caroline. It was not to be corporal punishment but instead, I was later informed, "a somewhat irrelevant lecture on the subject of the birds and the bees".

Jo turned to me in tears, "What have I done? I broke the hair brush in half, look! I have ruined everything."

Silence reigned in the bedroom for ten minutes whereupon a spritely voice bounced into the kitchen, "What's for supper, Mum?"

Jo regretted her outburst eternally. In retrospect, however, and in mitigation, I submit a plea; her sense of community justice led to her being offered the post of magistrate in her retirement, by the Winchester Judiciary; so, Caroline, your mother can be excused.

As to myself, I have to admit to being proud of my beautiful, charismatic daughter when seen together in public. She loved meeting people and had no 'side' in her deportment as did some private boarding school educated girls.

Jo and I began to discuss creating more children in accordance with our declared marital ambition to have six children, "to get free labour for your farm!" as my sister had commented regarding our ambition, at our wedding reception. We were still young at 36, and because of the Pill, Jo was now in charge of coital consequence. Maria Platt maintained that this German Pill was developed at Buchenwald human laboratory by the Nazis and "could have side effects". I can say in retrospect that the Nazis maintained their iron grip on Jo for five months after she stopped taking it. After that my parsimonious nature crept in, "Jo, we really can't afford it."

We became burdened by the weight of my survey work in the mountains at Kiwanda, and Cicely's theatre rehearsals. However, there were still days of relaxation and on one such occasion the Yacht Club organised a long sail seaward to the barrier reef, targeting the many teenagers on holiday. To picnic on the reef required careful timing against the tidal rise; get it right and the fascinating and beautiful marine-world of brightly-coloured fish became accessible by snorkel as did the rare very tiny cowry species much sought after by Tanga's cowry collectors. The numerous 'money cowries' were used by Arab traders in the C19th for currency along the African coast.

Upon our arrival at the coral reef, way out in the ocean, we found a capsized sailing cruiser, not from Tanga Yacht Club, with the lady crew member clinging to the reef buoy with a rising tide, and the helmsman struggling in the sea to secure his boat. The man, to our alarm, had only one arm but persistently refused our assistance. Such determined self-survival in a handicapped person impressed us all greatly. The harbour pilot boat appeared on the scene, by chance, and eventually succeeded in recovering the man's dignity, his yacht, and his wife.

We had two weeks' 'local leave' coming up. With Caroline alongside, our plan was to pick up the two boys from Arusha School at the end of term, leave Sally Spaniel with old friends Jean and Eric Wrintmore in Arusha and drive to Seronera on the Serengeti Plain. I had the Corsair fitted up with new replacements, for the worn out leaf springs, to help with the load of camping equipment, jerry cans of fuel, water and five humans. She also had her twin Weber carburettors tuned up by Riddoch Motors. We were then in good shape for the nine hundred miles round trip.

Approaching the North West region of Tanzania at the end of the dry season in Maasai-land, the road in those pre-touristy days was dusty but quite fast. We relentlessly became coated with white dust and then as we climbed into the Mbulu highlands towards Ngorongoro Crater, a layer of ochreous red. This sandwich became beautified by a layer of yellow as we traversed the old lake beds that led us towards Serengeti. I suspect that modern cars depending so much on electronics, might not survive such heavy coatings of dust?

Tanzania's record on wildlife conservation was already second to none, largely due to the far sightedness of its first President Dr Julius Nyerere. Tanzania has 19 national parks and game reserves. Our destination, Serengeti is the largest national park of some 5,700 square miles, the size of Northern Ireland. Serengeti carries an amazing population of three million wild animals, most of which take part in a seasonal migration to Kenya and back, governed by the bi-modal climate, of some one point three million wildebeest and two hundred thousand zebra, thus providing a world famous spectacle on TV. Along the route we periodically saw Maasai standing about leaning upon their six foot long deadly spears, gazing upon the spectacle of a four wheeled tin box overloaded with humanity and their 'things'. The Maasai seemed not to be in need of 'things', just a red blanket, belt and *simi*, a short sword sheathed in goat skin, copper earrings and necklaces, and a herd of cows. These warriors would think nothing of walking to Seronera, but then they do not live by clock and calendar as we do. They have time, and plenty of it.

As we drove relentlessly westwards, the sun overtook us and finally lay ahead of us in the windscreen, turning the dust cloud in my rear view mirror orange. We had covered five hundred and fifty miles from Tanga when we entered Tanzania's first National Park. The name Serengeti is derived from the Maasai word *Siringet* meaning 'endless plain'. Rainfall is said to average 20 inches which is very low and similar to Newmarket in the UK. In 1913 European hunters arrived to shoot Game. Lions were vermin and very numerous; it is recorded that hunters often shot one hundred on a single trip. In 1921 the Colonial Government proclaimed it to be a Reserve, and in 1951 a National Park. It was the height of the dry season so we did not expect to see the vast herds of wildebeest which by then had migrated over the Mara River into Kenya. The most fearsome and successful hunter of the plains is not the lion but the wild dog. They select a particular animal from the herd, and chase it until exhausted, then bring it down, eviscerate it, tear it apart and eat it, often within minutes. Compared with dogs, lions are poor hunters and succeed in only one in three attempts, wild dogs never fail.

One would need to be a poet to describe this animal kingdom with a pen. BBC cameras, were to subsequently capture this prehistoric place for the enjoyment of the human world over future years. *Homo habilis* thrived here over a million years ago, living on fish and meat when it was a lake. Our Ford Corsair GT was carrying a nucleus of *Homo sapiens* genes that might easily vanish in this vast wilderness and future generations of Dawtreys with it. No one in the car seemed to worry about our isolation, however. As far as traversing Africa goes, the motorcar is a miracle invention, as compared to 'footing' as the Maasai do. However, it is important not to overdo the challenge to the elements in some bravado moment and get stepped upon by a giraffe, or get a rhino horn stuck under ones' bumper, as we did in the Land Rover during a bush-whacking weekend with geologist Huw Jones back in 1962, with troublesome consequences!

A heap of rocks called a Kopje loomed in my headlights, Seronera was painted on the rock and, as if from outer space, there was a little wooden 'office'. We checked in – "Permission to camp"? An African in a green uniform said, "That's fine but be warned that there's a pride of lions around here. If you light a fire the lions will, probably, move away."

There was a well water supply so we were able to throw buckets of water over each other in the light of our pressure lamp hanging in the acacia umbrella tree. We erected our large tent but decided not to bother with mosquito nets. Mosquitoes were not a problem in the late dry season. We were up early the next day in the freshness of dawn, getting the kettle to boil for tea. Our whole family was together at last. We were so happy and all steamed-up for adventure. We had, in our family farming days, driven up and down the steps over the sea wall at Sea Paling beach in Norfolk and even driven up Mount Snowdon in our Land Rover, but this was REAL adventure. Caroline asked if I could teach her to drive the Corsair across Serengeti Plains. That was a good idea as there was no need to learn the Highway Code, only to look out for zebras crossing.

Caroline exceeded the speed limit chasing *twiga* = giraffe. The Game Guard explained to us that their 'horns' were in fact, soft tissue that absorbed blood "like a man's penis" when the head is lowered from the height of the acacia tree canopy to ground level to drink, which would otherwise cause concussion. "It equalises the blood pressure in the brain." he said. The children listened in silent awe to this piece of Serengeti knowledge. Jo and I were hopeful that the news didn't get back to school in too much detail. The anatomy of the giraffe is of absorbing interest, for example; that that long neck has the same number of vertebrae as the human. I read later that those 'horns' are called *ossicones*, which suggests bony tissue, rather than "soft tissue", "which inflates like a penis …"

"Look, cheetah! It's going to catch that Tommy." shouted Caroline excitedly, slamming her foot on the accelerator, giving us 0−60 mph in 12 seconds. The cheetah left us standing however, 0−60 mph in three seconds. Cheetahs have some doggy features like unretractable claws, lions do have retractable claws, and a sort of cack sound rather than a mewing cat, and it is most amenable to co-operation with mankind. Jo later raised a 'rescued' cheetah as a pet and carried it in the backseat of her car to deter thieves when she went shopping in township markets in Zambia.

After 10 days, we understood better how this ecological jigsaw fitted together. Biologists speak of the balance of nature, but it never quite gets there. There is flexibility in the forces that respond to any excess or shortage of a particular food or a particular species of animal or disease or over-hunting. If elephants destroy too many trees, grass responds to the absence of shade and becomes a sward, which attracts more buffalo and wildebeest and subsequently an increase in their predators: wild dogs, lions, jackals, hyena and vultures. Serengeti reminded me of a self-perpetuating mechanism for converting solar energy, via chlorophyll and herbivores, into meat. Hence *Homo habilis* evolved to become bipedal meat-eaters, unlike their vegetarian progenitors in the Congo forests, the pygmy *Bonobo* chimpanzees. Some refer to Serengeti as Eden, the 'cradle of mankind'.

Caroline took the wheel for our exit. She was doing well, she managed the three-point turn with plenty of room to spare, about 500 acres in fact; avoided hitting any kerbstones or gate posts or black buffalo or even one of those sump-breaking 'concrete' mini termite mounds. We said farewell to the cheeky 'rock rabbits' or *hyrax*, that inhabit the cracks in the rock of the Seronera kopje, and set off for Olduvai Gorge and pre-history. After some hours of choking white dust we reached the gash in the landscape, caused, it is said, some half a million years ago by horrendous flooding, as a result of seismic activity, which created a perennial stream flow creating this deep ravine through seven layers of sediments. These layers are visibly exposed in the steep walls, layer upon layer of fossilised animal and vegetable mutants that never made the grade against nature's everlasting challenge, death. Robert Ardrey wrote, before Leakey; "Chance proposes; death disposes."

Olduvai Gorge is one of the most important paleo-anthropological sites in the world and was a haven for fossil hunters in the 1950s and 1960s. The fossilised bones and stone tool discoveries of the Leakey family over several decades have dramatically revised prevailing religious ideas about the nature and location of human evolution, occurring some millions of years before Adam plucked his apple for Eve. I always pondered the validity of that legend, since apples are a temperate region crop and do not grow in the Mediterranean.

The Leakeys found evidence of the occupation of the gorge by *Homo habilis*, a million years ago, as well as *Australopithicus zinjantropus* (synonym *boisei*) about 1.7 million years ago, discovered in 1959 by Mary Leakey. *Homo erectus* of slightly more recent origin, about 700,000 years ago, was found further north in Africa, and appears to have been a more enterprising species of human, who reached the Balkans, Java and even China, adapting slowly to the cooler climate. It appears that all these species, and *zinjantropus*, our ancestors, were only four feet three inches tall.

Mary Leakey found 'Zinj', as my sons came to affectionately refer to him, in the lowest strata level. Jonathan Leakey found a *Homo habilis* jaw bone and other fragments in 1960–64 excavations, thought to date about 1.2 million years ago. More than twelve different skulls of early man have been found, together with stone tools, in the gorge. *Paranthropus boisei* the new name for 'Zinj', has been found to have occupied the site from approximately 1.8–1.2 million years ago. *Homo sapiens* remains, found elsewhere in East Africa in 1964 have been dated to a more 'recent', 17,000 years ago. Visiting Olduvai Gorge inspires serious reflection upon the origins of mankind; whether God created Man or was it the other way round? There was nobody working on this Palaeolithic site and no restrictions, we obtained a pamphlet from the 'hut' for one shilling from which the above info was extracted, plus some on-line updates. We waded ankle-deep in animal and plant fossils, some of which relate to an age of giant-sized animals, such as pigs as big as hippos.

Homo sapiens obviously learned to plan ahead and be inventive, in order to survive the cold winters in the northern hemisphere. His descendant, the *Bwanapima* a.k.a., master measurer/surveyor, had arrived back in square-one of the chequer-board of evolution, in his Ford Corsair GT., definitely one step ahead of the rest in the scramble for survival. Children do not have the same fascination with the past as adults do, so we did not stay long.

As we clambered up out of the valley, through millions of years, we reached a clump of wild *Sansevieria*. The sudden explosive leap of a cheetah from out of the clump almost sent us reeling millions of years backwards into the gorge with shock, as it streaked away into the distance.

Our next landmark in that wild landscape was Ngorongoro Volcano Crater. This is another natural wonder, which was created some three million years ago by an exploding volcano the size of Kilimanjaro, which then collapsed in upon itself, thus producing an enormous caldera. We took a photograph of a giraffe with Ngorogoro in the background; this really was, 'Wild Africa'. When we reached Ngorogoro we managed to steer the Corsair along a track taking us down the side of the caldera, descending 2,000 feet to the floor of the crater. We estimated that the crater must be ten miles across. We pitched camp in the bottom for a couple of days. It was cold after dark so we lit the Primus in our tent to keep warm. We spent the next day with the camera but failed to even begin, to capture an impression of the vastness of it all. It was teeming with every sort of animal including a high density of lions. The grazing must be rich to attract such a congregation into that amphitheatre.

Further on we entered Lake Manyara Game Reserve, later to become a National Park. As an Honorary Game Warden, I was permitted to camp there, near the lake foreshore, 'Amongst the Elephants', to quote the title of Ian Douglas-Hamilton's wonderful book, published in 1975 by Collins. I believe that it was in this same year, 1966, that Iain began his epic life there living on the shores of Lake Manyara, actually amongst the elephant herds. His daughter Saba was born there, presumably on the seventh month of the calendar, saba meaning seven in Kiswahili, and who is a well-known Presenter of BBC wildlife and tribal documentaries. Jo took Caroline 'on top' for a swim in the Lake Manyara Hotel "swimming pool in the sky", on the edge of the 3,000 ft. vertical escarpment which dropped down to our 'lost world' below. She waved down at us, she later said, "But we couldn't see you for acacia trees".

August 1965: The long summer school holidays in Tanga were memorable for young people; swimming in the blue tropical ocean; goggling in the coral reefs; sailing to Toten Island for a picnic; parties; late night restaurants; cinema, and for our boys; catching bats in the German WWI lookout tower; sleeping in the tree den; trapping weaver birds and, teasing the girls at the Yacht Club.

This latter exuberance led to a civil war between our ten and thirteen-year-old boys, and two pretty girls. The two pretty girls attracted the attention of our two young men who were diligently varnishing their Dab-Chick sailboard, by throwing sand upon it. This was the ultimate crime, by any standard of social conduct. The furious boys grabbed the girls behind the Club-house and frog-marched them up the steps to the street above. The street was lined with red-as-blood flamboyant trees. A rope was duly thrown over the branch overhanging the cliff, which it was declared to be "for hanging criminals". By this time, the proposed hanging had attracted a crowd of passive Africans and some white children. "We have got witnesses!" hissed Richard. I always puzzled why hanging was such a spectacle centuries ago. Richard decreed mercy like the gallant King Richard of yore back from the Crusades, and the two girls fled in terror.

It transpired that, unbeknown to the boys, the girls were daughters of the Yacht Club Commodore, Colin Beck. Colin never again spoke to Richard but did not expel him from the Club on account of his mother being on the management committee.

Late October 1965, half-term, found us in Arusha again. The two boys and their friend J. J. Crowder had been collected by our old friends Jean and Eric Wrintmore, thus ensuring a happy sojourn. Guests included two ex-Mbeya Forest Department friends, Lilian and John Bond. This mixture of disparate disciplines; the law, sisal/forestry, and land-use planning; plus the enterprising deviations created by five children, made for an eventful few days. The Arusha School Headmaster Mr Bryn Jones came to tea and surprised us by saying that Philip, aged ten, was not good boarding school material, but that Richard, aged 13, was well-adapted. We always thought it was the other way round. Philip had been awarded a Star for all round effort. Jo frequently expressed the view that Philip was highly emotionally sensitive like his father and was sent to boarding school too young. Very youthful parenting judgements can be intrinsically flawed, though errors may hopefully be recoverable with time.

Maasai Warriors: Eric had organised a luncheon expedition to Namanga Hotel, just inside the Kenya border. Our Corsair GT showed off her genius by achieving 'the ton' on level tarmac as we raced past the slumbering Mt Meru volcano on our right. There was no traffic of course, only guinea fowl and the odd *twiga*. After enjoying Kenya's best cuisine, we drove westwards across the plain towards another shallow soda lake, Lake Natron, the regular breeding area for some 2.5 million lesser flamingos. It is a safe breeding area as its caustic environment serves as a barrier against predators. We were in search of a supper and *kwali,* the yellow necked partridge was on our menu. I found my telescopic sight was skew, so it was once again 'corned beef for supper'. However, having expended 50 rounds zeroing my weapon, I discovered I had an audience of tall red men with 6 ft. long spears, Maasai. They were no good at killing *kwali,* either; they preferred the 'lesser' challenge, lion. This had been the traditional rite of passage to manhood and junior warrior status, along with circumcision, for centuries past; though strictly illegal today in Game Reserves they have no respect of boundaries. They are pastoralists and follow their beloved cattle, their wealth, wherever there is grazing. They believe that all cattle in the world were granted to them by God, which does cause a few problems at times! Also, woe-betide anyone who interferes with their bovine 'bank account'. I have previously related the Case of the British Vet being murdered for injecting the Maasai man's cattle against rinderpest. These men certainly looked the warrior part; powerfully casual, impressive apparel, with red plaited hair, copper ancient Egyptian-style earrings, colourful necklaces, and red robes tied round the waist with a belted *simi*, or sword. The *simi* is razor-sharp steel blade, weighted towards the tip, making it massively effective in a swinging chop towards an enemy's neck. I have one in my house; strictly for décor; not for 'cold callers', or theatrically-minded children.

We invited them, by gesticulation; they had no Swahili, to compete in a game of bush darts, Maasai-style, using their spears, and a cigarette packet, at ten yards, as a target. Huge hilarity was enjoined with this simple game. If only all human inter-cultural conflicts could be resolved so easily. Mind you, I would back my Corsair GT and .22 calibre rifle against a Maasai spear in anger. When the spear is thrown by a warrior, everything flies, his plaited ring pigtails, earrings, beads, blanket; along with the rest of his prized credentials. The blanket is their only garment and exposes a lean muscular thigh and buttock when they stand as motionless as Buckingham Palace guards, disdainfully observing gaggles of tourists. These men, fearful and envious of no one, are the ultimate image of freedom. They have access to huge 'estate' and immense bovine 'bank accounts' which self-generate.

On the 280 mile dash back to Tanga, my car had cause to complain. The transmission oil seal expired and we arrived with a heavy rumble in the prop-shaft. Our car was proving a 'welter weight' in the safari terms when compared to the two Land Rovers allocated to me by VSA, but Land Rovers are no one's choice of vehicle for doing long journeys. All cars suffer greatly on African roads and our beloved Corsair was showing signs of soldierly fatigue.

November 'the hell month': Heat and humidity invoked despair in the more unadapted white community; feelings were of a choice between murder and suicide. The decision was made for us in Tanga cinema, 'How to Murder Your Wife' by Terry Thomas. Murder was still in the air when I arrived in Dar es Salaam! The British Aid Funds were suffering a constriction somewhere along the administrative channel. The Commissioner said to me, "There just is not enough money left to implement all your schemes, Brian, economical though they are. Not to worry though, not unsurprisingly, the ministry is very keen to have you return for another tour of duty."

I again had that feeling of being a stone from which blood was extractible. There was yet a third piece of news from Dar that could prove to be a major threat to our ambitions for a career in Tanzania; the mishandling by the UK Government of the Rhodesian Crisis under Prime Minister Harold Wilson; about whose character we had no knowledge. This issue was the UK's refusal to grant sovereignty to Rhodesia until such time as there was majority rule. The Rhodesian Government was largely composed of members of Rhodesia's white minority. Given that Rhodesia had governed itself since 1923 more effectively than a number of recently granted independence, countries to its North, there was some sympathy amongst the expatriate community when the Rhodesian Cabinet's Unilateral Declaration of Independence (UDI) was declared, in November 1965. Tanzania's President Dr Julius Nyerere, condemned the UK Government for refusing to take military action against the illegal Smith regime, and subsequently broke off diplomatic relations. In 1966 Britain did, at President Kenneth Kaunda's request, send a squadron of ten Javelin jets to protect Zambian airspace. I never could work out exactly why, as there was no threat to Zambian airspace.

Iain Smith's mistake was to apply qualifications – 'One taxpayer one vote'. Even the Magna Carta in 1204 did not selectively discriminate between the Rights of only 'some' people. Surprisingly Britain only granted total Universal Suffrage, to include **all** women, as recently as the year I was born in 1928. The world had changed and Iain Smith had failed to grasp its significance. However, given the terrible bloodshed and economic trauma that has occurred in the renamed Zimbabwe, under lifelong President Robert Mugabe, history may be disposed to look more kindly upon Ian Smith than was previously the case.

At the end of November 1965, the Africa Area Commissioner pressed me for a Settlement Plan for the area to the south of Tanga where I had driven across the railway line, Mkalamo. I knew the area carried fertile black soils and good water supplies from wooded lakes. I needed to delineate the boundaries and prepare a layout plan for new settlers. The Corsair must now play 'second fiddle' to my Land Rover. Ali Chande was an excellent driver, he had a feel for the anatomical stresses and strains of his vehicle under virgin bush conditions and we rarely broke down as was the case with my other drivers who knocked the hell out of their vehicles, not to mention their surveyor passengers too.

We set off down the coast, traversing near the seashore, reaching Mkwaja Ranch without trouble, despite that nasty swampy *mbuga*. Once south of the ranch, we turned in land and spent an hour steam-rolling bushes and small trees verdant with the season of 'short rains'. We could see wooded hills to our right beyond the railway line, otherwise no sign of human life. To reach the Mkalamo site at dusk, we found an inviting-looking bush free grassy plain. We plunged into the short grass optimistically. It did cross my mind that it was odd, there being no woody growth and why was the grass only ten inches tall? Savannah grasses are usually four feet tall.

It slowly dawned on us that we were sinking in black clay, even in four-wheel drive. Why should an elevated plain be boggy? We later plunged the soil auger in and hit impermeable laterite iron pan one foot below the surface, 'soil profile drainage zero'; rice paddy, yes! It was too dark to attempt a retraction from our predicament so we huddled in the back with my Primus and a can of beans. We were going to need tea to replenish our blood supply as a result of being drained of blood by the female anopheles mosquito, not a few but multi-millions, female liberation certainly took place in Mkalamo. We sprayed the cab heavily with insecticide, slammed the doors and pranced about in the grass like monkeys, pending the settlement of fumes in the cab and hopefully genocide for the 'mozzy tribe'. We jumped in and slammed the doors, killing the few that immigrated with us with frenzied brutality. Stinging murderously, we grabbed the handrail and gritted our teeth. Gradually we regained our tranquillity and Ali produced a bag of bananas. "Here you are, Bwana, you always say that we can live forever on bananas. Just hope we'll not need to be here that long to prove it."

The temperature reading felt like approaching 100 degrees Fahrenheit, and humidity very high. With the windows shut, we were soon steamed up to gasping point. "We'd better get these ventilators mosquito-proofed, Ali."

"You mean, we will be coming back here again, Sir? I can see why everybody lives the other side of the railway line."

At first light we started the engine and gingerly churned forward through 'hell on earth', avoiding pools of water shining in the grass. Eventually we spotted shrubby growth at a lower level and headed for that with increasing speed. Once there we opened the doors for cross-draught – heaven!

We found the Mkalamo Lakes seen on aerial photographs, deeply shaded by evergreen woodland. They were beautifully secluded swimming pools, clear and blue where the sky touched them. "I must bring my wife here, it's a lovely place," I said to Ali, "Hmm – on second thoughts maybe that is not such a good idea."

After some study, I realised that the five lakes were sinkholes in a fissured limestone bed, hence deep ground water like a well, hence no mosquitoes, but surprise-surprise, there were, hippos! Hippos kill more humans than any other wild animal, so the potential as a future Lido was open to question. This conflict between humans and hippos created a worry for me, in view of the fact that they, being vegetarians, love fields of maize. Five hundred farmers growing maize might produce an explosion of hippos.

The local tribes, the *Wazigua* and the *Wakonde*, had heard from the Boma that the government would build a school here and TANU Youth League would build a road. They were ready to come they said and would 'sort out' the hippo problem. Do Africans eat hippos?

There is nothing quite like fertile soil and a road, or a railway! to draw in the legions. This scheme was going to cost very little beyond the regular provision of public services, education, health centre, agricultural advice, a storage building for inputs and marketing and above all, co-ordination and field management by the VSA. I felt elated and soon had the soil survey and farms lay-out plan drawn up for HQ approval, with the invaluable help of aerial photographs. In later years I learned that some 200 families had settled there, drawing food from their old villages to enable the move. The African Area Commissioner had organised a selection process and I really felt this could become one of the best of our projects in Tanga Region, and doubtless TANU would fly their flag for their self-help propaganda.

Some days later, whilst enjoying the cool air on the veranda at our mountain retreat, Amani, Jo and I discussed the implications of the fact that the British High Commission had been forced to close down over the Rhodesian debacle. President Nyerere's step in breaking off relations with the UK was an unusually principled, if not a wholly wise step, given that the UK was Tanzania's main aid donor.

"I am not sure how these VSA Schemes, and our salaries, will be affected, Jo," I questioned, "It's like a treasure ship without a rudder. There are 'sharks' about in the political depths of Dar es Salaam water."

The wild *Saintpaulia* or African Violets were in bloom everywhere under the tall evergreen trees. The forest echoed with the bark of Sykes Blue monkeys and 'bush babies'. It was such a wonderful place to retreat to after the humid coast. "Jo, do you think those *kima* are warning their families to keep away, or are they curiously calling their friends to come and watch these human lovers, sniffing the flowers?" The 'bush baby' is a tiny primate with large eyes:

"How about this new play you are in? Is Iain Kennedy in it? He seems to spend a lot of time with you these days."

"No, he's not. He does feel a bit out of it socially though; his lonely flat in the evening and the hospital operating theatre full of Africans all day. By the way, it's not a play, it's the Christmas Pantomime. Long way to go yet. We want you to paint the castle for Jack and the Beanstalk. What do you think?"

"Oh. Really. The boys will be home from school next week, perhaps they would like to give me a hand."

"I've got Caroline lined up to organise the children backstage and help with make-up. Let's all pull together like we used to on the farm, Brian."

"OK. I'd like that."

Jo went on to produce four plays, three of them comedies: *Strike Happy, Come Blow up Your Horn, The Bathroom Door and Trial by Jury,* a musical. Amateur productions were immensely hard work and usually ended in a riotous party which recharged everyone's batteries. Not being gregarious myself, preferring people in two's and three's, I had a problem with this. Jo used to say, "Brian, you will be in the loo for the next five days I am afraid, we are having a party on Saturday." She loved parties, I survived them.

It began to rain again so we retired for blissful rest. The following day we were destined to be trekking the cleared woodlands with my surveyors to organise the pegging out of tea scheme 'out-grower' plots. Tea just fitted like a glove into the rainy mountain topography, quite a joy to the eye, so much the opposite of boring sisal regimental lines, on the coastal plain, like a desert of 'spears'. To switch from trees to dense tea bush cover seems an amenable switch for Mother Nature to accept. Once established, the tea plantations just seem to perpetuate themselves, provided there is regular 'plucking'. The women who pluck tea do so in communal chatty groups whilst their men-folk occupy the shade to talk, they say, of urgent political businesses.

At the end of the week we headed downhill on greasy red clay to steaming Tanga in our Corsair GT. Humidity was 100% with thunder rolling around us all evening. The trouble with the *Masika* rains is that they are not heavy enough to clear the air. A crate of Tusker did help to add merriment to the atmosphere at No.46. In addition to theatre people we had guests from Dar es Salaam, medical people, invited by our Dr Iain Kennedy and also VSO John French, whose father was an Edinburgh surgeon. As I closed the shutters when our guests departed, I knocked down our English Country Scenes calendar.

"You had better get your hammer and nail out. Tomorrow, I mean!" said she in a culinary tone, "I'm whacked!"

She then undressed and stood beneath the squeaking fan to dry off the perspiration. It seemed like a good idea so I joined her. Perhaps there was something to be said, I thought, for having the children away at school. Jo always enjoyed sitting naked before her dressing table mirror brushing her long, naturally wavy hair, with tranquil charm and beauty.

"Have you seen my brush?"

"Well, as a matter of fact, I did catch a glimpse of it," I said perusing the hammer and nail tack. I sat down beside her. "What do you fancy this evening, master measurer, farmer or sailor?"

She took my hand. "Ready-about."

It was soon the 8th December 1965, the glorious 'arrival of the children day'. Tanga expatriate children were due to flock in from England, Rhodesia, and Kenya, and of course Arusha. Excitement was immense on Tanga Railway Station platform as hordes of junior school children leapt from the carriages even before the train halted. It was a flood of green shirts and grey hats, satchels flying; one of the most joyful events in our 'Tanga Days' life.

"Phew! It's a lot hotter here than Arusha," said Richard, stripping off his tie patterned with giraffe heads. "Has Caroline arrived yet?"

"Next week. How are you boys?" asked Jo, ecstatically happy.

"We're fine, Mum," said ten-year-old Philip, "I want to learn to sail the Dab-Chick this hols."

To celebrate, we had invited the harbour pilot, Peter and Annique Barefoot to tea, after which we all piled into the pilot boat and set off seaward to meet an incoming cargo ship. It was calm and cooler under the black night sky; a 180 degree dome of solid stars conveyed a feeling of cosmic awakening, a realisation of our insignificance in the Universe. This must have been how our Neolithic ancestors felt, needing to erect huge stone monuments to mark their existence on Planet Earth. I don't think our two boys saw the world that way; they felt very much here and now, determined to make their mark, not so much by erecting a stone marker but by becoming harbour pilots.

1ᵗʰ December 1965, TYC 25ᵗʰ ANNIVERSARY BALL.

Invitation said Red Sea Rig for men. Originally formulated by the Royal Navy for special occasions in the tropics, for me it was white long-sleeved shirt with red bow tie and red cummerbund, black trousers and no jacket. For Jo, it was blow the dust off her wardrobe of dresses, hoping they weren't mouldy. This was to be a major event, to be held at the finest building in Tanga, the Lead Memorial Hall. Of all the African dignitaries invited only one turned up, a Nigerian Magistrate. He made his mark, of which more to tell, later.

Over the weekend it was Tanga's turn to host Dar es Salaam and Mombasa Yacht Clubs in the annual tri-cornered competition. The visiting teams had to sail their Ospreys respectively north and south along the coast taking some 36 hours. The subsequent hotly contested racing left Dar es Salaam departing, sadly, with our coveted silver cup.

For the Ball Supper, Jo as Lady Member ended up catering for 200 guests, utilising 50 large crayfish from the bay. Two ships supplied us with gallons of rum, courtesy Iain Aitchison, shipping agent, which we made into four huge bowls of punch with mangoes, oranges and chopped bananas. All that gorgeous food and drink cost next to nothing. Then at coffee time, she dressed-up in sailor gear and mounted the theatre stage to sing, 'The Cutest Little Dinghy in the Yacht Club'. She was not only my darling that night, but that of 200 other guests too.

The two ships in the bay lit up 'over all' in honour of us, cast twinkling lights across the water under the palm trees. To add to this romantic effect, Laurie Bamford, Charlie Chapel of the Public Works Department and myself, had lined the whole hall with hessian painted grey like a cave with a view at the back of the stage, of the Bay and the yachts, projected by my Aldis projector and colour slides which because of the distance, projected a huge realistic image. The audience really felt like they were sitting in a cave looking out to sea. It was a great creative achievement.

For the cabaret Jo had created a backdrop of oil cloth at the side of the hall in black and white chequers, with glamorous girls dressed in sisal skirts and frangipani garlands. They danced to the John Barry theme tune of the 1962 James Bond movie 'Doctor No'. Jo then sang a solo about all the characters in the Yacht Club, dressed in her sailor boy outfit, followed by a clip from 'South Pacific' backed up with guitar music and the string skirted girls.

By this time, I was utterly overwhelmed with my bush-whacker soul-mate, stardom personality. Hysterical applause thundered across the bay. Some people are born to perform in the pulpit, on the green benches in Parliament, or on the stage. Jo broke away from quite a pious background when she was 17 years old, falling for a young soldier who aspired to be a family farmer. After 12 years producing beautiful talented children, caring for baby pigs, thousands of hens, calves and tractor driving in busy seasons, followed by long wild bush safaris during my last tour in Mbeya. It occurred to me again that she had definitely missed her natural vocation by marrying me.

The amateur play house was very much an expatriate cultural activity and did not attract the interest of Tanzanian people at all. The only one African in attendance at the celebration was in fact, an expatriate also, a Nigerian, who's role as it later turned out in retrospect, cast a dark shadow over that evening. The Yacht Club Commodore was in charge of the bar and he caught the African barman swigging the whiskey. The Commodore scolded him vigorously and twisted his ear in jest, "a wigging", which was thought to be the end of it. The Nigerian Magistrate next day filed a charge against the Commodore for assault which ultimately resulted in a two-month prison sentence. Since the Commodore was the Tanga Chief Customs Officer, this ruined his career, there being then no British High Commission then for support. This shadow did not appear until later in the week however, and dancing was the order of the night after Jo's cabaret. Ian Kennedy grabbed the pop star whilst the rum punch grabbed me and convinced me that I needed to sleep. I walked the lawns under the stars finally falling asleep under the palm trees. It was about midnight when a familiar face loomed above me.

"Hey, you, what about the last waltz then? Ian and I have been searching the Bay for you, what's going on?"

"Er; fresh air, knocked me out."

"Not like you to miss the dancing, Brian, you're a star performer on the dance floor. That cave you built! Everyone's asking who did it. Come on, I need you."

Christmas 1965: Dr Ian Kennedy, the young bachelor surgeon from the Isle of Lewis now had a half share with me in an Osprey called Jill. The Osprey is a well-balanced large and fast yacht that is sailed usually by a crew of two, or three in windier conditions, one of whom has to be nimble enough to spend time out on a trapeze. The fleet of Ospreys at the Tanga Yacht Club were predominantly acquired in the 1950s and renowned for their beauty and performance. An aforementioned man named Lead, the pioneer of the Tanga sisal industry, also manufactured some of these clinker built yachts in his workshops from native timber, to the design class Osprey. Joe Kerly was an elderly member of the sailing community, the only member to ever wear a life jacket, also the only member who never capsized. He owned an Osprey with a varnished hull, which added speed. Joe collected silver cups like lesser mortals collected cowry shells. He also collected jazz records. Jo and I were, you might say, Rockers, drawn to his house for sessions which led to the offer of sailing lessons.

Joe taught us how to win. What was the secret? "Don't get excited!" Imagine that! "Sense the wind shifts like a gull, clip the corners at the marker buoys and above all, convey calm confidence to your crew and time your start line accurately."

The *Kaskazi* had started. This Arabic word depicts the fierce monsoon wind from India which blows steadily into the Bay, the narrow entrance acting like a venturi. Anyone who could hold his Osprey upright was in for a heck of an exciting time. I mustered two trapeze artists, Jo and Ian, to risk their lives hanging out over the 'shark infested' ocean, and then I tightened up into a 'broad reach' catching the wind full on. Thus began the most thrilling experience of our lives. The yacht leapt into a 'plane-ing' mode, the bow lifting out of the water while the stern barely skimmed the water, literally flying. The ultimate attainable speed depended upon the wind strength and had been known to increase to, even above, 16 knots. The terrifying thing was that the very slightest error by the helmsman and everyone joined the porpoises; the sharks were further out, in an instant, with a cataclysmic inversion; the crew then cajoling the helmsman below the waves. On this first occasion honour prevailed.

Jo's naturally wavy hair had grown longer and longer with another contractual year to go before finding a professional hairdresser in England. Her wavy hair was now as long as when I first met her at the age of thirteen. She wore a shower cap on the trapeze. Looking at her flying in the clouds from where I sat at the helm, she was to me my princess of the tropical sea with the blue sky as her cloak and sea spray in her hair. Jo was my inspiration, leading eventually to us winning the TYC Silver Cup, without ever capsizing, like Joe Kerly.

On Christmas Eve, Santa Claus clad in red shirt and hat, arrived late. He was no longer a mystical spirit to Philip aged ten years but was as joyfully welcome as ever.

"I've been up to Mbeya looking for you boys, why didn't you let me know you had moved?" said Santa.

Philip shouted something about Tusker being left in the garden.

"Ah yes, I found it thanks. To tell you the truth that's why I'm a bit late. I was gasping in this coastal heat, my reindeers were too, emptied the crate."

Jo was heard to say, with a suspicious look, "Reindeers emptied the crate: O-oh yes!"

Sally Spaniel's tail was wagging overtime as a sack was opened, revealing plenty of gifts, by the standards of the day that is. We had sailed to Mombasa, and purchased an airgun, a 27inch model yacht construction kit and I found an ivory bangle for Jo. We couldn't find anything suitable for Caroline in Mombasa but she turned up from England on her short Christmas school holiday with lots of lovely gifts from the family in England. Traditional goodwill prevailed as ever and despite the un-Christmas-like environment of tropical Tanga, we achieved a roast turkey, ex USA, followed by The Queen's Speech on the Quarter Deck at 4:15 p.m. courtesy of BBC Overseas Service. We raised a toast to absent friends and tried to imagine how wonderful it would be to feel cold and cosy by the fire as we remembered it being on the farm in Norfolk. How life had changed for us all, we remembered the children caring for the animals over Christmas; laughing happy small children overjoyed with a small gift or two. One constant that prevailed was the understanding of the importance of love and trust in each other, in this expanding and hazardous world of Africa.

The Boxing Day shoot of farming days was forgotten as we all 'fell about' on the wind driven waves in the Plum Pudding Handicap yacht race. The reminiscent farmhouse log fire gave way to the joys of "Paradise Tanga".

Chapter Nine

Philosophy

New Year's Eve: The weekend saw us busy making *papier mache* heads of cows, giants, etc. for the Giant's kitchen part of the pantomime Jack and the Beanstalk. The children were all helping out whilst Caroline had been given the job of stage make-up. We invited Franky and Henry Dale, the harbour pilot, to dinner, and at 11:00 p.m. we agreed to bring in the New Year at the Bombo Club Wild West Party. However, the infectious African rhythms kept us dancing until 3:00 a.m. when we left Caroline and Oliver 'to it' and retired to the Oohms party until 4:30.

New Year's Day 1966: Tanzania had a commendable fifteen public holidays per year plus two weeks' mandatory leave for public sector workers to return to their native villages. This was also fed into my contract. Colonialism, amongst its several benefits, brought Tanzanians into the 20th century with employment holidays. When I was born, there were no annual paid holidays as such and in the colder north regions of our planet the human race has obviously evolved to endure unrelenting 'hard graft' in order to survive. Europeans seem to look upon a public holiday as an opportunity to catch up on all those home and garden jobs. Africans however have, enviously, achieved the art of maximum relaxation 'at the drop of a hat'. Historically, to the African, physical work had been looked upon as a necessary inconvenience rather than a lifetime aspiration. I suppose that 'tomorrow' had been somewhat of an irrelevance during the evolutionary process of the native African, genetically evolved from Olduvai Gorge and Serengeti 'the Garden of Eden', where food was available, in various forms, all year round and in an ambient climate. Nevertheless the modern African, in my experience, can be a very hard worker, given the right incentive.

African village women traditionally cultivate the land and grow cereals for storage towards the dry season, in addition to the more intellectual capacity of raising a healthy, cleverer, next-generation. The muscular male traditionally clears the land, builds houses, provides meat, and protects their families from wild animals, and enemy tribes. I have noticed that African men have exceptional vocal talent in the political field. It seems also that it is traditional for the men folk to create entertainment and music for dancing.

Tanzanians today have gained self-reliance and initiative through education and the provision of modern medical facilities. Today's Tanzanian is achieving the heights of competence. I did find that they were not so good at planning ahead and at stepping aside from the constraints of customary prejudices. This was something my African colleagues agreed with me about and was partly the reason why Jo and I were there.

"How is it that we *Wazungu* have lost that African talent to enjoy a workless environment, Jo? We went wrong somewhere; shouldn't life be about living, not working, about rhythm and dancing, about loving, about Tusker Lager?"

"Look who's philosophising, a crazier workaholic I know not! Okay, let's give it a go. Go and smarten yourself up, Brian, it's time for the New Year's Day Ball at Lead Memorial Hall. By the way, have you made a New Year's Resolution, Mr Land Planning Officer?"

"Yes ... to ramp up 'The Swinging Sixties'. The Kinks come to mind, and The Moody Blues, Tom Jones, Manfred Man, The Byrds, The Hollies." Primitive microphones meant projected voices and audible ballads in those days.

January 6th 1965: Another national holiday! This time it was to celebrate the Union of Tanzania and Zanzibar twelve months before. We celebrated by organising the annual race with the African *ngalawas*. These fishermen's canoes have two outriggers and the typical triangular sail of the Nile Arabs, called the lateen rig. They were very fast and really hard to beat in our ospreys but their weakness was, of course, beating to windward. So lots of good natured banter was the order of the day.

We were soon lined up on the town-side beach on the opposite side of the bay, hoping for a sense of urgency to emerge. I observed that my neighbour's bow rope was controlled by his daughter in her bikini. She was standing on the beach, a white-skinned, shapely girl contrasting sharply with the black congregation of onlookers, with her golden blonde hair shining in the sunshine. I could sense greedy native eyes homing in on her.

"Desmond! Just watch out for that young man in the water over there." I said pointing. He was wading briskly towards her. He wore long trousers and nothing more. His gait became awkward as he approached her on her blind side, his eyes fixed upon her. He dropped on her like a Kestrel on a field mouse. She squeaked as black muscular arms slid around her waist from behind. He lifted her off her feet and in an instant he had her face down across an upturned canoe minus her bikini. There was uproar from the beach and the osprey crews as they rushed towards the couple. An African reached them first with a paddle in hand. He dealt an almighty thwack to the bare bottom of the rapist from below, which sent him over the screaming girl's back. A further blow to the head left him senseless, his ardour wilting in the hot sand and the girl fleeing seaward with her heart in her mouth and her bikini in her hand. The event was a salutatory reminder not to ignore the stark realities of a possible clash between unrelated cultures, lying just beneath the surface.

On the last Saturday of the school holiday, everyone voted for that remote coral beach at Kigombe. Our teenagers included Oliver Delany and Caroline, declaring their aspiration for a "beach party in paradise." They chased each other in the warm blue sea the day long, exploring the coral reef and cooking bacon and eggs on a fire of old coconut shells. They genuinely preferred coconut water from green coconuts to ginger ale. After some BBC World Service 1960's pop, we recovered lying on the white coral sand listening to the casuarina pines whispering their tranquillity on the gentle ocean breeze. We decided to negotiate the road back before dark. It was rainy season and we were caught out by a heavy storm on way back which cut the road deeply. It took us an hour to cut wood and fill the gulley with my stock of, ever ready tools, from the car boot.

Back in Tanga, we opened mail from our Post Office Box; a school bill from Harrods. It was impressive; 340 Cash's name tapes (for Caroline, not the whole school), Scottish style tweed cape, a pair of men's pyjamas, for? *Homo erectus?* Single sex school? Should we be worried? Caroline was all too soon gone again into the northern skies at 500 mph, and poor young Philip too, chuffing uphill past Kilimanjaro at 30 mph. He was also to be on his own now since his brother Richard was 13 years old and enrolled at Karimjee Secondary School in Tanga. His teacher turned out to be Jerry Selness, a 'Peace Corper'. Our bereavement for the loss of

Philip, aged ten years, was heightened by the news that he had broken his arm upon arrival back at Arusha School.

April 1966: Richard grew to hate Karimjee School, being the only English boy in a form of Asians. Apart from school, however, life was exciting. He was mobile now with no bounds to his explorative nature. Fortunately his habitat was flat, fortunate because his Flying Pigeon Chinese bicycle lacked Sheffield steel reliability and the pedals bent when he pressed against an uphill slope. Richard, in his thirteen-year-old school-boy jargon, began to refer to his school contemporaries as "Chuts". In a moment of annoyance he said, "They treat the African boys like animals and they are trained by their parents to cheat and steal. I caught one stealing my bicycle pump today!" I was obliged to firmly suggest that some amendments to his terminology and attitude might be appropriate.

It was this prevalence of an 'attitude' by between Africans and Asians that, when a breakdown in law and order occurred two years before, known as the Colito Incident, in January 1964, some innocent Asians were killed by Africans, on the streets of Dar es Salaam. The incident in question was a mutiny by the Army based at Colito Barracks in Dar es Salaam, against the government. They occupied the city. Our close friends the Wrintmores and their two children Peter and Jane were departing on overseas leave and suffered the misfortune to be split up, rough-handled with rifle buts, and arrested, by rebel soldiers. The Vice President's intervention on behalf of Eric, who was a magistrate, may have saved their lives. Eric ultimately signed up for another tour of service.

President Julius Nyerere had called upon the British Government for assistance. This was before the breakdown in diplomatic relations. What provoked this attempted rebellion?

Despite their country's independence, the army considered, with some justification that the soldiers living conditions, pay and diet, had deteriorated. This contrasted particularly unfavourably with the living conditions of those British soldiers, predominantly officers, still serving with the Tanzania Rifles. The mutiny lasted three days and spread throughout the army who established control of most strategic points in Dar es Salaam. Moreover, there was the coincident unrest following the Zanzibar Revolution some eight days earlier and uprisings in the armies of neighbouring Kenya and Uganda. It was a potentially perilous time for the newly independent East African states. However, the mutiny was ended in less than an hour by Royal Marines off the British aircraft carrier HMS Centaur which was fortuitously patrolling in the Indian Ocean. They quickly responded to President Nyerere's request for help. The overall number of casualties from the three-day mutiny was mercifully small. The rebel soldiers surrendered when confronted by the British Marines.

John French, VSO, took Richard under his wing and taught him how to skin-dive on the coral reef, every Sunday. Richard eventually achieved a dive of 50 ft. We were proud of his achievement; also his talent as a junior sailor won him the Cadet Cup for that year. Richard had little chance of achieving academic heights but he was destined to make his mark in life through solid practical ability.

We were now in our fourth year in Tanzania, a young independent nation striving to find its own road to economic and social cohesion with an element of success. I enjoyed a respectful rapport with my staff and with officials of government and local tribal dignitaries. I did not notice any trace of racialism in post-colonial Tanzania amongst expatriates or Africans. Admittedly the boorish racialism between Afrikaners and Africans further south seemed to achieve short-term economic success, but Jo and I believed that development rooted in hatred, fear and sweated labour was, to coin a phrase, the route to hell.

Armed with a better understanding of the motivations of Africans and particularly of the rural strains and stresses, Jo and I had been able to establish five functional agricultural development structures, tied into local human and natural resources. Looming financial constrains in the administration of British Aid Funds, however, were to leave Jo and I feeling like victims rather than victors in our endeavours during the ensuing six months.

Another form of Aid was from communist countries, keen to exert influence upon Tanzania and its leader President Nyerere, popularly known as *Mwalimu* meaning Teacher. I had already experienced Yugoslavian Aid at Lupa Tinga Tinga hence my scepticism about the prevailing jubilation upon news of a coastal tarmac road to be built from Morogoro to Tanga by the Yugoslavs. These insular, solemn men were somewhat naïve about building durable roads under tropical rainfall conditions, thinking that the concept of soil/cement mixture would prove an adequate foundation for tar spraying. It certainly looked impressive and progress was rapid. I can say that my forebodings were proved correct. When Jo and I travelled the route one and half years later, our journey was very slow due to having to wind our way round thousands of potholes. Another year later there was no trace of a bitumen surface for hundreds of miles, not that anyone worried as it was just back to normal.

July 1966, *an introduction to caving.* One man who predicted the outcome of this showcase Yugoslavian form of Aid was an ex-Colonial District Commissioner who knew a thing or two about the dynamics of Africa, his name was John Cooke. John was a good friend of similarly adventurous nature to myself and was employed as a Geography teacher at Karimjee School in Tanga. He was a Yorkshire man with a comfortably extensive greying bushy moustache and an air of confidence, certainty upon the way the world worked. His wife Sylvia was of East African German descent and they were both committed to educating the African. John's Yorkshire background included potholing, hence his enthusiasm for exploring Amboni Caves near Tanga. Being something of an explorer myself and a surveyor, locally known as the *Bwanapima*, we teamed up well with some sixth form students. We set forth, equipped with compass, lamps, chains, helmets and climbing gear to explore the unexplored Karst limestone Amboni Caves. I was reminded to bring my rifle in case of an encounter with a leopard, renowned as guardians of the spiritual underworld.

Weekends spent underground would ultimately prove to be a gazetted revelation to the Royal Geographical Society and earned John some academic distinction in his later career at the University of Gaberone, Botswana.

Jo was not too happy about my planned excursion into an unknown world and had been told by Sylvia that there was an African legend that a "Deutsch entered the caves before World War I and was never seen again, probably a welcome meal for the resident leopard." We declared that we would keep a look out for any human remains to support the legend and so allay our claim to be the first human eyes to behold the wonders of the Amboni Caves.

We explored every fissure and cavern, at times very beautiful in tinted green light from the forest cover above. We negotiated a near vertical crack, edgeways on, our hearts in our mouths, finally reaching a tiny hole on the silty-soil bed deep down. We shone our torches through this aperture and beheld a wonderful cathedral-like cavern, hung with stalactites and illuminated with pale green light from a crack in the ceiling. We resolved to try and squeeze through. It was humid and the grey rock oozed with water. We were both tired but did not want to do this survey again. John volunteered to go first, thank goodness. I could not hear his instructions as his body blocked the hole completely. Suddenly he was reversing.

"I can't get my chest through. I will strip off and try again. I could see the mighty cavern beyond and it is definitely worth another try." I stripped off naked in unison. John lunged in again, inching forward by sliding on the bed of silty-clay and manipulating his toes. He paused and pushed arms to his sides. His fists in this prone position assisted in propulsion by lifting the body slightly and flexing the wrist muscles to give leverage. The atmosphere was stifling and claustrophobic. Suddenly he was through, his lamp light being visible.

I could hear him now, "Brian, listen, you will have to breath out when it gets tight and relax. Don't get excited, a rise in blood pressure will be enough to inflate the skin which will make it more difficult. Remember, relax, push, and relax, breath out, push. Tie a rope to your foot and the survey bag and clothes. It's amazing this side and really worth the effort."

I thought to myself, I am reputed to be a cool customer and this is going to be the ultimate test. I slid onto the mud like a sausage in a helmet. Fortunately I am a small person. *If Jo could see me now!* I muttered. The rock gripped me like a strait jacket. I could see John's torch ahead. Sweat poured off my torso, lubricating my muscles. I reached the point of no return and relaxed. *If I could just get my chest through, everything else behind me is smaller.* Suddenly it was all over. There we stood in the lamp light, smudged brown with silt and breathing ammonia-tainted air from putrid bat droppings. We hauled the bags through, resolving to find another way out through the roof. We found a basin in the rock, full of cool water for refreshment and a wash down.

We found a spider in the lamplight, flat against the rock, unalarmed by the bright light. It was blind. What did it live on? It was quite large and very flat, like poultry lice that live amongst the feathers, perhaps for hiding in cracks of rock. No web or mate. Upon careful examination, we found that its chitinised pedipalps had enlarged into wide spreading arms with a terminal claw. The spread of these arms when unfolded measured nine inches across.

"Do you know what, Brian; I reckon this spider catches bats!"

We left the creature to its blind world, rather than collect it and headed for our escape crack above. Out on top, I took photos of the surface. The surface terrain was hair-raisingly treacherous having been dissolved by acid rain over the millennia, into columnar needles and bottomless fissures, where a slip would mean oblivion in the bowels of the earth. Even a minor slip could render a ghastly gash to the leg or a posterior injection of elephantine proportions. Probably this was the most hostile terrain on Earth where even a snake could not cross, but nevertheless supported trees, sitting on bare limestone rock with their roots plunging down the fissures to the water table far below. We had encountered these roots below eerily searching; probing for nutrients in the darkness.

There were no fossils in this Jurassic limestone thus indicating its great age. Had we seen any other life forms? Yes, we had discovered two; one a pure white fungal growth of hairs, looking like a lavatory brush and the other, the flat spider.

The evening following found John and Sylvia, Jo and I at the Lead Memorial Hall for a live cultural exchange concert by Woody Herman. There was not a single African in the audience, they were obviously not into 'Jazz Blues', I'm not that keen either. John and I were reminded of that flat spider creeping in and out of cracks in the rock, suddenly pouncing upwards on its prey with its long reach arms like that sudden screaming clarinet, 'gotcha'!

During the interval; "John; I've got a job to do in your old haunt, Handeni."

"It is full of witchcraft is Handeni," John advised, "it has low rainfall there, which is a problem, and you would need water storage for any scheme of development. This made our efforts in the past, expensive. There is a government rest house there."

I seemed to have been transferred to the Ministry of Lands, Settlement and Water and they wanted me to survey the Handeni area for prospects of agricultural development. Whatever happened to that British Aid Fund my salary was to be guaranteed, for now.

Jo couldn't accompany me, Richard being at day school. I soon found myself occupying a hard wooden chair in the rest house with my pressure lamp hissing away. The door burst open to admit a stocky, black-haired, jovial-faced man accompanied by a Game Guard in a dark green uniform, an old Martini action rifle slung over his shoulder. He looked surprised and said in Welsh dialect, "Oh, I didn't expect to find anybody yer. Nice to 'ave company though. My name is Huw Jones. Geology!"

"How do you do. Brian Dawtrey, Land Planning Officer, Tanga. I think we met in Arusha in 1962."

"Ah, yes, the rhino weekend. Now that was somethin' boyo, I remember that! An impressive title you've got, Brean. I suppose you get out into the *pori (=*bush) then with your job?"

"True!"

"I thought you were a *Bwananyama* (= Game Warden) at first."

"I'm an honorary one."

"Are you now, there's a thing. You're a bushman reely then!"

He opened his camp chair whilst the Game Guard unloaded their boxes, food and bedding. "My Director insists I take a Game Guard everywhere I go round these parts. There are lots of rhinos. Look you at this, Brean."

He produced a large crystal of clear quartz with red crystals attached. "Beautiful, isn't it? I found a whole hill of it you see. Now I'm lookin out for some big crystals of garnet in that hill. I could take you there tomorrow, Brean. What d'you say? It is quite a way mind."

"I'd like that. I have got camping gear and a geological hammer, and a.22 rifle in case of … guinea fowl."

"Ah, there are millions of *kanga,* if you see one you'll see five undred!"

The next day, we aroused the Asian garage owner from his bed early to fill our metal 'peepa' with 45 gallons of petrol. We set off in Huw's Land Rover with the Game Guard in the back, and we were soon into the dusty plains of Maasai land. We met two Maasai herding their scrawny cattle. Huw had obviously developed a good rapport with Maasai despite their lack of Kiswahili, on account of his hugely expressive dialect, emotive manner and somewhat musical joviality. Imagine living in solitude and coming upon a 'Welsh clown'. It was an event. I was struck by the oddness of the trio standing there; two very tall red men and one very short black-haired man, exercising rapport like old friends, despite their presence in a barren landscape which supports only barbarous thorns and armour-plated rhinos.

The Maasai burst into song, a plaintive love song, about their beloved cattle, floating on the gentle breeze to eternity in that boundless theatre.

Huw, like so many British geologists, spent eight months a year under canvass in extremely remote areas seeking mineral deposits for the Tanzania Government, followed by four months at HQ in Dodoma, writing up reports and making maps. It was a hazardous life and lonely, without modern communications in case of snake bite, malaria, scorpion sting, and rhino or black buffalo bull encounter. I invited him to stay with us in Tanga and enjoy civilisation. He did so later, bringing me a gift of two very special rocks, one of red gold from Australia and the other a chunk of rock from the Rand in South Africa. I remarked that for all its reputation, it did not look much, just grey rock.

"That's the richest gold bearing rock in the world, Brean. Get your hand lens and take a closer look. Its lack of glamour is deceiving. You see that fine powder, that's gold. Gold means power. This rock has hidden power; like a certain lady I know!"

Huw was impressed with the power of the Osprey too. "Wouldn't mind livin in Tanga," he said later, "sailin ospreys is exciting; makes a change from being charged by rhinos."

September 1966: I was scheduled to spend five days of discussions with the Ministry in Dar es Salaam regarding finance for my four proposed settlement schemes in Tanga Region. Richard, now 14 years old, pleaded effectively to accompany me. He said, "I have always wanted to go to Dar Dad and I have been saving my pocket money for ages. I can buy something special for Mum there."

Richard had a special knack of persuasive phraseology which was surely suggestive of a career in sales. Jo agreed that Dar would be an experience, before it all changed with modernisation. An old Arabic and Hindu port, Dar es Salaam means Haven of Peace. However, it was not quite that for me because of the financial jiggery-pokery much in evidence that September.

Richard dressed smartly alongside his dad in pristine white shirt, shorts, socks and shoes, as we boarded East African Airways Fokker Friendship giving us fabulous views of the coastal coral reefs and the deep blue ocean. We touched down in Zanzibar. No one had been allowed to visit since the Revolution, hence trade had ceased. The cabin doors opened admitting hot air laden with the smell of cloves, so familiar to the explorers of the nineteenth century. This exotic atmosphere belied the stern reality of the welcoming committee of men dressed uniformly in grey serge suits like a necklace of Job's tears, a large tropical grass seed, uniformly grey and loaded with genes that means trouble for the farmer. The Chinese committee smiled uniformly and looked expectant, of what? Maybe there was a dignitary amongst us on the plane? I was uncertain and a little worried. If we disembarked we might not be allowed to continue to Dar es Salaam but instead to China!

I took a photograph and then thought; *mistake?* No one noticed and we were soon on our way to the tranquillity of Dar es Salaam, with a sigh of relief. Richard was charmed and took a keen interest in everything, the Arabic architecture the swaying palms along the coral beach, the street traders, the Askaris (African militia), the fishing canoes, the ships, and the black herons fishing along the shore line making their characteristic umbrellas to shade the water and attract the fish to the surface. Fish were on the heronry supper menu. Our supper menu was to be on the balcony of the New Africa Hotel, overlooking the bay, with refreshing drinks. Richard would remember this visit, and for another reason!

The next day we were again relaxing on that balcony which was a popular meeting place for friends and colleagues from all over the territory, when who should appear, clasping a Tusker, but my old friend and fellow hunter, now the Mikumi National Park Warden, Steve Stephenson. More to the point, he was accompanied by his boss, the Director of National Parks, John Owen. Having explained my anxiety over the loss of British Aid funds and my dubious prospects, Steve declared; "Brian, we have the solution to your problem; and ours as it turns out, we need a Park Warden for Ruaha National Park. You are definitely the right man for the job."

Where-upon Richard sprang to life. "Dad! That's it! Sign up. Yippee!"

Ruaha National Park was an old haunt of ours of course. It lies between Iringa and Mbeya in the Southern Highlands Region, and is very much a slice of 'old Africa', which together with its neighbouring Game Reserves extends to nearly 10,000 square miles. It teems with birds (400 species), and at that time 60,000 elephants. The Director acknowledged the offer and suggested I join the National Parks next year instead of returning to the Ministry of Lands and Settlement. We discussed technicalities at length. I had always aspired to join National Parks ever since seeing the film in England, 'Where No Vultures Fly', when the idea for wildlife conservation was born in Kenya by Mervyn Cowie. There was a problem however; wildlife conservation was not supported by the UK government in those days, which meant no school holiday air fares. I explained this to Richard.

"No problem really, Dad, we can all live in camp and help you do game counts in the plane, catch poachers and that. Mum says that correspondence courses by P.N.E.U. (Parents National Education Union) are a higher standard than Arusha School."

The Director expressed enthusiasm for this boy's devotion to the conservation ethic, "If only we had some African pupils with such aspirations then we would be much happier about the future for saving the elephants which are becoming threatened by the rising price of ivory in world markets."

I was now firmly put on the spot by Richard, again. "Let us know, Brian, when you have had a word with Cicely. The offer is on the table." It occurred to me that Steve's wife had abandoned him in favour of civilisation, once he turned to wildlife conservation as a career. Jo, much as she was an animal lover, might not favour the total isolation of life in the wilds of Ruaha, with only me and troublesome elephants for our evening's recreation.

My original employer the VSA, financed by the British taxpayer, was now defunct. Their offices were occupied by the ministry men and the atmosphere had changed. No one wanted to talk about work, much less settlement schemes, but only personal problems. The VSA was set up to overcome bottlenecks in administration and to enable the employment of staff from the private sector as well as civil servants. All salaries had been elevated to encourage hard work. Confusion and jealousy prevailed in the Ministry of Agriculture. Now we were under the Ministry of Lands Settlement and Water, there was no machinery for paying, private sector employees and expatriate VSA salaries did not fit the Establishment scales either. This ministry was much better organised than Agriculture, and I retained every hope of getting my schemes up and running by the end of the year, when my contract came up for renewal. It was explained to me that the Commissioner of Rural Settlement, whom I knew very well, by the name of Geoffrey Allesbrook, was now powerless. He must have felt like a museum curator with the title over his door, *Wazira Ukaaji wa Vijiji,* (VSA).

"Come in, Brian, I wanted to have a private word. Thanks for coming up to Dar."

I reminded him about my 'Assisted Schemes' of resettlement and how confident I was with the local support for Mkalamo, Kiwanda and the two 'out-grower' schemes for sisal and for tea, Kwangwe and Karimjee.

"I am afraid the financial position with this Aid Fund is hopeless. This VSA Department is in chaos and morale is low for the time being. I will explain why in a moment. He ordered some tea and we talked about my tobacco schemes in Mbeya region and the resettlement of the South African Apartheid refugees.

"Your schemes at Matwiga and Lupa Tinga are still functional thanks to OXFAM and WFP food from USA. I can pull those agencies in for your Tanga schemes but field organisation will have to be African, not expatriate. You do have local political support which is absolutely essential for any NGO, or other aided scheme to function long term. As far as VSA is concerned you are well out of headquarters because everyone is worried to death here. There is a certain minister who shall be nameless although I think you will know who it is, who has misappropriated British Aid funds to buy a fleet of Mercedes cars. The President has ordered him to repay the money in full to the Ministry of Lands, Settlement and Water. Our Permanent Secretary to the ministry, a young Cambridge graduate, is now being pressurised to recover the money from VSA. Our major Pilot Village Settlement Schemes that rely heavily upon loans, and capital finance, are destined to fall."

"There's worse, Brian, our expatriate staff will not get their air fares paid back to the UK either. The permanent secretary is threatening to make us pay back our salary supplements and there will be no contract gratuities. Leave pay will be normal for you because that is catered for within your ministry budget. The ex-Colonial Civil Service staff will not get their full pensions."

I reminded him that my three-year contract ends in December and I could not possibly pay the air fare home for myself, wife and two boys. "Come and see me here, the day before your contract ends and I will try to get you a ticket. I have a plan, not guaranteed. There is now no British Embassy to protect us from imprisonment as illegal immigrants when your work permit expires in six weeks. So keep this to yourself. Oh! By the way, the government is offering you a new contract for a further three years. Somebody thinks well of you at the top, I think it is the Vice President Rashidi Kawawa who originally pulled you into the VSA."

I called in at the Canadian Embassy to meet the British Affairs Representative. I complained to this auburn-haired young man that my contract had been illegally broken and I could not get home to Britain.

"I am awfully sowy, old chap, it is an awful mess I know. We do sympathise tewibly but I am afwaid we all have to gwin and bear it. With no diplomatic ties with Bwitain our hands are tied."

"You realise my family and me could all end up in prison!"

"I suggest that you keep in touch with your Commissioner for Rural Settlement in case he finds some money from somewhere."

I thought that maybe he knew something. I was not inspired with confidence however. There was a dearth of integrity in Dar es Salaam at this time, the 'graffiti was on the wall' with rumours of extreme left-wing socialism being the new philosophy of the TANU party.

The portents that I was seeing, heralded the Arusha Declaration of the following year, 1967. This historical event was President Nyerere's blueprint for an African model of development based on African socialism, otherwise known as *Ujamaa*. There were a number of laudable ethical elements to the Arusha Declaration which included the institutionalisation of equal rights, freedom of expression and religious belief, and compulsory free education. However, the application of *Ujamaa* to agriculture was disastrous. The Pilot Village Settlement Schemes of the VSA were converted to *Ujamaa* Villages based upon communal block farming and compulsion, on a massive scale. Over the ensuing ten years *Ujamaa* was destined to result in rising poverty. The production of food from the land is much too hard work to be undertaken without a personal incentive for profit, as 'The Soviets' found out to their cost. Additional factors came into play at the national level during these years; a war with Uganda, higher taxes, burgeoning bureaucracy fostering corruption, and a fall in the price of sisal and coffee. During this period there was also fuel shortages caused by the '70's Oil Crisis'. A later Iringa Declaration saw a soft pedalling of the 'communal' element of food production. Lessons learnt.

I called upon our permanent secretary, usually an affable intelligent personality but found him changed beyond recognition. He was hostile, illogical, emotional and with a primitive ferocity. His intellectual mind was not available. My enthusiasm for another tour of service in Tanzania was on the wane that day. Richard might have the right idea I thought.

Back at home in Tanga's relaxing ambience I said to Jo, "Would you like the good news or the bad news first?"

"Good."

"We have been offered a job as a Park Warden for Ruaha National Park, with flying lessons."

"Wow!"

I explained the horror story of the defunct VSA and the prospect of prison if we couldn't get out within six weeks. This was one of those transient moments when our eyes met, speechless, huge helpless emotion. Jo fainted. Later, after cups of sweet tea, we sadly sauntered down to the Quarter Deck, feeling that Tanzania was divorcing us, their devoted and loving friends. We clearly loved Africa and its people. Come what may, we would be back – that was our decision.

"We'll make out, Brian," Jo said gazing across the bay. "One thing I would say though is to ignore that permanent secretary and go straight to Geoffrey as he is our only hope. Hey! Cheer up, Brian; I've got some good news."

"You're pregnant!"

"Don't be flippant! I have organised a 'BRIAN'S PARTY' for your birthday, and I've invited all the Brians in Tanga, seven all told! I've got a birthday letter here from your daughter. Look at this."

It was a great success. Jo organised a gallery of baby Brian photos, requiring a guessing game for the wives to choose their men. The result was hysterically funny. The selected husbands inevitably weren't the right ones, and they were then required to partner their baby choices for the evening dancing too, as ever, Rock and Roll, not forgetting Dusty Springfield, and Sandy Shaw plus Ella Fitzgerald the Jazz Queen, from our record collection and the BBC Overseas Service.

Having no glass in the windows brought the neighbours around. They were greeted by candles glowing in paper bags lining the driveway. Adding to this merry scene was the glow of ships lights twinkling across the bay and the heady aroma of frangipani bushes around the house. The political nightmare in Dar es Salaam faded, but I did dream a lot, of life in the wilds of Ruaha National park.

"Let's be Tanzanians – don't worry about tomorrow," I philosophised to Jo later.

Eventually the candles flickered out, the Tusker bottles rattled empty and the gentle sea breeze became audible again, rustling the palm trees along the shore line. I had been, as always, very possessive of my wife on the dance floor, for which I had a reputation. She was the world's best dancer after all. Women are always very lightly clad in the tropics and cross-pollination was often a threat to marital stability. Female softness transmits across a yard of humid air.

The night was hot, humid and still, indoors. We dowsed the light leaving just the small bedroom inviting glow. With immense relief we removed our perspiration soaked clothes and stood naked beneath the squeaking fan, bathing blissfully in its torrent of air, fanning the passionate flames.

Jo muttered something about me being "the best of the 'Magnificent Seven' you are an alpha male."

I cannot say that those two titles had ever occurred to me. My mind was, perhaps over occupied, by an undaunted determination to get those four schemes off the ground before the end of December whatever became of us thereafter.

My time was now limited and I needed to plan for the Kwangwe Sisal Outgrowers Scheme initiated by the VSA, and organise the demarcation on the ground. The scheme could survive without British Aid provided I could get some support from the Yacht Club fraternity. That might sound odd! The fact is, that most of the sailors were senior employees of sisal estate companies, namely the British, Bird & Co. and the Swiss, Amboni Estates. In the outcome they proved willing to guarantee minor financial support for the Village Out-grower idea.

Jo and I were elated, for it meant that together with Oxfam and WFP support in Year One, a stable beginning was possible. Village growers would enjoy the key factor in producing sisal, to be within range of a decorticator machine. This essential mighty machine, invented originally by the Germans, is used for crushing and stripping the huge green leathery leaves, exposing the fibre which is then bleached in the sun and baled for export. The estate would purchase the raw material from the growers, and process it for export. Clearing the wooded landscape by hand is traditionally done by village men-folk felling the trees at waist level, piling the wood around the tree stump and burning it. This kills the tree stump and provides a pile of ash to fertilise the crop.

Sisal was, at that time, Tanzania's primary export earner, supplemented by cotton, tobacco, diamonds and corned beef from

Tanzania Packers in Dar es Salaam. Farmers the world over depended upon sisal twine for baling fodder crops and straw. From the Quarter Deck, the daily shipment of white sisal bales being hoisted from the lighters up the ships' sides was always a reassuring spectacle of prosperity and it seemed logical to me that peasant farmers should be able to benefit directly from its production. The settlement area was still wild bush. Would Jo be able to accompany me? Richard would shortly be on half-term holiday so we timed it to be together on what might be our last safari.

Tanga Region enjoys fifty inches of rainfall; hence a verdant agricultural region; so with rain threatening we needed our tent. My only remaining Land Rover was busy with my survey staff marking out plots of Kiwanda Scheme in the hills, so my Fort Corsair GT was conscripted to face some punishment penetrating the coastal forest belt. Timber extraction companies had left us some access tracks, albeit with the odd tree stump hidden in the grass looking for my sump guard. We set off in great haste with air photos, soil auger, Richard, Sally Spaniel and tent, 50 miles to go. I needed to plan for the delineation of some 2000 acres blocks on the air photos, with village sites along the sisal estate boundaries, for possible 800 settlers.

We made camp near some evergreen forest. Tall forest shades out the grass and hence no bush fires to destroy the organic litter than creates fertile soils. The old dictum that Africa burns annually from Cape Town to Cairo, thus creating infertile soils, is the result of man firing the dry season savannah grass, and not by lightening as is sometimes supposed. Most of Tanga Region is not a savannah environment, hence the fertile productive landscape along the coastal belt. A former Messerschmitt WWII fighter pilot, Dr G., whom I am reluctant to name out of courteously, and whom I conducted to Lupa Tinga Tinga Tobacco Scheme in the season of fires in 1963, spent hours lecturing me about the stupidity of Adolf Hitler turning to Russia in 1940 instead of invading Britain. He became quite rhetorical about Hitler's mistake, declaring that "Germany would now rule Tanzania and we would have put a stop to this fire mania with a bit of the *kiboko*." Of course he was correct scientifically, and one might argue that Teutonic rule might have also been agriculturally beneficial, as was the case with the establishment of the sisal industry. However, such a philosophy applied nationwide would have required willing farmers, and 'there's the rub'. However, he was an official guest of the government, with possible Aid funds in his pocket.

So; we were enjoying a profusion of butterflies, colourful avifauna and the forest echoing with primate calls as a result of the absence of bush fires. Much of the survey area had been heavily exploited by timber companies and the open areas now grew *Panicum maximum* grasses five feet tall in response to the extra fertility. Following a compass bearing next day we were blinded by tall grass panicles, with Jo behind me shielding her eyes from dust and flying seeds, watching my heels for direction. Richard and I reached an open *mbuga,* and turned to find that we were alone! We listened to the crackling heat of the dry grass and searched for any sign of disturbance. "Sally, where's your mistress?"

There were huge elephant dung balls in the *mbuga*, still moist, which meant they had passed early that morning. I did my two finger trill whistle as loud as I could. Silence prevailed behind the blanket of tall grass.

"Right, Richard, we will have to make a back-bearing and hope. Without a compass, you can't walk straight in tall grass. Your mum may have gone off at a tangent."

After a while, I climbed a *Combretum* tree, with some difficulty whilst Sally gazed up at me with some ridicule showing in the whites of her eyes. Suddenly alarm filled my spleen; there was a pall of smoke looming up. Fire was coming unpredictably and may be that elephant herd was also heading in our direction! I lunged into five minutes of shrill whistling. Sally thought I was calling her to climb the tree, poor dog. I thought I detected a disturbance not directly to windward, thank goodness. I could do nothing better than to continue being a 'whistling gypsy' as the sky darkened with smoke. There was a movement in that direction against the blackness, a white hand waving above the yellow grass. The fire had frightened Jo and turned her in my direction.

At last, "Why didn't you whistle or something, I could have been barbecued."

"Hello, my darling Cicely, I thought you were lost and gone forever."

"Don't be silly, I have got rehearsals at the Lead Memorial Hall next Tuesday!"

"It will be easier tomorrow when the grass has burnt off."

Back at camp, we made sure we were fireproof and brewed tea. The outdoor campfire evening was spoilt by the red chested cuckoo driving us mad, with its incessant call, way into the night, cak-cak-coo in a descending scale, repeated every five seconds ad infinitum. It is the scent of rain that sets it off, presumably asserting its male presence and commonly known as the Rain Bird. I tried firing off a few shots with my .22 rifle but each time the monotonous phrase returned a few yards further round, a circuit round our campsite.

Richard also marched around banging our tin water debbie and each time the cak-cak-coo came back a few yards elsewhere, well within earshot. "If only it appeared in the Red Book of Endangered Species, the world would be a happier place."

Jo responded, "How long do you reckon we will be in this little paradise, Brian?"

"Three or four days; if we can avoid getting lost."

We covered about 17 miles the next day and returned black as the Three of Spades. We found traces of old villages, two good earth dam sites and red clay soils on all upper slopes with sandier red soils lower down in the catena. "Those sisal estates pioneers knew what they were looking for, there are great soils here."

Jo said, "Those pioneers had the right idea too, about annexing the Yacht Club for their evening refreshment. I'm parched. How about we call it a day, Sambo?"

"Oh, you've been reading Richard's story book 'Little Black Sambo'. People think Sambo refers to a black man, don't they. He was an Indian actually."

"Yes, that's right. Go and get us something for supper."

A flock of *kanga* appeared boldly, having lost their grass cover. I managed to blend in with the charcoal and shoot one, out of the 200! They spotted me and flew off. Cooking guinea fowl on a stick over a camp fire, however, required a particular skill which was somewhat lacking. Consequently, we had to resort to, as ever, a tin of corned beef, from Tanganyika Packers.

We finally struck camp and drove into the sisal estate. We knew the manager, John Bond and his lovely Swiss wife Lilian. We enjoyed some decent food in good company; they even offered us the chance to recover our normal colour, and scent, in their shower. John showed us the decorticator shed and the washed fibre hung out to dry and bleach, like lines of washing. We felt that John and Lilian were tiring of the monotony of sisal production and political rumours about the future of the nation, and were 'considering their options'.

One other *salvete* call for us now back home in Tanga, was to visit Amboni citrus estate. Along the coastal slopes facing the ocean, we always enjoyed visiting this exotic farm. After a typical Dutch lunch of sliced cold meats and cheeses, the 'lady of the house' related her gruesome history. Her name was Wilhelm Van der Ploeg. We prompted her to tell us her traumatic life story. She told us of her horrific imprisonment in the notorious Japanese prison camp for women, near Kuching, which was, I think, the location of the famous 'movie'.

"The British bombed us with Red Cross parcels. That would have been our salvation, but the Japs collected them up and put them into store, where they rotted. When we were liberated, we were only 500 remaining alive out of the original 1000 women inmates."

She did not boast possession of the latest Japanese camera!

Boxing Day 1966: It really was just that, with our two boys packing enthusiastically. Having been offered a renewal of contract by some heavenly personage, we were entitled to put our crates into government storage in Tanga whilst Iain Aitchison offered to look after Sally Spaniel and my Ford Corsair GT. Since he had positive designs on our daughter Caroline, aged only seventeen, we felt we could trust him with our dog even if not with our daughter. He was a shipping agent and hence would be able to forward our possessions to wherever we might end up. The British element of society in Tanga now all agreed that it was unwise to work in any country where there was no British Embassy.

My Osprey Jill would remain with our co-owner Dr Ian Kennedy. I had every reason to believe that he would have liked me to leave him my crew, also!"

Our boys just took life as it came, but for Jo and I this was the end of a fabulous episode in our lives. So many friends we would never see again. There was a tear in Jo's Tanga Bay blue eyes when we opened our bird cage and left 'our' yellow weaver birds to fly away. They decided, apparently, that unlike us, they did not wish to 'flee the cage' and just sat there uttering just the odd chirp instead of their usual raucous singing to us over breakfast. Philip relented and threw them a bunch of long grass which they immediately began magically weaving into their impenetrable ball and entrance tunnel, impenetrable that is to all except the odd crafty tree snake which was agile enough to crawl up their vertical entrance tunnel.

Weaver birds had good reason to sing about their cleverness. "It beats me how they learn to construct such a complicated thing without a teacher," said Philip.

"They are self-taught," quipped Richard, "like we will be when Dad takes that job in the Ruaha National Park."

"He never lets up that boy," whispered Jo.

Chapter Ten

Escape?

27th December 1966: We all flew into Dar es Salaam and migrated to the Brigg's house in Oyster Bay. We always enjoyed their company and Dick was employed by the VSA like me.

"The situation has not improved, Brian. You had better go and see the Permanent Secretary again."

The Tanzanian Permanent Secretary was as hostile as before, almost neurotic with the pressure he was under from unscrupulous politicians above. He completely rejected any notion that he might be responsible for my family being held in detention if we could not get away within six weeks. I felt his 'ancestral spirits' were driving him into emotional disorientation. I became critical, verging on angry. "It takes a special kind of education to develop integrity as well as Cambridge University academic distinction. Sorry you missed out!"

My next step; look for my end of contract gratuity. The Department of Finance was run by Indians, I knew the Head of Department for Pensions and Gratuities, a Sikh. He said that they had received my message but "Your file is missing: In other words your file is hidden, so no action can be taken. I suggest you call in next year when things have cooled down and personally search for that file yourself. I will see that you get your cheque."

It looked like a write-off to me at the time, however, two years later, en route to my daughter's wedding to Iain Aitchison in Mombasa, I did as the Sikh said and got my cheque. Unfortunately it was in Tanzania Shillings which had been dramatically devalued by that time!

28th December 1966: I arranged to meet the British Commissioner for Rural Settlement armed with my assurances that I had genuinely tried everything legitimate to obtain my contractual air fares to UK. He explained that his authority was only functional for what was now unavailable to him; the Vote of British Aid Funds. He said that he considered my case was 100% legitimate as a charge against that vote and that he would write his usual Local Purchase Order for the airline tickets for me and my family to London. "There is a good chance that the booking agent will not counter-check the validity of the LPO with the Ministry of Finance, right there. If the trick works, grab the first flight out, TODAY; otherwise; with your Work Permit expiring you will become an illegal immigrant and subject to arrest."

We all filed into the plush East African Airways office that afternoon, trying to be a happy-looking family group, attracting the lady's welcoming smiles, and distracting her attention from, the technicalities. The boys made some prearranged enquiries about the type of plane from Nairobi to London – would it be the new VC10? How long does the VC10 take to reach London non-stop, etc? Soon she was writing the tickets happily and our eyelids ceased sweating. She franked them, VALID.

"There are plenty of seats. The Dakota to Nairobi leaves at 8:00 a.m. so be at the airport by 7:00 a.m. at the latest."

"We certainly will," we all chorused, thinking to ourselves, "*You bet!*"

We so casually, but tremblingly, slipped the tickets into my briefcase and filed coolly into the hot street after waving a cheery goodbye. Around the corner, the boys leapt into the air shouting, "Yippee! We've done it!" Jo fainted – only the second time in her life. We rushed to grab her and all hugged tightly.

Imbibing cool beer on the balcony of the New Africa Hotel, Jo pondered, "Could they invalidate these tickets before we board the Dakota?"

"No chance. They will be closed by now and they won't even think about it until 'settlement day'. By that time we will be in England." I said cheerfully, still shaking at the knees. "What say we go to the beach and buy some roasted *karangas,* which are roasted groundnuts, from the 'beach boys' and enjoy this wonderful country."

Jo echoed philosophically, "Wonderful country! Well, I suppose it is really. You just have to learn to live with it."

29th December 1966: The old Dakota stood stolidly outside the Departure Lounge window as we chatted with a surprising number of Dar es Salaam friends assembled to see us off. I thought we had suddenly become famous; probably notorious would be more appropriate.

Dicky Briggs said he would telegram my sister Joy and tell her we would be arriving at Gatwick at 2:00 p.m. tomorrow. As we left, one of the porters cheerily said, "*Safari njema*" happy landings, and another said plainly, "*Bwana. Utarudi?*" Will you return, Bwana? I thought for some seconds, staring him in the eye. He awaited my reply as though it really mattered. I thought of the last 24 hours of uncertainty and Jo fainting in the street. I thoughtfully suffered that 'steer –steer' moment.

"*Ndio.*"[Yes] shouted Richard.

"*Ah! Njema. Nenda salaama. Kwa heri wote.*" I hardly need translate; "Ah! Good. Go in peace. Goodbye, everybody."

Such is the draw of 'The cradle of mankind'.

The Dakota vibrated its way north along the coast, over our beloved coral reefs and shining blue ocean, finally turning inland and heading for Mount Kilimanjaro, flying low below its snowy peak into Kenya. We reached Tsavo National Park. No sign of human habitation just wilderness, hills and parklands of acacia thorn trees alternating with dense bush, and flood plain. Hundreds of zebra passed below us, and huge elephant herds walking purposefully, giraffe looking awkward, as always, dainty gazelles, and mighty black buffalo in hundreds. There are no words dramatic enough or lyrical enough to describe the country that was passing below us. How could anyone NOT wish to return to Africa?

Soon we were rumbling across Nairobi airport apron and then stepping out into the warm sun. The terminal was so much busier than Dar es Salaam, thronging with urgent looks from intending helpers shouting, "*Jambo, Jambo, Bwana. Nataka taxi?*"

The taxi driver carrying us to Nairobi was full of questions. "From Tanzania! Ah ... Kenya, Bwana, you will like more; THIS is modern country, CLEVER people here. Good farmers too Bwana." "In my village everyone has small farm and grow crops to sell in Nairobi; vegetables and milk."

"You are Kikuyu then?"

"Yes sir."

Kikuyu are renowned for their farming competence and enterprise. We booked into the New Stanley Hotel with the day in front of us to explore the markets. Our VC10 was scheduled to depart at midnight for London via Cairo. We fell in love with Nairobi. We sat at a pavement table, the sun glinting in the cool lager, excellent service, passers-by well dressed with happy faces. Professional 'white hunters' dashed in and out of the hotel attentively chatting with their American clients who were 'paying the earth' to be staged as the greatest hunters of all time. That was actually money hard-earned by the 'white hunters'.

Visitors somehow felt important in Nairobi; expected guests. One immediately made contact with the Kenyan and with probing a little he became companionable. There was a sunny atmosphere of expectancy everywhere, not only of exciting safaris, into mankind's cradle of wildness, but of the surprises round the corner in this new-born modern African city.

We explored the Asian *dukas* for craftwork. They preferred sterling they said "to help them settle in the UK", so we made good bargains with elephant ear shoes for Uncle Tom, a black-mane lion handbag for Jo, zebra skin wallets and belts, elephant tail hair good-luck bracelets. These goods all carried licences from the Game Department.

Our VC10 was much faster than the Comet 4 on our last trip home, in fact it still holds the world speed record for crossing the Atlantic I am told. It was quite heavy on fuel and hence our touch-down in Cairo.

Unfortunately our plane carried goods for the locally hated Israelites and so we were delayed for an hour or more by officialdom searching the plane; the Six-day War was to break out six months later. Gone were the colonial days when you could travel from Cape Town to Cairo without even a border check. We were finally released only to be delayed by fog until 11:00 a.m. The heat was oppressive. The whole consignment of liquid refreshment was consumed before take-off.

We finally arrived at Gatwick Airport at 3:00 p.m. emerging on the top step was a shock. Philip said, "Its dark here, Mum, it must be night time."

Jo replied gloomily, "No. It's always like this here, in winter."

We managed to find a grumpy porter after a search, who took us to a coach destined for London Victoria. From there a taxi took us to Paddington Station. We had no idea about tipping London cabbies who obviously expected the earth, for what? We couldn't make it out. The driver was not the least bit helpful, in marked contrast to the Nairobi taxi drivers who cheerfully couldn't do enough to oblige one.

As we pulled out of Paddington Station on the train to Leamington Spa, we heard our names called on the public address system, "It's Uncle George. There he is, Mum, on the platform." shouted the boys excitedly.

"We can't stop now. Give him a wave." We all waved madly at his happy smiling face, a welcome contrast to those miserable porters and taxi drivers. Now the race was on; which of us would get to Leamington Spa first? In the outcome, we beat George, but only by five minutes, even though this pre-dated the M40.

Interlude: – Life in England, between contracts

1ˢᵗ January 1967: Our family celebrations were cosy and jolly, as compared to our rather riotous Tanga parties, but we had the over-riding joy of Caroline being with us. She had finished school. Our two boys who had hoped that they might end up living in camp in Ruaha National Park were instead facing secondary boarding school entrance examinations. It was a nasty shock for them but a challenge that they accepted as a part of living, and they would be at home with us as day-boys for six months on our friend's farm at Woolston in Warwickshire. Our hired farm cottage was called Hill Top. It did in fact command a fine view over the verdant countryside of Leicestershire. Our future at this stage was uncertain, which, it must be said, was normal.

We purchased an ex. Police-car, a Ford Popular, a terrible degradation from our Ford Corsair GT but good fun for our boys to drive across the farm fields. Since the pastures were the medieval ridge and furrow type, the sight of these two boys driving hump back style, across the corrugations, in fits of laughter made up for the loss of their prospects for flying across Ruaha National Park looking for poachers. Their inherent enterprising nature revealed itself in the creation of Fred's Workshop, set up in a farm shed. This was where the two collected bicycle parts from a scrapyard and made two bicycles. This was just what native African boys would have done.

Our three months' 'leave pay' was modest and we had £6 per week rent to pay plus 30/- per week for coal and the prospect of school fees, subject to whether or not we returned to Africa on an Overseas Aid contract. In the latter case the County Council were obliged to settle boarding school fees. Soon we had a knock on the door by a Social Worker. We were amazed at his insistence that we should accept weekly money as unemployed and homeless, from the taxpayer. We absolutely refused. He left feeling dejected having, as he explained, failed in his duty. We did not have television at Hill Top but we did have family visitors from everywhere, including Jo's father, now accustomed to being widowed, all wanting to enjoy the lovely countryside, the shooting, and in some cases wood pigeon pie. This alternated with rabbit pie and rook pie. Rooks and wood pigeons were in great profusion and the local farmers welcomed our 'services'. The boys learned to shoot safely too with the borrowed farmer's shotgun.

"Why don't we just go back to Home Farm in Norfolk, Dad?"

This dreaded question now received a scolding from Mum. "The local farmer here says he hasn't made a penny profit for three years."

Richard was close to getting his ear clipped when he said, "Too many pigeons eating his crop, that's his problem. We didn't have a pigeon problem at Home Farm because we used to poke out their nests with those long poles."

Jo now loved having her own home with three children and "no nuisance servants". Richard lit the fire daily at dawn while Philip made morning tea for his mum and dad. Caroline found a boyfriend, Geoffrey Friswell, who was a young racing car driver.

"Er … why don't we look for a house, just in case," said Jo one day, "£5,000 would get us a good house in the Cotswolds, your sister Joy says." That tail-piece was intended to add weight to the idea, and secure Caroline's support too.

I felt tears welling up. I had two passionate loves, Jo and Africa and they were, sort of, inseparable in my psyche. Would Jo really prefer to stay in England? She would be with her children of course. Caroline found a job in Coventry as a dental nurse with Geoffrey ferrying her to work each morning in his MGB. There had been no letters from Iain Aitchison in Tanga and we had high hopes of this new 'natural' teenager relationship with Geoffrey. This was surely a perfect family setting for resettlement back in England, farm managing. I wandered off across the fields literally trembling with uncertainty and fearful of doing the wrong thing by my family. It was cold and dark and I selfishly dreamed of the African sun. I knew that Africa, in the end, would not let go of us.

One event remained to complete our culture shock of hitting the UK in 1967 and that was the hairdressing salon. Jo emerged in due course with two inches of hair all over, clutching a carrier bag of lovely locks reminiscent of the Cicely I first met, as an evacuee, when she was thirteen years old and had long ringlets. She was now the brisk charismatic Jo, plus a new concept in hair styling, coloured, reddish-brown. Tanga certainly disappeared that day. The two boys had also become somewhat anglicised; they slotted back into the rural farming scene as though they had never left it.

Springtime charmed us as ever, Africa has no such season; the countryside was merry with the music of the dawn chorus, early lambs bleating, raucous rookeries in the elms, and distant tractors busy with spring cereal drilling. The woodlands were embroidered with bright primroses, catkins dusted the breeze with pollen, and the hawthorn struggled to get some fresh green leaf out to make some sugar from the rising sun. The cuckoo arrives in April, sings its song in May, changes its tune in June, and then in July it flies away. Now I wondered; will that be our song too? It actually was.

In the meantime I had to admit to enjoying my life at leisure as a country sportsman with our boys 'at foot'. Jo and Caroline faced a challenge in the kitchen with Mallard ducks, pigeons, rooks, rabbits and the odd pheasant shot as a guest of Lord Aylesford's shoot at Meriden, courtesy of 'old' friend Arthur Coleman.

Easter was cold and snowy, often is, and Caroline began pining for Tanga. Iain was now writing to her charming her into the idea of marriage and living in 'paradise' Tanga. My leave pay ceased, crunch decision time loomed.

13th May 1967: The Grand National had captivated us that year. Only one horse survived the melee at fence 23 – having been so far adrift of the field and it went on to win at 100-1. Jo lost her bet.

A brown envelope appeared on the doormat emblazoned with the letters OHMS.

The three-year Overseas Services Aid Scheme Contract enclosed was a Provincial post in the Copperbelt of Zambia, ex-Northern Rhodesia. Zambia was described as being in "urgent need" of staff in the rural development sector. I was offered all the usual Aid support, with holiday air fares for children and terminal gratuities on offer, plus training for me within the Ministry of Overseas Development in London, in the use of modern technology for aerial photo interpretation and land resource analysis. For a country of 300,000 square miles, equal to France and Germany together, this seemed an appropriate discipline rather than measuring the land with a chain and compass as I had done in Tanzania. With the salary of £2,085 per annum as compared to the Tanzanian offer of £1,750. I signed up for Zambia.

The political and economic background to this contract is worthy of note; Rhodesia declared UDI in November 1965, and became isolated by the other African States which refused to trade with them. Hence as Rhodesia was the traditional supplier of maize and domestic goods to Zambia plus staff to run the copper mines, Zambia suffered more that Rhodesia. Although the border between the two countries did not formally close until 1973, it became so when it was initiated by the white government of Rhodesia to inhibit the passage of guerrilla forces. Zambia's plight became worse. The cutting off of the trade route to RSA, to the south of Rhodesia, caused catastrophic shortages of food, fuel, staff and domestic goods in Zambia. Zambia urgently needed to increase its production of food, and actually had the money from copper to invest. Better than Tanzania, Zambia enjoyed valuable land-use and agricultural technology learned from the, more advanced, Rhodesia.

So, sorry Tanzania, the Dawtreys were destined to move south to Zambia. The National Parks idea also flew out of the window. Richard was grief-stricken. He had always been top of his class in Nature Study. "He loved caring for his farm animals," Jo commented "and his heaven would be living amongst the creatures of the wild. Wouldn't surprise me if he ended up as a vet."

Back to Work: Two months paid employment with the Land Resources Division of the Ministry meant working in Tolworth Tower, south of The City. I took the recommended lodgings in Ewell to share with a notorious white-bearded gentleman named Bill Verboom. With a name like that, he had to be Dutch and with a very loud voice 'to boot'. He had spent many years in the Indonesian jungles during the rebellion before realising, he told me, that he was on the wrong side. He had acquired the habit with which he continued later in Zambia, of carrying a long knife and a Colt .45 revolver. He commented that with that calibre you did not need to be a marksman because whatever part of the body you hit, he was done for.

Bill was a keep fit survival fanatic. Tolworth Tower was very high and everyone needed the lift, except Bill Verboom who insisted that he, and me, climbed the stairs up, and took the lift down.

The other distinguished man I was to meet in my 'field' was Jim Mansfield whom I continued to work with in Zambia later. Both these gentlemen were a mine of knowledge on tropical soils and vegetation. The three of us were to acquire skills in the modern use of air photography and stereoscopic imagery to produce land resource maps and plans, to scale both vertically and horizontally. The Directorate of Overseas Surveys, the DOS, continue to provide an invaluable service to the Commonwealth of Nations. They were sited close by in Tolworth at that time and would demonstrate to us how contour maps were made from air photos, using stereoscopes, an amazing achievement inherited from WWII. I hoped that this skill would reduce enormously, the endless trekking through the 'bush' with land chains, compasses and Dumpy levels in order to make contour maps for land planning purposes. The Wilde Stereoscope was like low flying, except that you could stop and do detailed analysis of landscape features. Selected landscape features that is, that promised good soils, dam sites or road alignments, and which could be scaled off with acreage measurements, thus hugely minimising fieldwork.

I was now a weekly London commuter. I had never before experienced life in a crowded urban environment. On Derby Day, HM The Queen and the Duke of Edinburgh passed within ten feet of me on their way to Ascot as I stood on the pavement. I felt some personal pleasure in her impassionate wave. This was a three-dimensional image of royalty, almost personal, certainly appealing. I kidded myself that the Head of State now knew that I existed. The huge variety and quantity of people around Ewell and Tolworth was mesmerising at first. Everyone was rushing, something that I had never aspired to or experienced. When I stood still, observing the scene, suspicious glances came my way, *"He's up to something."*

There was a relieving feature to this grim environment of noise fumes and concrete; the miniskirt had arrived. It seemed to me that as the population density had risen, so had the hemline from ground level Victorian skirts to one foot above the knee! It seemed to me that London girls wanted to attract the male eye and double the pulse rate of wild country boys and still be cool and aloof as though they did not even know that they were showing their knickers when climbing the stairs of London Transport omnibuses ahead of me. Was I supposed to ignore it in the name of fashion or was it cheese for the field mouse?

After a couple of days missing my stop and being late for the office, I must have become hardened somewhat. Come the final weekend back at Hill Top, the "raging alpha male" as Jo called me once, faced me in a new miniskirt: "It's time we had another baby, you. Caroline is out with Geoffrey until midnight. It's now or never – you can choose your style, I've chosen the weapon!"

"You are thirty-eight years old, are you sure about this?"

I took her out to supper at the quaint Dun Cow Inn in beautiful Dunchurch, ten miles out of Coventry, and after that we 'called it a day'.

Just before our departure for Zambia, we enjoyed three glorious days at the nearby Royal Show, Stoneleigh and all the family loved it. The following week came the ghastly separation. Fred's Shed was ceremoniously closed down, the tadpoles all hopped away, the boys were signed up for boarding school at Princethorpe College, Rugby. They were to stay on the dairy farm of our friend Philip Frost near Newark, until school term started. Caroline, now the dental nurse, fell into Geoffrey's arms. No one complained to Mum and Dad, but when Caroline picked up a new song by Dusty Springfield on the radio, we all collapsed in floods of tears. Here are a few lines of this emotive song:

If you go away, on a sunny day,
Then you might as well, take the sun away,
And all the birds, that flew in the sky…
If you go away, if you go away… as I know you must
Then there'll be nothing left, in the world to trust,
Just an empty room,
Full of empty space,
If you go away; don't go away, don't go away, don't go away

Jo and I silently asked ourselves, *might there be a 'day of reckoning' for us two?*

10th July 1967: My sister Joy and "Uncle George" drove us to Gatwick airport together with Caroline who was to live with my mother in Leamington Spa, next door to my sister Joy. We managed to stop fretting with this huge support and the thrill of the new EAA Super VC10 on the tarmac waiting for us. It was our philosophy that we could achieve anything together. Our teenage love affair had already proved enduringly that. Shakespeare's Juliet was only 14, yet their love is still an epic after 420 years. As the Maasai say; "first love lasts forever". Our other love our Ford Corsair GT awaited rebirth in Tanga, which was where we were heading.

We reached Nairobi non-stop! An expanding travel world was dawning. We changed planes in Nairobi for the EAA Focker Friendship flight to Tanga. Two old friends joined us, John Osborne and Ramus Lyatuu whom we knew as the District Agricultural Officer in Chunya in 1963. He was now Chairman of the Moshi Coffee Co-operative Growers Association. We were BACK. With joyful tears in our eyes, we were now flying low over the Tsavo Park, close by the snows of Kilimanjaro, down to Mombasa, then low along the tropical coastline to Tanga. As the aircraft door opened we were enveloped in the welcoming warmth of the coast, and of smiling Yacht Club friends who were accompanying Iain Aitchison.

Outside the gate awaited our Corsair, and on the backseat Sally Spaniel. She was not sure of us at first. Maybe six months stretches a dog's memory? In no time we were enjoying a cool beer on the Quarter Deck, and can you believe it? We were already entered for the Monthly Mug race on the morrow. Were we missing our children? In every slack moment in the conversation our tears flowed, desperately wishing they were with us, and that pervading thought *what the hell are we doing?* This was going to be really hard. Zambia had better be good to us.

I actually came in first in our Osprey with Ian Kennedy as crew, though I think they excused my error at the last buoy. Jo said later, "Brian, I've got that feeling again. We belong here. Shall we stay?" We did.

Ian Kennedy declared, "There's a chap here offering you fifty pounds for your share of Jill. I'll have to sell mine as well, I'm leaving shortly. I've decided to head for Canada. I am a bit disillusioned with the lack of a sense of responsibility and integrity here, and I need to further my career in surgical skills."

"Tanzania is a very young nation, it will take time. I can understand that you need to get on with your career, Ian, best of luck. So you are not going back to Lewis in Scotland then?"

"My mother lives in Glasgow now."

"Lots of people leaving!" I remarked to John Cooke and his wife Silvia at dinner. They were, also, leaving, for Botswana University, to teach Geography. John told us that the British Headmaster of Karimjee School had just left. The new African Headmaster of the school had cancelled afternoon lessons in favour of pupils growing food. This seemed to be a reflection of the broadening socialist impact of President Nyerere's Arusha Declaration, made four months earlier.

My Ford Corsair GT had been checked over by Riddoch Motors in Tanga, in readiness for our 1,300 mile drive to the Zambian Copperbelt on corrugated murram roads. They claimed that I owed them money from last year. Good try. The fifty pounds from the sale of Jill paid for the installation of two extra loud horns for overtaking in heavy dust clouds.

When saying goodbye to Dick Oohms, he declared he was also leaving and would we like to take his Colobus monkey, "a treasure" with its long black and white coat and happy face with bouffant hair style. I suggested he released it on Karimjee Tea Estate in the Usambara Mountains.

We said more goodbyes ending with Caroline's suitor, Iain Aitchison. He would forward our boxes to Zambia. We thanked him for looking after Sally Spaniel.

We drove to Morogoro and on to Iringa, arriving by 6:15 p.m., 420 miles, and checked in at the White Horse Inn in the cool highlands. Meeting old friends everywhere kept us happy. We learned that Tim Harvard from Kitulo Plateau had become engaged to his mountain girlfriend at Njombe Wattle Estate.

We managed to say cheerio to a whole round of expatriates from the Department of Agriculture in Iringa before leaving for Mbeya at 9:30 a.m., 240 more miles of murram road to go.

16th July 1967: Being the dry season, the road was quite good and we reached 70 mph, however, when overtaking a truck, fifty miles short of Chimala, my engine seized. There was nothing for it but to settle into a long roadside wait for a possible bus. After a couple of hours we were in luck and I managed to flag one down and get Jo on board.

Jo reached Chimala where there was an American Mission Station we knew. They provided hospital facilities which we much approved of instead of just collecting souls. The three-hour bus journey had been, Jo said, "Insufferable with the stench of menstruating women adding to the terror of the lunatic driver, who drove at break-neck speed on downhill slopes in order to get enough momentum to get his over-loaded bus up the next hill, puffing thick black smoke behind him."

Not one saloon car passed me all day. I chatted with some local elderly curious villagers. The headman said, *"Pole ya safari, Bwana."* "Sorry about your journey, Bwana."

"Saidia itakuja." "Help it will come," I said optimistically. *"Habari yako?"* "What's your news?"

"*Ah-h-h, Bwana*", he continued to say, "We've had enough of this *Uhuru,*" Which is the political slogan for freedom, "when is it going to finish? Too much cheating and you can't trust nobody. We need you British come back, run things properly, treat everyone fair."

I thought to myself, that's the word of the 'common man'. I wish that it could be heard by certain UK intellectuals who frequently preach about the evils of colonialism.

A Land Rover drew up and offered me a tow. God was on my side after all! But no, the driver fell out; drunk. I had the greatest difficulty in persuading this compassionate African that really I could manage.

Darkness fell at 6:00 p.m. The Chimala Mission car arrived to collect me. I recognised the two young men. "I think we've met," one said blushing.

"Yes, on Usangu Plains. You were hunting lion with a shotgun from the back of a motorbike. It must be four years ago. I trust by now you understand better how things work out here."

"Ah-h-h. Yes."

Jo and I were soon reunited and enjoying the eerie halls of Illinois Church of Christ social circles. Over a game of dominoes, American version, we learned that their nurse at Igalula Mission Health Centre, up on the Matamba Plateau, had been sent home to USA with her vocal chords cut. She had fallen victim to the denigrated *Wambuda,* the leopard cult that terrorised villagers by dressing in a leopard skin, and purporting to be a reincarnated ancestral spirit descending from Kitulo Plateau, to administer punishment for some social misdemeanour.

A new 'player' was emerging in the economic field, the Chinese. We learned that the grandiose United Nation Development Programme managed, irrigation scheme, on Usangu Plains, near the Mission, known as the Mbarali Tenant Scheme, for growing groundnuts for export; had "folded". This was due to technical design errors, by the UN Experts, leading to extra unplanned heavy constructional costs for extracting water from the river into the canals. The Tenants became overburdened with debt in the form of loans, such that they had all run away in fear of prosecution. President Nyerere had just visited Mbarali and declared that the Chinese were arriving to take over the scheme to grow rice "for The People". The senior surveyor there, whom I knew, a Cape-coloured man named Mr C. Kirchestein, was to be promoted to Manager to work under a Chinese Director.

The following day our two young 'heaven-sent' gentlemen were detailed to tow our Ford Corsair GT the 50 miles to Mbeya with the Mission truck. Far from making reparations for their past poacher misdemeanours, they turned out to be terrible drivers and gave Jo and I a missionary experience of what Hell must be like. Our lovely car, as well as Jo and I, arrived in Mbeya in a shattered condition.

Mbeya is quite near the Zambian border, a mere 65 miles, so near yet so far!

Our Italian mechanic friend Mr Sossi said he'd try his best to fix the car. He said a piece of metal had flown off the "V" belt drive wheel which had sliced the radiator hose and caused loss of water, thus overheating the engine. There were minimal Corsair spares in Tanzania, certainly not engine components, he said, and it might take some time. We enquired about trucking it down to the Copperbelt in Zambia, but the quoted cost was more than the car was worth with the damaged engine.

"Thanks, old friend. We'll stick around and enjoy Mbeya as we used to. We can stay at Nessi Stead's place until you get some news from Nairobi, then we can decide the best course of action."

We wrote to Caroline pressing her to be firm with Iain and that he had not even enquired after her whilst we were in Tanga. Jo said to me, speaking from heartfelt experience, "You know, at 18 years, old passion is pretty insurmountable – it's emotional rather than logical. You can understand why Asians favour arranged marriages."

We met the new United Nations manager on my Kitulo Wool Sheep Scheme in Mbeya, and he loaned me the official car to visit Kitulo Plateau. Amazingly they had built a new road up, but from the south side where it was less steep, though much further round. As to housing for U.N. staff, he told us that they thought it was too cold up there and they were living in Mbeya. Maybe the *Wawanji* ancestral spirits had once again exerted their influence? The traditional "no human has ever lived on Kitulo" prevailed.

The vicar loaned me the parish car for the two hours' drive to the border post at Tunduma. From there I sent a telegram signifying my arrival in Zambia which would trigger my salary and hopefully signal the need for a government house in Luanshya to be made ready. I was not even asked for my passport. I then turned round and drove back to Mbeya. I put my feet up at the Golf Club. "Was it busy?" asked Jo.

"There were no cars going to Zambia at all. The roadside was littered with those crashed lorries that were used for carrying smoked tilapia fish from Lake Rukwa to the Copperbelt. The kipper smell was everywhere. I think that's the only trade between Tanzania and Zambia. The trouble with these African drivers, driving such huge distances, is that they seem to think that alcohol is a survival tonic."

The following day Mr Sossie declared that he'd managed to contact Nairobi by phone and that there were no engine spares in stock. If we could get the car to Riddoch Motors in Iringa, it could be restored with parts from the UK but obviously it would take a considerable time.

"We have to take up my job in Zambia, not stay here for weeks and weeks. What shall we do?"

"Looks like a tow back to Riddoch's in Iringa either way!"

We gathered from gossip at the Golf Club in Mbeya that the U.N. staff at Kitulo Wool Sheep Scheme was not too popular. There was evidence of a resentment of their high flying tax-free salaries. Mbeya dignitary, farmer, Ivor Bayldon, had said to Kitulo Manager John Williams that, "The real work was done before you arrived, by a certain government officer on a fraction of your salary." Doubtless this had helped in achieving such a kind gesture from him in resolving our travel problems. He was certainly popular with me.

After some discussion with John he kindly loaned me his driver and their four-wheel drive truck to tow me to Iringa. Leaving Jo in Mbeya I eventually struck a deal, with some financial jiggery pokery, and arrived back in Mbeya two days later with a used chocolate-coloured secondhand Ford Zodiac Mark IV to get me to Luanshya, Zambia. I was to sell it shortly afterwards to a copper miner at a profit, which enabling me to buy a brand new Land Rover – made in Ndola, for £840. The Zodiac comfortably spread itself luxuriously across the bumps in the road, like a rich man's car. It did not have that perky stylish performance of our beloved Corsair and was certainly not a safari car. It was *Kwa heri* to our B reg., two-and-a-half-year-old Ford Corsair GT which had given us pride in its style, comfort, and bold performance. It had suffered no body rot, as cars do from salted roads in the UK. Its mileage I cannot recall but it was only high relative to its two and half years 'youth'. It had skipped over hellish roads with a certain 'fleet of foot', shod with a total of 17 new tyres. The suspension had managed the thousands of miles of corrugations with supreme fortitude, and one set of new leaf springs. We did not arrive at our destinations with hard bottoms and covered in dust as we did when travelling by Land Rover. If we did get stuck in the mud in the rainy season the car was light enough to be lifted back onto the road by willing villagers, for a few 'bob'. I sincerely hope that the Ford agent thought it worthwhile to ship her back to her home country and 'fix her up' for some classic car collector. With that thought Jo and I were able to pocket our tear-soaked hankies and consider our future in the more modernised country of Zambia.

Nessy Stead charged us the equivalent of £5 per day for full board plus Sally Spaniel. Gold miners used to hang out there in the 1920s and 1930s so it was pretty rugged, both the building and the proprietor-ess. We met Mr and Mrs Mervyn Hillier who were still living in the bush managing my Oxfam Matwiga Tobacco Scheme after three years. He surprised me by saying he was the cousin of my colleague, the Regional Agricultural Officer Bob Silcock. So, that was how he came to be posted there as manager!

"I hate to say this of Nessi, Jo, but there are fleas here. There are too many dogs."

"Funny you should mention fleas, Brian, I was just reading in Reader's Digest that there are 80,000 fleas to the ounce! I wonder if they are edible, we could make some pin money selling them to the Africans – they will eat anything."

"I expect Sally Spaniel will have collected a sample to take to our house in Luanshya!"

Bunny Brown came by and pulled up a chair by the fire. We met him before when he was living with Geisela Sergeant at the Lime Works where they made a living selling bat guano from the cave nearby. Bunny hailed from the Gold Rush days and earned his nickname, Bunny, from being promiscuous. He was 85 years old and did not need a walking stick. He announced that he was leaving Tanzania "like everybody else" and I enquired where he was going to. He told me, Rhodesia, and that he had no money and was therefore going to have to walk.

We packed our bags. "Jo, we have got two passengers – Sally Spaniel and Bunny Brown."

1st August 1967: We had left England on July 10th. We now faced a 740 mile drive on a deserted murram road, into the unknown world of recently independent Zambia under its new, pioneer President, affectionately known as K.K., Kenneth Kaunda.

--------------o-------------

'Jo Dawtrey' as Mrs Puffin

Tanga players

TANGA Theatre Group's hat trick of three one-act productions in one evening certainly confounded the critics.

Yne Stiel's production of Charles Vites' drama, "The Barrier", Gertrude Jennings' farce, "The Bathroom" produced by John Jones, and Gilbert and Sullivan's one-act musical comedy "Trial by Jury," produced by Dennis Chanter, were received with applause by an appreciative audience.

"The Barrier," if somewhat heavy going as a play was superbly produced and acted. Three new-comers to the Tanga stage —Jean Wolley as Ruth Simons, Tony Mitton, as Dan Simons and Ulli Von Ungern-Stenberg as Mrs. Kalman—showed great talent, each one giving a creditable account of themselves. Hans Stiel's superb performance as David Simons will long be remembered.

Though old and oft-performed, Gertrude Jennings' farce, "The Bathroom Door", was excellently produced with good characterisation and got its fair share of laughs. It came as pleasant relief after the tenseness of "The Barrier."

A scene from the Gilbert and S

John French and Graham Matten, both new-comers, more than did justice to the parts they took. Judy Duff as the "Young Lady" acted with exceptional charm while that versatile artist, Jo Dawtrey, was up to her usual standard.

Tanga's pet comedian, Charlie Powell, did not have much of a

THE STANDARD
TANZANIA

279

Cicely in Arusha, Mt Meru at the top of the High Street

View from our safari camp tent in Amboseli Nat.Park

Amboseli; popular with honey-mooners

Caroline, age sixteen

Jo, ex. Cicely, age thirty six

Caroline on school 'hols' at TYC

We met some Maasai

We set up camp at Seronera in Serengeti Nat.Pk.

*Centuries old look-out site for our speed competitor,
0-60 mph in 3 seconds*

The immaculate Thomsons gazelle

Wild dogs never fail to kill

The beautiful serval cat

Australopithecus zinjantropus, 1.8 million years (Photo courtesy Dar es Salaam Museum)

Wild country, driving towards Ngorongoro Crater

Our tent in the crater was an object of some curiosity

Road; Tanga to Amani in the Usambara Mountains

Brian loves his soil pits

Impression of Karimjee tea estate

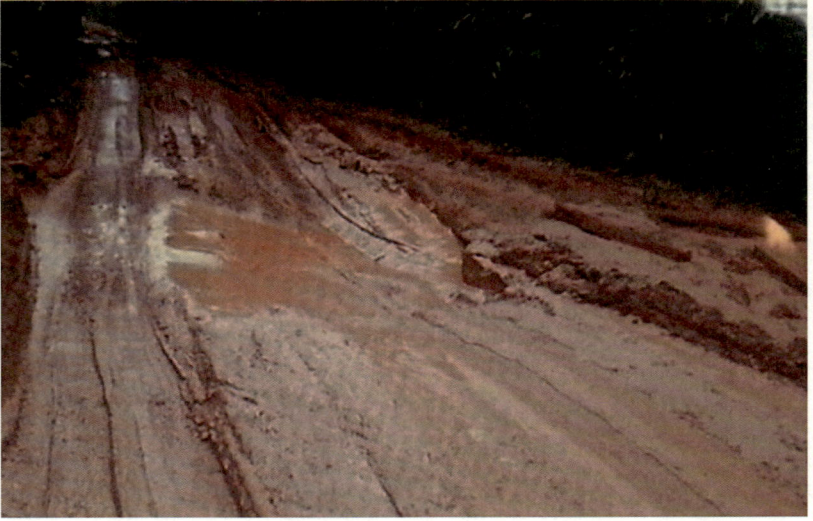

Road down from Karimjee tea estate

Road to Kiwanda Scheme

Road to Kigombe

Road to Nkalamo

Coast Road to Pangani becoming road to Nkalamo, going South from Tanga

A Tanga ngalawa fishing canoe with lanteen rig

Brian won the Monthly Mug at last, in his Osprey with Ian Kennedy crewing

Brian's collection of cowrie shells from the Tanga reefs

Richard won the Cadet Cup

Richard in Dar es Salaam

Jurassic Karst Limestone, sculpted by acid rain

Peering down a terrifying crevasse in Amboni Caves

Back in England, the 'Farm Kids'

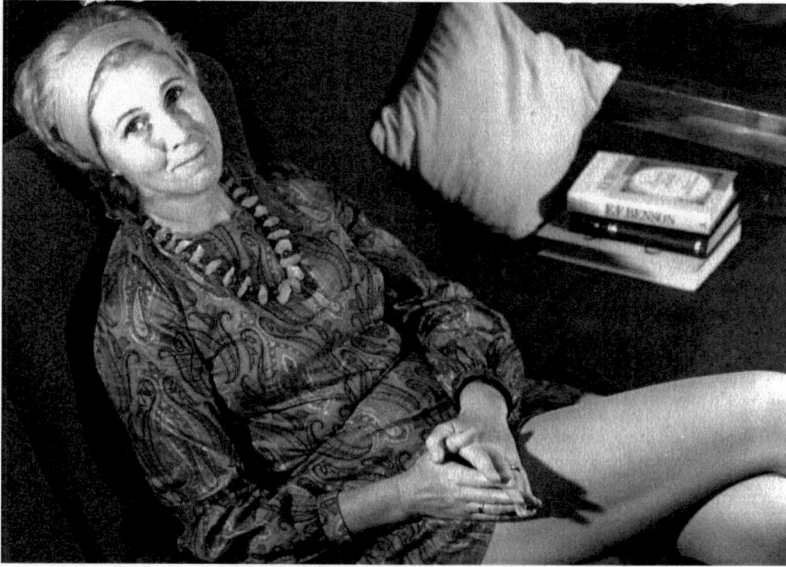

And the mini skirt!

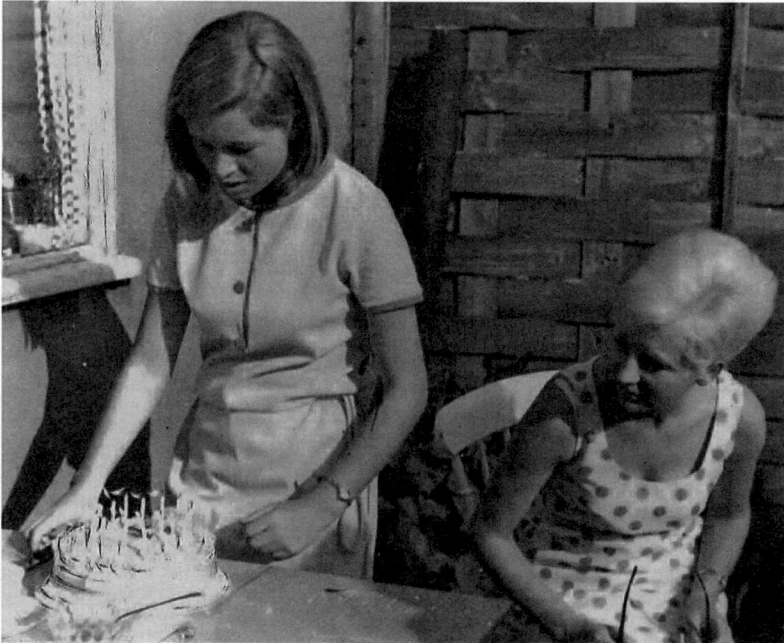

Caroline, 18, with my sister Joy in 1967

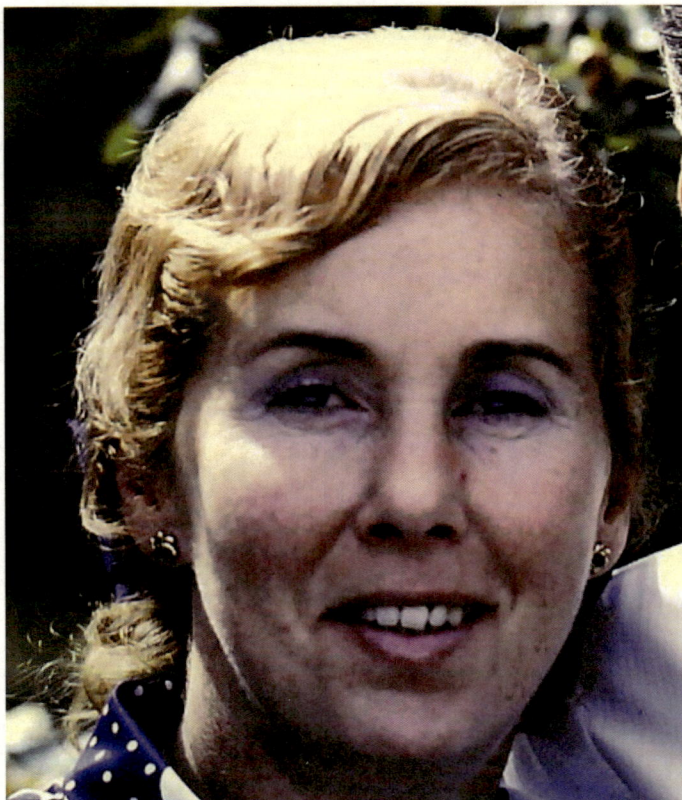

Jo looking English with Tanzanian ruby earrings

Super VC10 awaiting us at Gatwick

Here we go again

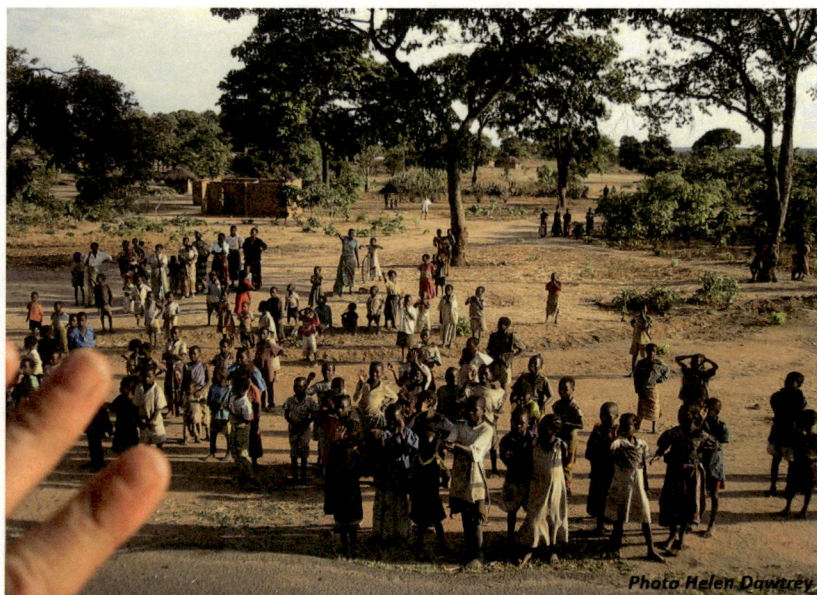

Road to Chimala, Tanzania, en route to Zambia.

*Engine seized; cause; chip off the fan v-belt drive. End of the road
for our beloved Ford Corsair GT?*

Post Script

A 1998 Government Report on Chunya District, in Mbeya Region: Surveyed by a Danish Company, has revealed some amazing development in this, in my time, remote poverty stricken, tsetse fly ridden, back water, about which I wrote in my book **'Voyage to Wild Africa'**, published Dec 2014, and in the early Chapters of this book. These locations were originally uninhabited miombo woodland and the cattle population was nil due to tsetse fly.

Matwiga (Oxfam Scheme): now has a population 5,066 people, 3,000 cattle, and children at school 141.

Lupa Tinga Tinga (tobacco farm): now has a population of 10,023, 7,000 cattle, and children at school 397.

Kipembawe area: overall tobacco sales for export 1,467 tons p.a., cotton sales 6,000 tons p.a., one (private) secondary school, 17 primary schools.

Lukwati is now a Game reserve with three air strips.

Ngualla volcano crater which I described in my book as the remotest place in all of Africa has attracted mining surveyors from Perth Australia. They have found oxides of a range of very rare minerals, used in modern mini electronics technology, more valuable than gold. Also traces of uranium. They were to set up a mine there at the time of the report, 1998.

Chunya District: '29,219 km sq with population of 7 per km sq.' (This compares with UK over 257). 'Average temperature 21 –23 degrees centigrade, rainfall 1000 mm'.

----------o----------

Richard was married in Luanshya, age 20 yrs, to the Mine Captain's daughter, Ann Hartley. He became an NHS hospital manager in Yorkshire.

Philip went back to College in England, and married age 23. He became an engineering designer with a company that manufactures stair lifts.

Caroline married Iain Aitchison in Mombasa, age 19 yrs. She lived in Kenya, Hong Kong, Japan, Seattle, San Francisco, Los Angeles, Bedford New England, and currently Atlanta Georgia USA.

Jo and Brian continued working in Overseas Aid for 24 years, in Tanzania, Zambia and Nigeria, before retiring to the wilds of the New Forest in Hampshire, UK.